Discovering the Magickal Mysterious Character

Empowering Teens and Women of All Ages Using a Journey of Native American Teachings

Dancing On the Edge Series

Book 1 – Discovering the Magickal Mysterious Character

(coming soon)
Book 2 – Becoming the Magickal Mysterious Character
Book 3 – Living the Magickal Mysterious Character
Book 4 – Legacy of the Magickal Mysterious Character

Phyllis Cronbaugh

Artwork Property of Phyllis Cronbaugh
Cover Photography by Dave Atkins, Atkins Photography

ISBN 1-4515-0038-6

Published by:
Dancing On The Edge, llc
11108 E 59th St
Raytown, MO 64133
USA
www.MagickalMysteriousCharacter.com
http://blog.PhyllisCronbaugh.com
816-353-2691

Printed in the United States of America
Published April 2010

Acknowledgements

I thank the numerous indigenous elders who have so willingly shared the teachings of their particular path over the years. You have helped me to find the Magickal Mysterious Character within myself and have and given me reason to celebrate my life.

Many thanks go out to Chloe, my beautiful granddaughter, whose picture is on the front of this book and to Dave Atkins of Atkins Photography who took the photo of Chloe. Thanks to Kris Marvel who was so helpful in manifesting the attire for the picture.

And finally, I thank my mother, Beverley Murphy, who at a very young age instilled in me the desire to put my thoughts down on paper.

4

Dedication

This book is dedicated to my beautiful granddaughters, Chloe and Bailey. My wish for you is that you find the Magickal Mysterious Character that resides in you early in life and always cherish her.

All my love, Rock'n Roll G-Ma

Prologue

I have witnessed the abominable conditions that are present on Indian reservations in our country today. Most people at some time have been subjected to what we call *the ghetto* in some city in the U.S. Conditions in ghettos are horrendous, but do not compare to what our government believes is adequate living conditions for many of the indigenous First Americans of our land.

On reservations, unemployment can reach as high as 85% and the median family income may be $3000 a year, with 97% of the population living below the federally acknowledged poverty level. Teenage suicide on most reservations is 150% higher than the national average, infant mortality 300% higher, diabetes 800% higher and more than half of the people may suffer alcoholism, cancer, heart disease, tuberculosis and malnutrition. In some communities, 30% of homes lack basic water and sewage systems and *over* 30% have no electricity[1].

It is very easy to see why many indigenous people feel they are victims with hopelessness consuming their lives, but many do not. What makes the difference in their attitude and approach to life? I have had the privilege of learning from a number of native elders who saw the glass as half full instead of half empty. They stood as the proud people that once enjoyed beautiful lives on the plains and in the mountains of North America. I pray that all native people will find the courage to stand in this place again.

It has to begin with the children and the teens. Just maybe this story will reach some of those teens and help them to break free of the *box of limitations* they have been conditioned to believe has to be their existence. Additionally, my hope is that other teens of all nationalities will benefit from the amazing wisdom that comes from the teachings of ancient peoples.

This book was initially intended as a short story with a few simple truths for my granddaughters, but as I wrote I discovered that I wanted to follow Samantha Playful Autumn Wind through her entire life to show how these truths can benefit any age. This is the first in a

---

[1] For more information on reservation living conditions, go to http://www.nativevillage.org/Messages%20from%20the%20People/Hidden%20Away%20in%20the%20Land%20of%20Plenty.htm.

series of four books that will tell the story of the Magickal[2] Mysterious Character inside all of us.

[2] The word magic is what magicians refer to as *slight of hand*. The word magick is the spelling of old and means *change at the cellular level*. It is used in this book to indicate the intuitive side of ourselves that has been suppressed by the modern world.

8

Chapter 1
The Story of My Name

It was only the middle of the Budding Trees Moon, but today the radiant sunshine warmed Samantha's body and soul as she strolled through the meadow. The fringes of the woods ahead were peppered with the brilliant white flowers of the early dogwoods and the rosy pink of an occasional redbud. She inhaled deeply taking in the scent of the flowers along with the fresh smelling earth below. Her long blond hair reached the middle of her back and danced with the gentle gusts of wind and her sea green eyes sparkled with anticipation. A huge hawk soared overhead; the creamy underbelly and the reddish tail feathers were easily visible. With a slight wave Sam projected her wish for the raptor, "Good hunting my friend." Then, returning her focus to her mission Sam headed for the trail that meandered southeast into the woods. She had high hopes of finding her new friend, Grandmother Wisdom Keeper.

Sam had seen eleven winters since her birth and was so caught up with loving life that she seemed oblivious to the delicate changes in her slim young body that indicated she was maturing. Joyfully, she leaped over a log and then realized her quick movements had startled a couple of does who bounded from the path to take cover in the denser brush. She wondered why they weren't sleeping as they usually did in the middle of the day. As she approached the spot where they had been she noticed bloodroot flowers poking though the soft dirt. *Ahhh, they had been eating lunch.* The flowers hadn't been there two weeks before when Sam had passed this way, but were now showing their faces even before their foliage appeared. She stepped wide to avoid a three-leafed plant that at first looked like poison ivy, but with closer scrutiny she discovered a small greenish-yellow flower. It wasn't the toxic plant after all. She lifted a tiny flap revealing tell-tale purplish stripes and peeked at Jack snug in his pulpit. Signs of spring were everywhere. A rabbit suddenly bolted from the underbrush and ran ahead reminding her that she shouldn't dawdle any longer.

She walked another stones throw into the woods and began calling, "Grandmother, Grandmother Wisdom Keeper. Can you hear me?" No answer. After another fifty paces a small gurgling stream intersected the path. It too seemed to be on a mission and Sam's intuition told her she should follow it. Stepping on several large boulders, she hopped across and made her way down a cliff trail to where the creek joined a larger stream. Rounding the next bend she laughed out loud.

"Hi, I've been looking all over for you."

The Indian woman sat on a fallen log amid spears of sunlight that streamed through the still leafless branches of an enormous cottonwood. Her tan deerskin garment was beautifully beaded around the neck and hem with intricate designs in colors of the rainbow. Suspended from a long silver chain hung a pendant of beautiful turquoise. Beneath the greenish stone numerous strands of beads and silver feathers dangled. Her snowy white hair was pulled back into a long thick braid that hung over her right shoulder.

The Grandmother swiped at a few loose strands of hair that had come loose and fluttered in the breeze around her dark face. "It is good to see you too, Samantha. I'm glad you and your parents came from the city again so soon."

"Well, we hadn't been home more than a day, when Mom started talking about our next trip to the cabin. She says all the snow we had this past winter has really given her *the fever* to be out in nature. So, here we are."

"I know exactly how she feels." Wisdom Keeper held out her hand to Sam. "So why have you come seeking me?"

"Well, I was reading a book about native people this week and I realized everyone has a beautiful name, like yours… Wisdom Keeper." She let it roll off her tongue. "How did you get your name?"

"Ahhh, I've had a number of names over my many winters." She raised her face to the sky thoughtfully and then brought it back to Sam who had flopped at her feet. "The medicine man or woman, or you might say the shaman of a tribe generally asks the sacred ancestors for a baby's name shortly after its birth. My mother's name was Gentle Deer and I was still rather red and blotchy several hours after I arrived, at least that is what I have been told, so I was given the name Spotted Fawn."

"That's cool."

"At around your age when I went through my Becoming Woman Rite of Passage, I was given the name Star Maiden Rising, but all my friends just called me Star." With hands wrapped around one knee, she began rocking back and forth fully absorbed with the tale now. "When my son came into this world, I used to walk with him every night under the silvery moon and my name became Moon Dreamer."

"Wow! You've had names just like in my book."

The Grandmother raised her eyebrows and smiled, "And, finally in a rite of empowerment ceremony I realized it was my destiny to pass along the ancient knowledge of my people to the next seven generations. That's when I became Wisdom Keeper."

"I knew it would be a neat story. How can I get a name like that?"

"So, you think you are ready for a *medicine name*?"

"Medicine name?"

"Yes, an Indian's name represents their *medicine*. It has meaning and describes something about them, maybe their personality or their talents and skills... their medicine."

"Yeah, I can see how your names described you, but I don't know what kind of talents I have."

"Well, if you are asking for a name, I will be glad to do the ritual to find it for you. You know, the name does not come from me, but from the Great Mystery and the Universe."

"Can you do it now? I don't think I can wait."

Sam had such enthusiasm, the old woman grinned from ear to ear causing the sun-baked skin of her cheeks to crinkle. "Usually, I smoke my sacred *chanunpa*, my pipe to help me set my intent, but I believe I can draw on my powers to do something for you right now. Come here and let me look into your eyes."

Sam stood to face her and their eyes locked for several seconds.

"Good. Did you know that the eyes are the window to our soul?"

"No."

"Well, they are and I needed to memorize your eyes so that I could visualize them when I ask the ancient ones for your name. Get comfortable and I will journey."

Wisdom Keeper rose and moved to the center of the small clearing between the cliff and the creek and Sam sat back down and leaned against the log. As she watched, Wisdom Keeper stretched her arms up to the heavens. Her necklace jingled with the movement, a cheerful tinkling sound.

"Great Spirit, Sacred Ones, this is your Wisdom Keeper, and I ask your guidance in discovering the medicine name of this beautiful one, now known as Samantha." She paused taking a deep breath, "As Above energies, I call to you and marry you to the energies of the So Below." As she made this decree, she brought her raised right hand down in front of her left shoulder, across her chest and then down her right side, creating a spiral.

Samantha gasped as she saw a wavy light of some kind follow Wisdom Keeper's movements and then disappear into the earth. She continued to stare as the older woman reversed the process by creating a sun-wise spiral back to the sky as she ordered, "So Below, I marry your energies to the As Above."

Samantha wasn't sure. Was the sunlight playing tricks or was she actually seeing Wisdom Keeper doing some kind of magick? Before she could decide, the woman turned to face across the river and spoke. Then she turned a quarter of a turn to her right and repeated her words and gestures and then again two more times making a complete circle; each time asking the ancestors for assistance. Sam realized she was gawking with her mouth hanging open when Wisdom Keeper glanced her way and chuckled under her breath. Sam tried to regain her composure as the grandmother sank into a cross-legged position and closed her eyes.

After a few moments Sam changed positions causing the sun's rays to hit her squarely in the face, blinding her for a second. Her natural reaction was to squint and... and then she knew she hadn't been imagining anything. With the slightly out-of-focus vision created by narrowing her eyes, she could definitely see what looked like a glowing bubble surrounding around the seated figure. *This had to be her aura.* Sam had read somewhere that every living thing was surrounded by an energy field, but she'd never dreamed she would be able to see such a thing. Wisdom Keeper was deep in meditation and as the minutes ticked by Sam sat mesmerized watching the subtle colors of the field change. First it was a clear sky blue and then for a few seconds parts took on a turquoise hue. A pair of ravens caused a ruckus and drew Sam's attention to the top of the cottonwood and when she looked back several areas of the grandmother's aura had become a light indigo and then changing again, she was surrounded by iridescent, pearly white.

Finally, Wisdom Keeper raised her head, rose and moved to sit on the fallen tree again. She patted the log indicating a spot for Sam. "Samantha, I had a vision and I would like to describe it to you. I believe the story of your name is just as important as the name itself. The story can help you understand who you really are. The ancient ones call this discovering our *magickal mysterious character*. Are you ready?"

"This is going to help me discover a mysterious character?"

"Yes, it's a way to begin. Everyone has an amazing magickal mysterious character inside them. Let me go back a little ways. Before you were born your soul was pure energy. It resembled a big ball of light that shown like the sun." Wisdom Keeper extended her arms out in front of her and using her hands with outstretched curved fingers created an imaginary ball shape about six inches in diameter in the air. Sam could almost see a shimmery white glowing sphere. "This energy was surrounded by the Great Spirit's or God's love day and night. When you were born, you were thrust into a completely different world. Some of it was filled with love, but some was not, and from that initial moment your soul has tried to go back to the light and find that unconditional love. When things happened and you didn't receive the love you thought you should, you wondered if something might be wrong with you and you changed a little to see if that would help. You became like an actor in a play. Over time some people start acting like pussy cats when inside they are really tigers and some act like tigers when they are really pussy cats, and it isn't long before they completely forget who they were originally. They go through life wearing a mask believing that is who they are when it's not truly them at all. Wearing the mask and trying to be someone else all the time is very stressful and even painful. The teachings of my people can help individuals take off their masks and shed a lot of baggage they have been carrying around and find that magickal mysterious character that they once were."

Sam didn't know if she was carrying around a lot of baggage or not, but the idea of finding something magickal and mysterious inside of her was intriguing.

"Okay, I think I understand. I'm ready."

Grandmother laughed. "Well, my dream took place during the Duck's Fly Moon. I know with the beautiful rebirth of spring all around, it may be hard to picture the reds, oranges, and deep burgundies of the changing-time of fall, but I want you to go there if you can."

Sam closed her eyes and then they flew open again.

"There's nothing to fear. Close your eyes now."

Sam relaxed a little. "I can see it. There are lots of leaves on the ground."

"Good. Now, what I saw was the Wind Spirits playing with a large pile of leaves. They created a little tornado whirling the leaves high and then the leaves playfully glided back down... and then they were hurled into space once again. Can you picture that?"

"Yeah, cool."

"Open your eyes."

Sam turned with anticipation.

"At first I thought the name you were given was Playful Autumn Leaf, but then I realized I was missing something. You were not merely a leaf that floated on the wind... you were the wind that sent the leaves soaring. You are Playful Autumn Wind, Samantha."

Sam's eyes became as big as saucers. "That's good, I think. Isn't it?"

"Yes, very good. It means that you are going to become a woman of great power, a leader that others will look to. I was told at the end of my vision that in the years to come, you and I will be spending a great deal of time together. I am to pass on to you the ways of the ancient ones and you are to become Grandmother Wisdom Keeper one day."

Sam sat speechless staring at the old woman's face.

"When a name is given, the receiver always has the opportunity to accept or reject it and its message. If you choose to accept your new name, I want you to face each of the four cardinal directions and announce it to the world."

"How do I do that?" Sam slid off the log, all her nervousness had vanished.

"Face the south."

"Which way..."

Wisdom Keeper pointed in the direction where she had begun calling in the powers. "Now raise your arms and feel your connection to the element of water and to the energies of the south direction. When you have that intent, let me know."

Sam lifted her arms, fingers reaching as if to grab a nearby cloud. Suddenly she felt a gentle motion that caused her to sway slightly, a rocking, like lapping waters on a beach. "Uhhh, okay. I think I got it."

"Repeat after me. Great Mystery, I, known to you as Samantha, accept this new name of Playful Autumn Wind. Awanestica."

Sam repeated the words and then turned, "What's awanestica?"

"It means *I have spoken.* Now turn sun-wise and face the west. Once you have made your connection to the element of earth, repeat the process you have just gone through."

In the west Sam felt a new connectedness to the Earth Mother. There was stability and a centeredness in her physical being that she had never experienced before, like the strongest wind could blow but never topple her off her feet. Aligning with the element of air and the wind of the north brought sensations of flying and she felt she could see what was happening around her from all directions at once. At last she turned to the east and Wisdom Keeper directed her to find alignment with fire. This was the most amazing experience. A warmth, a spark began to grow inside her heart and expand until she thought it would burst right through her chest. She actually looked down at her shirt to see if she was glowing.

When Sam was done, she and Wisdom Keeper together thanked the powers that had helped them find her new name and then Wisdom Keeper raised her arms one last time and announced, "This ceremony is finished in beauty."

Sam made her way back along the creek, feeling that she was in a dream. *Could what Grandmother Wisdom Keeper said be true? Would she be able to ask for medicine names?* The responsibility of a wisdom keeper seemed overwhelming even if it was years in the future.

Where the stream crossed the trail she turned and headed back toward the meadow. She stopped a couple of times, puzzled. It had only been a couple of hours, but there seemed to be many more Jack-in-the-pulpits guarding the pathway. And, the bloodroot flowers she had seen now had tiny leaves appearing on their red-orange stems and

15

more flowers were pushing through the soil reaching for the light. When she thought about it, she actually felt taller herself and she pushed back her shoulders and stood straighter.

As she neared the meadow she paused, seeing a Red-tail hawk deep in the tall grass about twenty paces away. He remained utterly still, but his amber eyes followed her every movement and she wondered if this could possibly be the same bird she had seen in the sky earlier. In passing, she nodded a greeting and was positive her gesture was returned just before the rapture pumped his mighty wings and lifted off. Free from the grass, she could see he carried a small green snake in his talons. She laughed with joy and headed for the cabin.

Chapter 2
Sneaking a Peek

"Well, Grandmother Wisdom Keeper likes her. Let's go watch her play soccer," said Abril, gently twisting a lock of her jet black hair.

"Yeah, I want to go," exclaimed Luna, who was always up for any kind of escapade.

"It's not even going to be a game," complained Dash. "It's only practice, the season hasn't started yet."

"Then don't come with us, you old party pooper," said Tinga. "We don't need you along anyway."

"If you go, make sure you don't cause any trouble." Wisdom Keeper looked up at the quartette sitting on ledges high above the river. "I know what kind of mischief you can get into."

"Yeah, yeah."

"No sass from you Tinga. Samantha doesn't even know you guys exist. I'm counting on you to be good. She'll be able to see you one day, but right now you better stay invisible." Grandmother rose from her log and began walking away down the trail, the deerskin fringe of her dress swinging in time with her hips.

The quartette consisted of two elves and two faeries. The ringleader was Abril. She was a petite figure with silky, milk-chocolate skin and gorgeous, wild, coal black hair. You never saw her without beautiful gold hoop earrings and a golden armband that circled her upper right arm. Standing, she was twenty-eight inches tall and today she was wearing a tight fitting coral top and brown leggings. Her feet were bare. She lounged in the shade of the old cottonwood, knees crossed, and golden iridescent wings gently moving in the breeze. "So it'll just be us girls today. Fine with me."

"I'm ready," said Luna. She was the second faery and Abril's best friend. She was taller than Abril by a whole two inches and her hair consisted of short blond ringlets. Her trademark, if she had one, was her green pointy slippers. Her pale pink wings shimmered in a ray of the sun that had broken through the tiny new leaves that were showing themselves.. Her outfit was a hot pink sweater and green and pink striped leggings.

Tinga was an elf. Her greenish skin sparkled like diamonds even when she was in the shade. Pointy ears poked up through short, curly bright red hair. She had high cheekbones, deep dimples, and almost always a devilish grin. Of the three she was the least fashion conscious and loved wild, mix and match outfits, which drove Luna and Abril crazy.

"Are you going to wear that?" asked Luna.

"What's wrong with what I have on?" Tinga smirked, looking down at her Capri blue jeans and tie-dye t-shirt. "No one is going to see me except you two, if we follow Wisdom Keeper's instructions."

"Maybe I need to go with you," said Dash, "and, keep you in line." Dash's mother had been an elf and his father had been a leprechaun. He looked more like a leprechaun. His favorite thing in the world to do was eat and he could have been a jolly Santa Claus, except he always wore green and he wasn't that jolly at times. A poufy green hat usually covered most of his long white hair, and a fluffy white beard and moustache covered most of his face. He considered himself a father-figure to the girls.

"No, we know you want to stay here," said Luna, sending a message to the other girls to make a quick exit. "See you after while."

They were just leaving the clearing when they saw Gideon. He was a gnome and could have doubled for Yoda in the *Star Wars* movies. His eyes slanted at the corners, and his small mouth and turned up nose were dwarfed by his enormous, pointed ears, which stuck straight out from the sides of his bald head. What you couldn't see was his huge, loving heart.

"Where are you off to," he asked.

"To a soccer game. You don't like soccer, do you?"

"Sure."

"Well, okay, you can come, but let's hurry and lose Dash."

A tree close to the soccer field provided the perfect bandstand.

"I do love soccer," exclaimed Tinga as she wiggled to get comfortable on a branch. "That must be Samantha over there with the long blond hair, number seven. I don't see anyone else that meets the description."

"My gawd, she's beautiful," exclaimed Gideon, getting high enough off the ground to see down on the girls. He stared for several seconds before settling himself in the crotch where a branch met the trunk.

Abril and Luna hovered another minute and then lit on the fat limb next to Tinga.

"I'm not much of a sports fan," yawned Luna, "but I was certainly curious to see this new apprentice of Grandmother's."

"You're right Gideon, she sure is pretty," said Abril, "I bet she is going to drive the boys crazy when she gets older. I remember when I..."

"Cut it, Abril, we don't want to hear about your many exploits today," groaned Tinga.

"Just thought I would entertain you. But, look, they're ready to start."

Sam and nine other girls ran onto the field. One remained behind on the bench. Sam and four of the others had on red shirts and the other half was wearing blue. They all wore tall socks and shin guards. The two groups lined up across from each other. The coach dropped the ball in the middle of the two lines and the race was on. A short Hispanic girl on Sam's team got the ball and easily began maneuvering it through the short grass. She passed to Sam, but a girl with auburn hair and lots of freckles managed to intercept and passed the ball to one of her blue teammates.

"Look at that! The freckled girl took the ball from Samantha," exclaimed Luna.

Abril, Tinga and Gideon gave each other side-long glances.

The blue team headed for the goal, but then one of the red team managed to steal the ball and took it back in the other direction again. After about twenty yards, she used a banana kick to send the ball to Sam who dribbled expertly on toward her own goal. Getting close to the goal, one of the blue team tried to take the ball and fouled her.

"Well, that serves her right. That'll teach her to beat up on Samantha," said Luna. She was off the branch now and hovering.

The referee got the ball and set it up for a free kick. The other girls backed away ten feet and Sam looked for the dark Hispanic girl, but kept her eye on the one with auburn hair. When the whistle blew, the Hispanic girl got the drop and headed down field. Sam was beside her and when another girl got close, she was ready for the pass. The two managed the drive and got the ball close enough for a goal shot, but the goalie managed to block it and the auburn haired girl retrieved the ball and then reversed the direction. With a lead pass, she sent it on to another player and it looked like they might score, but at the last second the goalie for Sam's team grabbed the ball.

"Hey, that girl just plucked the ball out of the air. Is that legal?"

"Yes, its legal, Luna. She's the goalie. You really don't know anything about soccer, do you?" said Tinga.

"Well, no."

"That's obvious, Tinga," exclaimed Gideon. "Come over here and sit down, Luna. You're making me nervous with that hovering."

The game continued for about ten minutes and then the coach called all the girls over to the bench. After a short talk, they lined up again. The one girl who had been on the bench went in as a substitute on Sam's team. She walked with a little bit of a limp and it appeared that one leg might be a little shorter than the other.

When the game started again, the new girl got the ball and push passed to Sam who took it down the field for a ways before sending it over to another one of her teammates. The receiver was making a mad dash, when the girl with the flying auburn hair slipped over and managed to steal the ball. She handed it off to a blue teammate who spun and headed in the opposite direction. They almost scored when the new girl with the slight limp on the red team made a valiant effort to get the ball away and got run over in the process.

"Hey, that blue player ran over that girl with the limp. I don't like that," cried Tinga. "What's her number?"

"Ten. Where are you going, Tinga?"

Tinga did not answer, but jumped out of the tree and headed for the field.

"Oh, geee," said Luna. "I smell trouble."

The next time number ten got the ball, Tinga moved in. The girl looked around feeling someone's closeness, but couldn't see anyone near. The distraction was enough though to cause her to lose the ball.

Tinga laughed and moved off to the sidelines and then turned and waved at the others in the tree.

"Wow, that looks like fun," exclaimed Abril, as she flitted from the tree leaving Luna and Gideon in the branches.

Abril joined Tinga and they watched the girls run up and down.

"Looks like Samantha might be getting a little tired," winked Tinga. "Think she might need some help on the next play?"

"Why not. It's not a real game. And, Samantha deserves to have a goal today. What's the plan?"

In the next minute or so they saw the girl with the auburn hair, which they were now calling Freckles, coming down the sideline with the ball. Sam was right on her tail, but couldn't quite catch up. Tinga slipped onto the field and as Sam passed, she did a little wavy motion around her legs. Within a second, Sam put on a burst of speed and stole the ball and passed it to her teammate with the limp. Freckles stopped dumbfounded, wondering where on earth Sam had come from. The limping girl reversed the drive and took off for the red goal. Abril was right beside her.

When one of the blue team tried to steal the ball away, she suddenly tripped and the handicapped girl continued her drive dodging several other players. Getting close to the goal, she saw Sam to her right and made a perfect pass. Sam caught the ball on the inside of her foot, kicked, and it whizzed right by the unsuspecting blue goalie.

The red team surrounded Sam and the girl who had assisted and cheered.

Abril and Tinga met Luna and Gideon back at the tree.

"Grandmother hadn't better hear about this, Luna," said Abril accusingly. "She'd probably scold us."

"Mums the word," said Luna.

"Boy, she sure is pretty," sighed Gideon.

Chapter 3
Gifts from the Great Mystery

Sam had only known Grandmother since her previous visit to the family cabin in the Missouri Ozarks a couple of weeks ago. At that time it had been too early in the year to go swimming in the lake and Sam hadn't felt like sitting in a boat and fishing with her father and brother. Her brother, Tyler, was eighteen months older than her and she thought he was the most obnoxious person in the world. It didn't matter what she did or said, he made a nasty comment. His favorite was, *you're just stupid*. She couldn't stand to be around him.

That morning her mother had been curled up in a lawn chair reading a novel, so Sam had wandered down the gravel road and found a game trail that she'd never seen before. She'd followed it and as it opened onto a large meadow, Sam had seen a woman with her reddish-brown face turned upward toward the sun. She'd looked like she was praying and Sam had held back not wanting to disturb her, but then the woman had turned and looked directly at her sensing her presence. As the old woman had beckoned, Sam had cautiously approached. Getting closer, any fear Sam had had changed to curiosity. She felt like she'd stepped back in time maybe two-hundred years. The woman had been wearing a rust-colored deerskin dress with wide earth-tone colored stripes of vertical beads that started on one sleeve and found their way across her shoulders and down the other arm. The lower part of the dress had been plain in comparison having only a few long fringes of golden leather that danced at knee length and were anchored by white cowry shells. She'd worn beautifully beaded moccasins, but the object that had mesmerized Sam had been a turquoise necklace with silver feathers that sparkled in the sun.

That night after meeting Wisdom Keeper, Sam had lain in bed wondering how old the woman might be. Sam hadn't seen her grandma in California for several years, but she remembered her mother saying she was now fifty-eight and Granny in Montana was somewhere around sixty-five. She thought Wisdom Keeper might be about the same age as Granny. Lying there Sam had realized she didn't remember much of what was said after their introductions. She'd probably monopolized the conversation again, like her mother was always reminding her not to do. She'd regretted that she hadn't even asked where Wisdom Keeper lived when something strange had happened. Her mind had flashed back to the meadow and the whole scene had replayed in slow motion. She'd seen Wisdom Keeper turn and gaze at her and Sam's skin had prickled a second time as her eyes connected with the old woman's. And, in that instant Sam had known the Grandmother had been waiting for her.

But, when Sam took off to find Wisdom Keeper today, the day after she'd been given her medicine name, all those thoughts were forgotten. Sam left the cabin right after lunch promising her mother that she would be back in plenty of time to help load the Toyota RAV4. It was Sunday and her parents would want to leave the lake to return to Kansas City around 4:00 in the afternoon. That would leave her plenty of time if she could find the grandmother.

"Hey, know what I saw yesterday on my way back to the cabin?"

Wisdom Keeper was down by the river again and had her moccasins off, dangling her feet in the cold stream.

"No, what?"

"There was this huge Red-tail hawk in the tall meadow grass and I just know that before he flew away he actually nodded at me." She twirled on the bank with arms outstretched imitating the hawk's spiraling takeoff.

"Why do you think he would do that?" asked Grandmother.

"Well, I don't know if it was the same bird, but when I was coming to find you yesterday I saw a hawk gliding on a wind current high in the sky and I sent him a wish. I said, *Good hunting, my friend*, and the Red-tail that I saw in the grass had caught a garden snake and had it in his huge claws."

"He was probably thanking you for your prayer."

"Really? You're joking with me."

"I like her, she's got spunk," said Dash.

Gideon sat in the crook of the old Cottonwood tree with Dash not far away on a branch. Luna hovered close by gently flapping her tiny, shiny, pink wings. When the gnome had seen that the McLaughlin's had come to the lake again this weekend, he'd brought his leprechaun friend over to see Sam. For the past week, Gideon had talked about little else. Luna had decided to join them.

"Samantha, when is your birthday?" asked Wisdom Keeper.

"April 15th. It's next week I'll be twelve."

"Hey, a fire sign. I'm compatible with a fire sign. I'm a Sagittarius," said Gideon.

Sam heard a murmuring in the trees and glanced up, but the wind wasn't blowing. She dismissed it as some kind of bird or animal.

Grandmother flashed the gnome a warning look and then turned back to Sam, "Ahhh, I thought so. The Red-tail hawk is your animal totem, your ally."

"What's an animal totem?"

"Have you ever heard of astrology?"

"Yeah, sure, the sun and the moon and planets and stuff. My mom told me that I was an Aries. That's a big sheep."

"The ram, yes. She is absolutely right for astrology that deals with the zodiac. But, my people also work with *Earth Astrology*. It is believed that the Great Mystery gave each of us eight animals at our birth and each one has a different message for us."

"You mean the animals are going to talk to me?"

"This gnome will actually talk to you too," Gideon laughed, but cut it short when he caught Wisdom Keeper's glare.

"I'm gone," said Luna. "You guys are in such big trouble. You know Wisdom Keeper told us to stay out of sight." Her tiny wings went into overdrive and she disappeared in a flash.

Wisdom Keeper cleared her throat and tried to remember what she was saying. "All animals will talk to you if you will listen, just like the hawk did yesterday."

"Wow!"

"Would you like to learn about your allies?"

"Yeah!"

Wisdom Keeper rose and then knelt down and drew a circle in the soft sand and then glanced around. She took a position and sat down cross-legged. "Sam, have you ever heard of a *medicine wheel*?"

"No."

Sam plopped down when the grandmother patted the ground next to her.

"Well, do you remember yesterday when you gave away your name to the four directions?"

Sam nodded up and down.

"This circle that I have drawn is a medicine wheel. It is actually like a map. There is a north and south," she pointed across the circle when she said north and then directly in front of her when she said south. Then she pointed to the left side, "This is west and this is east." She indicated the right side of the wheel when she said east. "My people don't think linearly, ahhh, which means in a straight line, as most in western cultures do, but in circles or cycles." Sam looked very puzzled. "A line is something that has a beginning and an end. We see cycles all around us in nature and believe there is no beginning or end to anything. An example is the seasons. In the spring the days grow longer and warmer bringing the trees to life. Tiny leaves and flowers appear, like right now. In summer, the sun shines its brightest and the flowers on the trees turn to fruits and mature. The fall brings cooler weather and the days grow shorter. It is time to pick the harvest and finally in winter the sun almost disappears and the trees have a time to rest. They loose their leaves and hibernate. It has been a full cycle for the seasons. By spring when the Grandfather Sun shows his face for a longer time, all the plants are rejuvenated and ready to begin the process all over again. Cycles have been going on since the beginning of time. We say *since always and for always*. We believe our lives go around and around in cycles just like nature."

Wisdom Keeper paused and thought for a minute. "But we will talk more about cycles another time. Right now I want to introduce you to your animal guides." With a twig she drew an outline of a hawk that was easily recognizable directly in front of her in the south of the wheel. "Across from your Red-tail in the south, sits your raven in the north. Raven is a bird of magick." Wisdom Keeper drew a bird with a long, slightly rounded bill in that direction. "In the west," she moved to the left of the circle, "is a Thunderbird and to the east on the other side of the wheel is an eagle. The animals in these directions for you are all birds, but everyone has different animals on their wheel."

"I know what an eagle looks like, but not a Thunderbird."

"Well, there are many legends of the Thunderbird. Some say it had wings that were longer than a grown warrior is tall. Feathers on its wings were the length of my arm." She extended her arm and indicated from shoulder to fingertips. "They say this huge raptor was so powerful that it could fly up and touch the sun." Sam's eyes grew wide. "The Grandfathers say that lightning shot from its eyes and when it flapped its wings it created thunder. So, the Thunderbird helped to bring the rains that nourished the earth. It was a friend to the two-leggeds, the humans, and a source of great wisdom."

"And, this bird is my ally in the west?"

"Yes. It is your Clan animal. You belong to the Thunderbird People. The eagle in your east is your Spirit animal and is also very powerful. Eagle flies higher than any bird, well… maybe except the Thunderbird," she chuckled. She moved her drawing stick to the southwest between the Thunderbird and the hawk and began to sketch again. "Your guide in this direction is a Flicker. Do you know what a Flicker is?"

"I'm guessing it's also a bird."

"Right. The Flicker is no legend though. It is a type of woodpecker, but instead of having a red head the way so many do in this area it is speckled black and white with beautiful coral on its tail and wing tips."

"Oh, I've seen one of those. I know I have."

"Good. In the northwest between your raven and Thunderbird is a rattlesnake." Wisdom Keeper made a squiggle in the dirt and then went back and added a heart-shaped head and a rattle tail.

Sam drew back a little and made a face.

"What's the matter?"

"I don't like snakes."

"What a coincidence. You don't like snakes either, Gideon," laughed Dash.

"Ssshhh," warned Gideon. "Luna is right. Grandmother is going to be furious with us. Let's go."

Wisdom Keeper glanced after the pair as they hurried down the trail. They were definitely going to get a talking to. "Uhhh, Sam, you thought it was fine for the Red-tail to have caught the snake yesterday. Why are you upset that a snake is on your wheel? Snakes are vital to the cycles of nature. The snake that your hawk caught had been eating mice in the field and then it sacrificed itself and provided a meal for the hawk. That's another type of cycle that we will talk about in the future. The snake has many great messages for you, especially the rattlesnake. There is a beautiful pattern on the rattlesnake's back, but snake reminds us that not all the patterns that we have established for ourselves are in our best interest. Sometimes they keep us, what I call, *locked in a box of limitations.* Snake can remind you when it is time to change your patterns or habits. The snake can also teach us about timing. The rattlesnake is very patient. He waits until just the right time to strike his prey. If he is too early or too late, he will go hungry. But, let me finish with your animals and then we will talk more about discovering what each totem's message is for you."

Sam watched her sketch an animal in the northeast between her raven and eagle. When she saw the long flat tail and two bucked teeth, she immediately knew what it was.

"Beaver."

"Right, and your southeast animal is the Snow Goose."

This time Sam watched Wisdom Keeper draw several of the birds in a *V* shape.

"Cool. I love to hear them honk-honk as they fly overhead."

"So now we are only missing one animal," said Wisdom Keeper.

"Where would another animal fit? We have animals in all eight of the directions."

"Ahhh, in the center, Wind. It is there that you will place your Power Animal. But, *you* will have to discover who *your* power animal is."

"How do I do that?"

"Well, the animal actually chooses you. You don't choose it. We can find out who it is by doing a *Drumming Down Ceremony.*" Wisdom Keeper nodded toward a small drum and beater that was sitting on the fallen log close to the cliff. "Would you like to do another ceremony?"

"Yeah, sure."

"Okay, get comfortable. Here you can lay on this over in the shade."

Sam spread out a colorful blanket and lay down, looking up at the silvery branches of the old cottonwood above.

"Close your eyes and follow my instructions. I am going to take you on a journey. Listen to my drum. It mimics the sound of Grandmother Earth's heartbeat."

After a little wiggle to avoid a protruding root, Sam lay still. "I'm ready."

"Close your eyes. We are going to travel to one of my favorite places. You will see many animals, but all will be your friends. They may venture out to meet you because they are curious. Trust me that in no way will you be harmed. You must tell me what you see and I will direct you. Do you understand?"

"This sounds cool. Yeah."

Sam began to hear the soft thump-thump-pause, thump-thump-pause of the drum and then Wisdom Keeper's voice.

"Samantha, known as Playful Autumn Wind, I want you to take a deep breath and let it out slowly. Let the earth cradle your body and feel yourself sink into her. In your mind, I want you to see me and take my hand. Not far from here is another old, giant cottonwood tree. It is just down this path. Walk with me."

In her mind, Sam pictured Grandmother holding out her hand and she took it and together they began down a trail lined with yellow daisies and indigo blue Gentian. The drum sounded far away now. They hadn't gone far when Sam saw a huge tree that she knew had to be the one Grandmother was referring to. It was the largest for a long distance.

"Is that the tree, Grandmother?"

"Yes, now notice the hole tucked between the huge roots. It is a tunnel that goes deep into the earth. Can you see it?"

"Yeah, it's right here."

"Do you think you can fit in there? I want you to go inside, kind of like your tale of *Alice in Wonderland*. Do you know that story?"

"Sure. Alice follows a rabbit down a hole."

"Good. Don't be afraid. Go inside and then tell me what you see."

The idea of going headfirst down into the hole made Sam a little nervous, but Grandmother had said that nothing could hurt her. She gathered her courage and told herself that this was just another adventure. She imagined herself crawling on her knees and within seconds she found she could stand inside the hole. "I'm in the desert, Grandmother. It looks like a place I went on my way to California to see my grandmother. It was Arizona, I think. There's a giant cactus with big arms and tall, skinny bushes that look like they have red flames on the tips of their branches. Oh, wow! I can see a bunch of horses and one is walking toward me. It's white with big reddish brown blotches on its flanks. It's right up beside me now and I can actually see myself in his big amazing brown eyes. He has the longest eyelashes I've ever seen."

"Good, Sam. Keep going. The mustang may follow you or he may not. Tell me what you see next."

"There's an eagle soaring high above a tall flat-topped mountain and there are a couple of rabbits and, oh, there's a big yellow and black lizard crawling across the trail. He's really fat and has these horns that come off the back of his head. He kind of looks like he's wearing one of those Viking helmets. He was staring at me, but now he is waddling off. I can see a couple of raven's pecking at something shiny over by one of the big cactus. Now they have stopped and are watching me too. You said raven was my north ally, right?"

"Right. What do you see around the next bend, Sam?"

Sam waved to the ravens and continued down the trail and the terrain changed dramatically. "Well, now I seem to be in a forest of humongous trees. They look like Redwoods or what do you call them, Sequoias, I think. Oh, this is cool. A deer just came out from behind one. It's close enough to touch. It's licking my hand, but now it's jumping and running off into the trees. Oh, my, here comes a bear. Are you sure I don't need to be scared, Grandmother? He's coming right at me."

"No, Sam. The bear is just curious. What color is it?"

"It's kind of a cinnamon color and has a hump on his back. Wow, he just rose up on his hind legs and is sniffing the air. He's enormous, but I guess I'm not afraid. He... he doesn't look mean."

"That's fine. It's time to move on. Where would you like to go next, Wind?"

Sam's attention was drawn to a creek and she began to follow it, marveling at the clear sparkling water that bubbled over rounded stones. Before she realized it, the scenery changed again.

"Grandmother, now I'm walking along a beach. I'm at the ocean. No wait, I'm under the ocean. I can see a whale and some dolphins. There's fish of all colors everywhere. This is absolutely amazing. I can breathe under water. Do you think there are any Mermaids down here? The dolphins are offering me their fins and I'm going for a ride. Wow! They are so fast. Now, I see a huge sea turtle swimming just ahead and I think he wants me to follow him. We're back on the beach now. The bear is here too. I guess he followed me. I don't see the turtle any more, so I'm going to climb up on these rocks. Geee, now I'm up in the mountains. How cool. Actually, I'm in a valley and looking up at snow-covered peaks. I think I just disturbed a moose that is chomping on some bushes. My Dad always said that moose can really be mean, but this guy's not paying much attention. It seems he's more interested in dinner. I'm going to follow this stream and see where it leads. There's ice along the edge, but I'm not cold. Wow, a beaver, Grandmother. He slapped his tail on the water and now his whole family is looking over. One is close to a round lodge and another is on the bank eating some bushes. I can't believe how cool this is."

"You're doing great. Let me know the next time you see an animal."

"There's a path here that leads up the mountain. Oh, he's so cute. It looks like a weasel, but he's all white."

"That's an ermine, Wind."

"He popped up out of a hole in the snow. If I hadn't been looking in that direction, I wouldn't have even seen him. Wow! There's an eagle sitting in that old dead tree over there."

"Eagle is your Spirit Animal, Sam. He's in the east of your wheel. Can you get close enough to look into his eyes?"

Sam crept a little further up the trail and the eagle's head rotated to follow her movement while his body stayed still. The head was as white as the snow and looked like it had been stolen from a completely different bird. "He's gigantic, Grandmother. Geee." Sam's green eyes riveted onto the eagle's golden orbs. "He's talking to me like you said. He just told me that I could look through his eyes any time I wanted. What does that mean? Oh, my gosh, he's flapping his wings to fly. I guess that cinnamon bear is scaring him away. He's still following me."

"I don't think you have to go much further, Sam. Do you see anything else?"

"Yeah, I can see some sheep up above me on a cliff. The horns on one almost make a complete circle. That's neat."

"Wind, I want you to walk a little further on your trail. Around the next bend, you should see the hole that you went down. You've made a complete circle. Do you see it?"

"Yeah, it's right where you said."

"Is the bear still following you?"

Sam glanced behind her. "Uh huh."

"Ask him if he wants to come out with you."

"He's nodding and bobbing his head up and down. I think he's saying *yes*."

"He has a name, Sam. It's only polite to ask his name. I think you will be working with this bear in the future."

"Uhhh, okay. What's your name?"

The huge brown monster jerked back his head showing all his enormous teeth and growled. For a second Sam was petrified and then she looked deep into his gigantic brown eyes and saw only a teddy bear. "Griz," she said. "Okay. That makes sense. So glad to have met you, Griz." She stuck out her hand and the grizzly raised a paw. Sam took hold of a claw that was about the size of her longest finger and shook it. The bear threw back his head and roared again. "Those teeth will take some getting used to," laughed Sam.

"They look kind of scary at first, don't they? Make your way through the hole and come on out. I'm here waiting for you."

Sam heard the last few beats of the drum as she opened her eyes. The sun was staring her straight in the face and she used her hand to shade her eyes from the glare. She glanced around and realized she was still lying on the blanket and the sun had just shifted while she was on her journey.

"Welcome back, Wind."

Sam sat up expecting to see the bear. Wisdom Keeper laughed, reading her thoughts. "So, you have a new friend, a grizzly bear. He is your power animal."

"Well, if he is on my side, I don't have to worry about anyone ever hurting me," laughed Sam.

"Ah, true. Bear is a powerful ally." Wisdom Keeper's eyes sought out the position of the sun. "It is almost time for you to go. I want to give you some instructions before you have to leave."

"Wow! I didn't realize it was so late."

"When you get back home, I want you to find out everything you can about your totems and your power animal. Use that new computer that your dad bought, but make sure you follow his rules."

"Okay. How did you know about the new laptop?"

Wisdom Keeper laughed, ignoring Sam's puzzled look. "Especially look at four things. Are you listening to me? The first one is how and what the animal eats to survive. Like you saw your beaver eating willow branches. And, you already know that a hawk eats mice and snakes. Does your animal chase after its prey or does it hide and wait for it to come along?"

Sam nodded.

"Next I want you to find out who the animal's enemies are and how it defends itself. Some animals may freeze like the rabbit, while others run or take flight. Then look at its family. You'll discover that both the mother and father eagle help to raise their young, while that turtle you saw lays eggs and when they hatch, the young are left alone to fend for themselves."

"Got it."

"One last thing. Where is the animal most comfortable. Does it just fly around the sky and land in a tree once in a while, or is it a bird that likes the earth and has a hard time flying, like a roadrunner. Is it like a deer that can make its home in a meadow and also on a desert? Your beaver is a great swimmer, but comes out of the water to find food. Your snake is never going to fly, but some snakes like water. Find out your animals favorite habitat. Can you remember all that?"

"I will." Sam was already on her feet knowing she was going to have to hurry to get back. "When will I see you again?"

"Oh, Playful Autumn Wind. Maybe I will find you next time."

Note: If you are interested in finding out more about your own animal totems, go to Appendix B. You will also see all of Sam's animal allies on a wheel.

Chapter 4
The Totem Book

During the next week, Sam's anticipation over her Friday night sleep-over birthday party took up most of her free time. She and her three best friends were going to start the evening with pizza and her mom, Kari, was renting two movies for them to watch. And, she had requested her favorite birthday cake, red velvet with cream cheese icing. Sam thought her mom made the best cakes in the world.

Sam's friends had arrived about an hour earlier.

"Open mine first," exclaimed Abriana as she handed Sam a white sack with Happy Birthday written on it in every direction. Sam had met Abriana years before when the girls were still in Brownies. Abriana had sprung up and was taller than the others, but still had a very boyish figure. Her hair was light and she wore it with the sides longer and a wedge in the back.

Sam peeked through the red tissue paper to find a small box. I bet I know what this is," she exclaimed, as she opened it. "Wow, thanks, Abby." The box contained a pair of dangly earrings with purple stones. Sam had just gotten her ears pierced and was starting a collection of earrings. "I love purple. What kind of stone is this?"

"They're real amethysts."

"I love 'em. Thanks so much."

Chloe slid a flat package toward Sam. "Mine next." Chloe had been Sam's best friend since the second grade and lived two houses down the block. They did everything together and their friends said they must be joined at the hip. Chloe envied Sam's long blond hair and was trying to let her auburn hair grow long. The only problem was a natural curl that created silky waves. Chloe hated it. Her mother had told her that someday she was going to love it. She didn't believe her. In the summer when it got hot, the short hairs that grew out around her face formed sweaty little curls and while in the sun you could almost see new freckles pop out on her nose and cheeks. The one thing she did love about herself was her bright blue eyes that her father told her twinkled when she grinned.

Sam could tell the gift was a book by feeling through the paper. She loved books. The paper tore easily revealing the title, *Totem*

Animals. Sam stared at Chloe unbelieving and then back down at the cover. A beautiful silver wolf stared back just beneath the lettering.

"How did you know?" stammered Sam.

"How did I know what?" Chloe asked, puzzled.

"How did you know this is just what I wanted?"

"Well, I didn't. It just kind of jumped off the shelf at me the other night when my mom and I were shopping in Border's Books. Mom tried to get me to buy you something else, but somehow I knew this was the one I wanted."

Goose bumps popped out on Sam's arms as she studied the wolf. He appeared to be smiling at her. "It's perfect. Thank you, Chlo," said Sam slowly as she stroked the furry beast on the cover with her thumb.

"Here's mine." Jennifer pushed another gift bag across the table tearing Sam's attention from the picture. She put the book down, but couldn't shake the feeling that the wolf was still watching her.

Jennifer was Sam's second best friend. She was about Sam's height, but it was obvious that Jen was maturing earlier than the other three. She'd been wearing a bra for quite sometime and was pretty self conscious about her voluptuous, budding figure. She had inherited black hair from her Hispanic parents and wore it in a short wedge that she proudly proclaimed didn't require any attention.

Sam open Jennifer's present and did a little dance. "Great, now I can get some new tunes for my I-Pod. Perfect. Thanks, Jen."

Three hours later, plates with cake crumbs littered the dining room table and the girls were in the middle of the second movie. Jennifer was already snuggled into her sleeping bag on the family room floor and Chloe was yawning. When the hall clock chimed twelve times the TV screen had gone to snow after the last movie and the goal of staying up all night had long been forgotten. Just before Sam had crawled into her own bag, she had tucked her new book under her pillow.

She didn't know what time it was, but sometime in the middle of the night Sam woke to the sound of a soft jingling noise. She turned on a table lamp and saw Wisdom Keeper sitting on the hearth of the fireplace toying with her necklace. "How did you get in here?" Sam looked around. Everyone else was asleep.

"Oh, I have my ways," said Grandmother. "It looks like you got a new book."

Abril and Luna sat perched on the blades of the ceiling fan above. "Hey, isn't that Freckles in that sleeping bag?" asked Abril.

"Sure looks like it and I think that other one is the Hispanic girl that was on Sam's team. Maybe we shouldn't have been so hard on Freckles."

Wisdom Keeper glared at the two and they clamped little hands over their mouths. They had promised to stay invisible and quiet if they were allowed to come along.

"Yeah," said Sam. She pulled the book into her lap and it fell open revealing a glossy color picture of a mountain lion. "Am I dreaming?"

"You'll have to decide that. I like to think that all of life is a dream. Have you looked up any of your animal totems yet?"

"No. Are we going to wake my friends?"

"I don't think so. Why don't you look up your Red-tail hawk?"

Sam glanced at the other sleeping lumps and then checked the index and flipped through the pages. Suddenly a magnificent mottled-brown bird appeared. Its darkish head had a reddish tinge, but the real rusty red was on the tail feathers. Creamy down covered its belly and its legs ended in scaly feet with huge talons that gripped the branch of a tree. A short, hooked beak extended out from between dark amber eyes.

"This one looks just like the one I saw in the meadow."

"What does the book say?"

Sam read for a couple of minutes while Wisdom Keeper rocked back and forth, her knee held in clasped hands.

"Well, Red-tails mate for life and both male and female care for the young. I remember you telling me to find out about family habits. Uhhh, it says they have the keenest eyes of all raptors, that means it's a bird of prey," she said proudly, "and they are protectors and visionaries. The Red-tail is supposed to awaken my visionary power and lead me to my life purpose. Wow. This book says it will teach me how to fly to great heights while still keeping my feet on the ground. That sounds good. It generally stays in one area all its life and doesn't migrate, which it says here, means that it will always be with me as a totem. That's neat. Uhhh, in the wild a Red-tail can live between fourteen and twenty years. It eats rodents, rabbits and snakes. I knew that. The book says that most of the time, while other birds soar until they see their prey and then dive, the Red-tail generally sits on a post or in a tree and waits. I guess he is kind of lazy."

"You might say that he is conserving energy."

"Yeah, that's another way to look at it. Hey, it says the hawk reminds us to be observant and to know when the Universe is sending us signals. That's cool, but, oh wow, this is sad. It says that their main enemies are pollution, particularly from pesticides, and habitat destruction. That means that humans are the Red-tail's greatest enemy."

"You are learning a lot, Wind. Those are all good facts about hawks in general. Native people believe that every direction on the wheel carries a different energy. Among other things, the power of the south is the understanding that we, as sacred humans, have the ability to do anything we choose in life, if we will only step into our circle of power, step into our own essence. My people say that the Red-tail, being one of the highest flying birds, is able to see the big picture, but never miss any details. Since the hawk sits in the south direction for you, when you see him it may be a reminder that you need to be taking your power on some issue or it could mean that you aren't seeing the big picture. For someone else with a birthday between the middle of May and the middle of June, a Gemini, their main animal ally would be a deer and the red hawk would sit in the direction of northeast for them and the hawk's message would be different."

"Jen's birthday is June 1st," said Sam.

"Good. The energy of the northeast direction is how we choreograph our lives."

"What's choreograph?"

"It is kind of how we act in our lives or how we create our lives. Some people are very spontaneous and jump right into things and others have a tendency to hold back and be more shy."

"Okay."

"For Jennifer when she sees a Red-tail, the bird's message may be that she needs to slow down a little and focus more on what she really wants. Be a little less spontaneous. Like you said, the hawk is known for sitting on a fence and waiting until its prey comes along and then attacking. Instead of just jumping right in, Jennifer may need to think more about the consequences of her actions."

"Amazing!"

"What can you find about ravens?"

Sam flipped until she found a black raven. "Ravens may be the most intelligent of all birds. That's interesting. It says they are clever, cunning, fun-loving, smart and witty and love to solve puzzles. They love shiny things and will pick up glistening items and carry them back to their nests. It says that if you are missing a ring or something else shiny and ravens nest nearby, it might be wise to take a look in their nest. They may have stolen it. That's funny. It says they have been known to steal golf balls right in front of a golfer and they love to play in the snow rolling over and over. Ha! They are considered birds of mysticism and magick and are supposed to remind us that we have *magick* or psychic powers and can even shapeshift. What does shapeshift mean?"

"It means they can help you shift your perspective, see from a different point of view, or it might even mean you can shift and become a raven."

"Hmmm. Let's see, some Indians think of raven as a trickster, like the coyote. I heard a story about a coyote one time where he tricked a bunch of people. It was really funny. Pacific Northwest tribes, say that raven stole the sun from a being that wanted to keep the Earth in darkness, so they think he's a hero. Huh, that's interesting. Ravens are scavengers and will eat most anything. They have been known to crack open nuts with a rock and a lot of times they hang around other birds of prey or carnivores and wait for a handout."

"What about their family life and habitat?"

"It says here that they have a *complex social dynamic* and that they sometimes forage for food in large groups and other times by themselves or in pairs. They are found all over the world and live ten to fifteen years in the wild. They are supposed to have interesting courtship rites and then mate for life. That's like the Red-tail. They are very vocal and have a number of different calls and can even copy human speech. Wow! Imagine that. Maybe a raven really will talk to me."

"Wind, your raven sits in the north on your wheel. One of the aspects of the north is our *mind*, how we think. Do you find that sometimes you spend a lot of time in your head analyzing something and then find you have waited too long and missed an opportunity?"

"Yeah, sometimes I just can't quit thinking about something. Is that what you mean?"

"Well, it is good to think things through and not be *too* spontaneous. But, we need to find a balance. If we are in our heads too long and don't listen to our intuition, our inner feeling that is telling us to go ahead and act, then we may find we aren't in the right place at the right time to take advantage of a situation. Being at the right place at the right time is called *catching minimal chance.* When you are playing soccer you don't have time to think, you just have to act and follow your intuition about where to take the ball. If you spent a lot of time thinking, someone is going to steal the ball from you."

"You're sure right about that."

"Well, as you read in your book, ravens are a sign of magick. For most native people *your magick* means your psychic powers, your intuition and your ability to see things that other people may not be able to see. When you are spending too much time in your head, your raven can remind you of the power of your psychic abilities and help you get out of your head to catch minimal chance and find those sparkly things that make your life shine."

"This is great."

"For someone with the astrological sign of Libra, the raven would be their main animal totem, so it would sit in the south of their wheel. Seeing a raven for them might remind them that taking their own power meant they needed to be more resourceful and creative. You remember that ravens are great puzzle solvers. I think you are going to enjoy your new book, Sam. I need to leave and let you get back to sleep. Remember to lock the front door after me."

The grandmother rose from her spot on the hearth and glanced toward the fan before walking toward the hallway. The faeries flitted after her. Sam looked around, amazed to see her friends still fast asleep.

Chapter 5
The Red Road

Sam's 6th grade class had just gotten home from an end-of-the-year field trip to Hannibal, Missouri and even though it was late, she spent an hour recounting the events to her mom and dad.

To help the kids understand more of what they were going to see in Hannibal, her teacher, Mrs. Murphy, had had the class do a book report on *The Adventures of Tom Sawyer* and then they had watched the Disney movie *Tom and Huck* before they left. While in Hannibal, the book had really come to life for the kids. Chloe, Jennifer and Sam had watched as actors in period costume mingled with the crowd in Hannibal's Historic District. Tom, Becky Thatcher, Huck Finn and Indian Joe had acted out familiar scenes.

Becky, dressed in a long pink and white ruffled dress and a pink lacy bonnet, had autographed a brochure for Chloe and just as she'd finished, Tom had come along and pulled Becky's pigtails, and she'd chased after him yelling, "Your going to be sorry, Tom Sawyer."

The acting had been fun and had seemed almost real, but Sam had figured they probably did the pigtail routine a number of times each day. The character Tom had looked very presentable, even barefoot and with holes in his jeans. Chloe had commented that she thought he was cute. Huckleberry had been another animal entirely though. He'd worn a tattered black coat that hung almost to the ground and when he'd slung it open, it was obvious that his disheveled clothing had been made for someone much larger. His pants had been held up with rope and his feet had been muddy.

After the pigtail routine they'd watched as Tom had prepared to paint his Aunt Polly's fence. He'd actually handed Jen his paint brush and tried to coerce her into doing his work for him. She'd gotten into the act and had given the fence a couple of swipes, before everyone got distracted by Indian Joe's arrival. He'd swaggered down the street trying to terrorize the onlookers with a huge rubber knife and had played his part so well that Sam and her friends had sought protection behind a wrought iron fence. As he'd passed them, he'd glared and snarled and then he'd grabbed an older woman tourist and threatened her with his blade. His hair had been stringy and looked dirty and he'd had a long red scar down his cheek. The woman had screamed and he'd shoved her away, laughing and saying that she wasn't worth getting blood on his knife.

From there they'd gotten to ride the three-tiered paddle-wheeler riverboat, the Mark Twain, and had marveled at the mighty Mississippi, which had seemed to stretch for a mile across. On the boat, they'd listened to a marvelous banjo-playing story teller recount more of Tom and Huck's adventures. He'd been telling the one about Tom and Huck in the graveyard and Sam hadn't realized how much she'd been taken into the story until the teller had jumped from his stool, grasped an imaginary knife and plunged it repeatedly into an imaginary Doc. She'd almost screamed and when she'd looked over at Chloe, her face had been flushed under her freckles, her eyes bugging out. A horrible kid named Chad in her class had teased them unmercifully as they'd boarded the bus to go to the actual scene of Indian Joe's demise, McDougal's cave.

The enormous cave had been amazing and a tour guide had explained the difference between stalactites and stalagmites and other formations. He'd said there were over a hundred tunnels that intersected at different points and stretched on for miles. That had been his intro to Tom and Becky's *cave adventure* story. To make his point about how easy it would be to get lost in the cave, he'd turned off all the lights and it had been completely pitch black. Jennifer had just commented that she couldn't see her fingers in front of her face even thought she knew they were only two inches away, when Chad had jumped at Sam out of the darkness. Sam had screamed for real this time and so had nearly everyone else in the room. When the lights had come on, Sam had thought about punching him. Just like Tyler, he always seemed to have fun making her life miserable.

Her story ended and she crawled into bed exhausted and began dreaming almost as soon as her head touched the pillow. She was back in the cave, candle in hand, exploring the myriad of chambers. She walked along amazed by the beautiful formations and made several smoke marks on the walls so that she could retrace her steps, just like she'd heard the guide say Tom had done. Around a bend she found Tom's waterfall and climbed the natural steps along side. For some reason she wanted to find the source of the water. Entering another room, she heard a swooshing sound and felt a slight breeze over her head. It had to be a bat, but surprisingly, she wasn't afraid and instead felt the same excitement that she'd experienced on her quest for her power animal. She wondered about the medicine of the bat and made a mental note to look up bats in her totem book. She squeezed through a tight passage into a chamber filled with numerous curtains of stalactites. A light much brighter than her candle illuminated the drapes, but hey, this was a dream. Intrigued, she made her way through the maze of wavy stone and coming out the other end she found what she had been looking for. It was a large pool of sparkling blue-green water. She bent down and using her cupped hand retrieved a drink and then kicked off her flip flops and drowned her toes in the cool water. Thoroughly enjoying herself, she didn't hear the approach.

"You're going to get lost, scare-dee cat."

She wheeled on the intruder of her dream, "What are you doing here, Chad?"

"I can go anywhere I want. Don't be weird, Samantha."

"Weird. I'm not weird."

"What about all that Indian stuff you're doing?"

"How do you know about that?"

"I just know and it's weird. What do you think that old woman can teach you anyway?"

"Leave me alone."

Suddenly it was dark. Sam felt around on the damp stone trying to locate her candle, but couldn't find it. "Chad? Chad? Are you still here?" There was no answer. She found herself stumbling down a long corridor that split again and again. It was as black as it had been when the guide turned out all the lights. She began to sob and finally sat down on the cold, wet stone unable to contain her fear.

"Samantha. Playful Autumn Wind."

"Grandmother! How did you find me? I'm lost," she wailed. "I can't find the marks I made on the walls."

"I'm with you aways. You're not lost, Wind. Stand up and look around. There are several ways to go."

"Where are you, Wisdom Keeper?" She wiped her eyes trying to see and got to her feet. She realized she was at the junction of several tunnels. She squinted to see down one of the passageways, but beyond the entrance it was dark. She saw Chad waving to her a short distance away down another one. "Come on, Sam. I know the way out of here," he laughed and then began walking away.

"Wait, Chad."

She turned to study the third tunnel. It looked like a road of some kind. In fact it looked like the yellow brick road in the *Wizard of Oz*, but the bricks weren't yellow, they were dark red.

"It's the Red Road of the ancestors, Sam. You'll never be lost if you follow the right path."

"Grandmother, I can't see you. Where are you?" she cried, tears still streaming down her cheeks.

"You have to make a decision as to whether to listen to people like Chad or your own heart."

There was a rustling overhead and she thought the bat had returned. Flapping wings came close to her head and then took off down the tunnel with the bricks. It wasn't the bat, but her Red-tail hawk. She remembered Wisdom Keeper saying that her hawk could help her see the big picture. Her decision was made. She began running after the large raptor.

"Sam, wake up. You're dreaming. You're okay honey. It was just a dream."

She opened her eyes to see her mother sitting on the side of the bed. "I... I was lost in that cave, but it's all right now. I know how to find my way.

Chapter 6
Walking Around the Wheel

School was out and Sam was looking forward to a wonderful summer. She'd played soccer for several years and when her games fell on a Saturday or Sunday and her parents were going to the lake, she'd spent the weekend with Chloe. Most of her games were evenings during the week though. This year she realized the one conflict where the lake was going to win her vote was the 4th of July. No way would she miss the 4th at the Ozarks. And, since she'd met Wisdom Keeper, soccer seemed to be moving to the backseat in her mind. This weekend she really needed to talk to Grandmother.

She'd been hearing her mom and dad argue night after night. The problem seemed to be money. Last Thursday night had been the worst. She'd overheard her dad say that they might have to sell the cabin at the lake. This was inconceivable to Sam. How could they think of selling this place she loved so much? And, now that she'd met Wisdom Keeper...

This morning when she woke in the cabin, she wondered how she was going to find a way to lose her nosy brother and keep him from following her. Sam never planned to introduce Tyler to Grandmother. Grandmother was her secret.

Right after lunch she found her chance. She'd helped her mom make pancakes for breakfast and now it was Ty's turn to help with the dishes. As soon as his hands went into the soapy water, Sam stole quietly out the back door. She raced as fast as she could through the meadow, her blond hair flying out behind. She hopped across the creek and ran down the trail. Rounding the cliff wall, she was disappointed. Wisdom Keeper was nowhere in site.

"Grandmother. Wisdom Keeper. Grandmother," she shouted. After a couple of minutes she plopped down dejectedly on the old log not knowing where else to look. A trail of ants scurrying around carrying small bits of leaves caught her attention. They approached a hole in the ground and suddenly disappeared. They were fascinating. She wondered how on earth the tiny creatures could carry something that looked like it weighed more than they did. She'd have to look in her book to see what messages ants had for people. A few minutes passed and then Sam thought she heard the swishing sound of buckskin. Her spirits lifted as she saw a woman coming up the path. A grizzly bear was right on her heels.

"Grandmother, I didn't think I was going to find you today."

"I'm right here, Wind. You seem to be upset." Wisdom Keeper handed her a bouquet of daisies that she had been gathering.

"Thanks. These are beautiful. Hi, Griz."

The bear's enormous head bobbed up and down in a greeting.

"I thought you might like them, Sam. Daisies always cheer me up."

Sam stuck her nose deep into the flowers and sniffled and then turned her face up to the old woman, tears brimming in her eyes. "My mom and dad have been fighting a lot the last few weeks. In fact Dad didn't even come with us this weekend. He said he had to work and I heard him say the other night that they might have to sell our house down here."

"Ahhh. I see. Their fighting makes you sad."

"Yeah, my dad says money is tight and he needs to work more and mom is unhappy because he has been missing my brother's baseball games and he's never home for dinner. They've been yelling a lot."

Sam's dad, Jack, owned his own alternative energy company. He had converted their Toyota RAV4 to be an electric car. Instead of an engine in the front, it was filled with batteries. Pryor to the Toyota he'd converted a Porsche and there was a lawn mower and several other appliances that ran on batteries or solar energy. They had solar panels on the roof and collected rainwater. Jack's goal was to get them as much off the *grid* as possible in the next few years. Getting off the grid meant they wouldn't have to rely on utility companies for natural gas or electricity. His schedule had been pretty flexible and quite a bit of the time he'd worked from home, but recently he had been working with another company that required his presence at their office, which was causing problems.

Wisdom Keeper sat down on the log and pulled the young girl close. The bear nuzzled her leg and then lay down at her feet. The intimacy opened the flood gates and Sam began to sob, "I'm afraid they might get a divorce."

"Wind, stay in the present and do not worry about the future. No one knows what the future will bring and worrying about what might happen, never helps."

"But, who is right? My dad says he is doing the right thing for our family and mom thinks she is right."

"Well, it is time for another teaching. It is called *Walking Around the Wheel*. Can you listen to me?"

Sam nodded but continued sniffling.

Wisdom Keeper rose and walked over to a big piece of wood that had washed ashore the last time the creek had flooded. Someone had evidently cut down a tree years ago and it had died. The roots were no longer able to hold the soil and the stump had finally let go of the earth and begun a floating journey. In the stump's new home now on this shore instead of the roots being in the ground, they stretched up towards the sky.

"Come and stand here, Samantha." Grandmother indicated a spot about six feet away from the driftwood. The grizzly's eyes followed the grandmother.

Sam laid her flowers on the log and used the bottom of her t-shirt to dry her face.

"Imagine a large circle with that piece of wood in the middle." Grandmother used her arm to sweep a wide arc. "We are now standing in the south of this wheel. What do you see Playful Autumn Wind?"

"A piece of wood."

"Is that all, Wind? Look deep into the spirit of the driftwood."

Sam wrinkled her face and squinted like she had when she'd seen the aura around Wisdom Keeper before. Suddenly she could see it. "Wow! It looks like the head of an elk. Yeah, it's either an elk or a big deer and those are the antlers," she said pointing at the roots.

"You are absolutely right. But, do you know what I see? I see a lazy octopus lying on his back with his tentacles waving above him."

"Where?"

The grandmother knelt down and Sam looked over her shoulder to see exactly where she was pointing. "See, there's his round body, and his tentacles float upward in the sea.

"Yeah," exclaimed Sam, getting into the game.

"Let's see what we will find in the north. They walked so that they were standing opposite of where they had been.

Immediately, Sam said, "I see dolphins like the ones at Sea World."

"Show me."

Sam pointed to swirls that had been left when some of the softer wood had rotted away creating what looked like giant waves. "See, they are jumping out of the surf."

"You are absolutely right, but I see a face. In fact it looks like a friend of mine," she laughed.

"I don't see any face."

"Look there's his nose and his eye is right above. It looks like he is having a bad hair day."

"Yeah, it's blowing in the wind. This is fun." Thoughts of her sadness had completely vanished.

"If you look from the west you will see something else and the east will reveal something different also."

Sam moved to her right and squinted again. "Over here I see a cougar crouching and that piece that goes up is his tail."

"Good, Wind. Now listen carefully. What you saw in the south was absolutely right, but what I saw was also right, for me. It is the same in the north. We were looking at the same piece of driftwood, but we both saw something different and that's because we have different perspectives. A perspective is a point of view and we have different perspectives because we have had different experiences and have lived different lives."

"Okay," Sam pondered.

"Wind, your mom is standing on one side of the wheel and your dad is standing on the other. They are both looking at the same issue, but have different perspectives. Both of them are absolutely right from the place they are standing. But, neither of them can understand what the other is seeing, because they are unwilling to walk around the wheel."

"But, I always thought that if someone was right the other person had to be wrong."

"You can see that is never true. Neither you nor I could see what was in the north while we were still standing in the south. You couldn't see my octopus till I showed you and I couldn't see your dolphins. And, I still can't see your cougar in the west because you haven't shown me exactly what you are seeing. Wind, my teachers and the elders of my people have taught me that one of the steps toward becoming a *balanced two-legged* is to develop *flexibility of mind*, in other words to be able to see another's point of view. This does not mean that the person has to change his or her own opinion, it just means that they honor where the other person is standing. They accept that the other person believes he or she is right. Sometimes this is called *walking in another man's moccasins*.

"So my mom is right and so is my dad?"

"Yes. Your dad believes the only way to solve his money problem is to spend more time working. He believes his willingness to do this is showing his love for you and your mom. Your mom on the other hand either isn't as worried about the money or wants to solve the problem in another way. She feels that your father's absence is showing that he doesn't care about his family any more."

"Wow! They are fighting and it's only because they are on opposite sides of the circle. Do you think I can help them straighten this out?"

"Maybe. Indian people have used what is called a Talking Stick for hundreds and hundreds of years to solve problems and I will teach you how to use one."

"Great. What do I have to do?"

"Dig around in the pile over there and find a stick that really *speaks to your heart*. You may have to ask several sticks if they want to work with you. Find yourself a strong branch and bring it here."

The grizzly rose and followed Sam to the pile. As she began rummaging around, Griz used one of his enormous paws to uncover some debris that had been hidden. With one swipe he rearranged half the pile. When she found the stick she wanted and held it up, the great bear threw back his head and bellowed his approval.

Chapter 7
The Talking Stick

Wisdom Keeper spread out the same colorful blanket that Sam had used for her Drumming Down ceremony and sat down cross-legged at one end.

"I found one." Sam came back with a stick that was about eighteen inches long. It had a good number of knots and the river had washed it for some time before depositing it on shore, leaving it gnarly and mysterious looking."

"This is perfect, Sam. Later you may want to paint or decorate it and make it a permanent medicine item, but remember that if you need to do a Talking Stick on short notice any item will actually do. It could even be a pencil or pen. A Talking Stick's power comes from your intent." She pointed to a hole where a branch had once protruded, "I can see you gluing a big piece of turquoise here or maybe adding a piece of leather or fringe and feathers here," she indicated a place further down.

Sam dropped down on the other end of the blanket and listened intently.

"Talking Sticks are wonderful because they do two things. One, they create respect and promote self-esteem for the individuals involved, and two, they guarantee that a person is understood and not just heard. Do you know what that means?"

"Kind of. I bet you mean that when someone is talking a lot of times we don't really pay attention."

"True. Many times we are thinking of what we are going to say next and don't really hear, or maybe even if we are listening the meaning of what someone is saying is misunderstood. It's kind of like that game you used to play when you were very young where a message is whispered in someone's ear. Then it is whispered to the next person and when it gets to the end of the line, the message is something completely different."

"Yeah, I remember. It was always funny to hear what the last person said. Even though we thought we were listening, the story got all messed up."

"Communication is hard even when we want to understand and it's even more difficult when we are sad or angry and our emotions aren't balanced and get in the way. We have a tendency to hear what we *want to hear* instead of what the other person is really saying. Having a Talking Stick can help."

Grandmother thought for a minute while she lovingly stroked the stick Sam had chosen and then she handed it back to her. She pushed her long, snowy white hair that hung loose today, back off her shoulders. "Long, long ago, there were two chiefs named Hiawatha and Deganwidah and they created a document called Kaianerekowa or the Great Law of Peace. At the time that George Washington and Benjamin Franklin were fighting your Revolutionary War against the British, the Indian people of the Cayuga, Seneca, Onondagas, Oneida, and Mohawk tribes had been living in peace for over seven-hundred years, because they honored and allowed themselves to be governed by the Kaianerekowa. The tribes were known as the League of Five Nations or sometimes the Iroquois Confederacy. By the end of the Revolutionary War after battling for eight years, Benjamin Franklin, who was a great friend to the native peoples, said he wanted some of that peace too. He was very tired of fighting. He got George Washington to send Thomas Paine to work with the Iroquois Confederacy and Thomas created your Declaration of Independence using the Kaianerekowa as a guide."

"Cool. I wonder if my teacher at school knows that."

"I don't know, but here is how it worked for the Indians. All decisions that affected the five nations had to be agreed upon by a Council of Elders and there were representatives from all the tribes on the Council. When they met, they sat in a circle and no one was more important than anyone else. If there was a fight between two people, the disagreement was resolved using a Talking Stick."

"Seven-hundred years of peace. That's a long time, huh?"

"It sure is. There are some basic rules that must be agreed to when two people are going to do a Talking Stick. Are you ready?"

Sam nodded.

"The first one is that the people involved must come to the Talking Stick session with a desire to solve their problem. This is not the time to attack another individual or try to make them feel bad. It is a time for expressing feelings. Because of that, a person must always speak in *I* statements, like *I had my feelings hurt* or *I need to tell you that I think something is unfair.* You can't speak for someone else by saying something like, *Tyler told me this* or *All the kids at school are doing this or that*. It can't be used for tattling on someone. Understand?"

"Yeah."

"Next, a person can only speak when they have the stick. When the other person has the stick, they must sit and listen and they can't make a lot of faces or gestures, either in agreement or disagreement. There are some other rules, but those are the main ones. So, here is how it works. The person asking for the Talking Stick is the one who begins. It helps for the two people to be facing each other like we are doing right now. The first person has the opportunity to say what they want to say. When they are done, the second person *repeats back to them* what they heard. And it has to be done to the first person's satisfaction. If the second person repeats back and it is not what the first person intended, then the first person gets to restate what they said and then the second person has to repeat again. So the second person really needs to be listening. When the first person believes they have been understood, they pass the stick to the second person and then it is their turn. The second person says what they want and now the first person has to do the repeating back to the second person's satisfaction. Have I made myself clear?"

"I think so. Can we practice?"

"All right. What do you want to discuss?"

"Uhhh. You be my brother and I will be me."

"Hummm. I will have to go back quite a few years to try and think like your brother."

"You can do it. Can I go first?"

Grandmother nodded.

"Tyler, you really make me feel bad sometimes..."

"Wait, Sam. *I* statements, remember. Take responsibility for what you say."

"Oh yeah. Uhhh. *Tyler, I really feel bad sometimes when you talk to me the way you do. Lots of times I am just asking a question and you make fun... I mean, I feel that you are making fun of me.* How's that?"

"Very good. Now let's see if I can be Tyler. *Sam, what I heard you say is that what I say makes you feel bad sometimes and that you think I'm making fun of you.* Now, Wind, you have to tell me if you believe I really understood what you said."

53

"Yeah. *You* really understood me, but I can't imagine he would ever say anything like that."

"Well, we can hope. Now it's Tyler's turn to speak. Let's see. *Sam, I don't really want to make you feel bad. I guess I don't have enough patience with you. I hear Mom say the same thing about having patience with me. I guess I need to try and understand that you are younger than me.*"

"Wow! That'll be the day. Do you think he would take the Talking Stick seriously?"

"Amazing things happen when a Talking Stick is used. Remember, seven-hundred years of peace."

"I can't wait to get home and try this. But, I guess I still have to repeat back to Ty. Ahhh, *I heard you say that you are going to try and have more patience with me and that you don't try to make me feel bad.*"

"Perfect. Good luck, Playful Autumn Wind."

While Sam and Grandmother had been role playing, the grizzly had gone back over by the log and fallen asleep, but now that she was leaving he raised his head and stared at her. Sam went over and gave him a bear hug and then waved to Wisdom Keeper and started up the path with her stick.

Chapter 8
The Little People

"Hi, Grandmother. Guess what. When I got back to the cabin yesterday, Dad was there. He said he'd been missing us and came on down. Isn't that great?"

"It sure is."

"Well, because he was in such a good mood, I asked him about doing a Talking Stick."

"Well, how did it go?"

"You know something strange happened while Mom and Dad were talking." Sam gave Wisdom Keeper a suspicious look and laughed. "I'm positive I heard the jingling of your necklace. Were you there? I couldn't see you."

"You make it sound like I can appear and disappear, just like the *little people*."

"Oh, you're fooling with me. I'm talking about *you* and there's no such thing as little people."

Wisdom Keeper raised her eyebrows, glanced up at the overhanging ledges of the cliff above and smiled. Looking back, she said, "Well, then, tell me how your mom and dad are doing."

Sam sat down and continued, "The hard part was figuring a way to tell them how I knew about a Talking Stick. I finally told them I got a book at the library," she laughed.

"Ahhh, you haven't told your mom and dad about me yet?"

"Not yet. I'm not sure they will believe me and I don't know if I will ever tell Tyler about you. I kind of like it just being you and me."

"That is fine."

"Well, I finally got Dad to agree and then Mom said she was willing to do anything to stop the fighting. So, I got this blow-up doll thing that we used to play with in the lake. It has a clown on one side with a smiley face and on the other side the clown is frowning. I put it between them, just like you did with the driftwood."

Wisdom Keeper had been sitting cross-legged on the blanket creating a long strip of beading that looked like the kind on her dresses. Sam watched her fingers, all seeming to do something different at once, and wondered if part of her training would be to learn to bead. It looked very difficult. When Sam paused, Grandmother looked up and then turned to lean back against the fallen log stretching out her legs, her hands relaxed for a moment in her lap. She glanced up to see a hawk catch a thermal and then turned her full attention toward Sam.

"Uhhh," said Sam, "I tried to give them the same lesson that you gave me and I think they got the idea about having different views and understanding that everyone is right. So, then I gave them my Talking Stick and since Dad was the first one to agree to do the stick, I got him to start." As she spoke the last she proudly held up her stick and Wisdom Keeper saw that it was now decorated with beautiful stones and some other items that she couldn't make out.

"Good."

"It was amazing how quickly they caught on. Dad told a story that I had never heard about his father and a time when he had to start school without any new clothes or shoes. He didn't even have a notebook and had to borrow one. I guess they were really poor. He remembered Grandpa, his dad, going away and being gone a long time. He only came home a few times a year, but they did have more money and Grandma always told Dad that Grandpa loved them very much. So, you were right about that. I'm really glad he has more money now."

"Hmmm."

"Mom was almost crying when he was done and had a hard time telling Dad what she had heard, but I know she was really listening. When it was her turn, she told about her childhood when her father had gone off with different women that he worked with. Mom said there were times when he would go on a business trip and say he would be home on Friday night and he wouldn't come home till Sunday or Monday. And, Mom said he never would explain where he'd been. While my grandfather was gone, Mom said Granny cried every night in her room. I never knew him, because he died when I was two years old, and I'm really glad that I never met him. He sounds awful I hate him for making Granny cry."

"Sam, I don't want you to hate this grandfather of yours because of something that you just heard about him. Remember, there is always a different story across the wheel. That doesn't mean that I am defending your grandfather; it's not my place to judge anyone. And, it's hard to get the other view when someone has crossed over and you can't talk to them. So for now just remember that everyone has a different perspective. In the future you will learn to do an *Ancestor*

Speaking ceremony and you will have the opportunity to ask him questions about what he did yourself. Can you wait until then?"

"I'm really going to talk to him?"

"You can if you wish."

"Boy, you sure see things differently. I was feeling all tied up inside just talking about grandpa, but now that is all gone." She paused and stared up at the sun. "Do you think he felt what he was doing was right?"

"I don't know, but at least you are not tied up with hating someone. The bad energy we carry around about someone, even if they are alive, doesn't ever hurt them, it only hurts us. It is good to get rid of it. And, you should think about that when it comes to Tyler. What happened next in your Talking Stick?"

With the mention of her brother's name, she stared at Wisdom Keeper and then thought a minute. It had never occurred to her that Tyler would be right about anything. "Well, it didn't last really long. Dad said he understood Mom's feelings better and promised to work less hours or at least call Mom when he was going to be late. He also said he wouldn't miss any more of Tyler's games, and then Mom said she understood he was only trying to protect our credit, whatever that is. She said she didn't really mind doing some of the chores that Dad usually does around the house and I think *Tyler* is going to have to start mowing the lawn," she laughed. "and I told Mom that I could do more of the laundry to help too. I think it really worked."

"My heart is glad. I know you have to learn your own lessons in life, but when I see your tears my heart aches for you." The grandmother paused for a moment then said, "I see you have dressed your Talking Stick to make it your own. May I see it?"

Sam glanced over to where she had laid the stick, but it wasn't there. She scooted to the left and then to the right and finally got up on her knees and looked where she had been sitting. "It's… it's gone. I know I put it right here." She continued looking around as Grandmother smiled and chuckled to herself.

"Where did it go?" exclaimed Sam completely baffled. "It couldn't just walk away."

"Well, maybe it had some help from those *little people* we were talking about. They have been known to steal things from humans, especially those that don't believe in them."

"What? Don't joke with me. I know it was right here."

"I'm not joking, Wind. They have even taken things from me when I was careless with them."

"Oh, Grandmother. I'm being serious."

"So am I."

Sam stopped her searching and studied the old woman's face. "Wait a minute. You're saying that leprechauns or faeries or something really exist?"

"Oh yes, quite real. My people say that the *little people* were the first to inhabit the Earth. In fact, they were the ones that prepared the Earth for human habitation. They are feisty and love to play tricks on people, especially when people take themselves too seriously; when they have forgotten the value of humor in their lives."

Sam watched Wisdom Keeper intently, sure that there was going to be a punch line. She had seen her dad tell jokes before. He was usually very serious when he started and then he would come out with the punch line and everyone would laugh, realizing they had been fooled. But, Grandmother finished and there was no punch line. Sam finally noticed she was staring up at the cliff face. "What are you looking at?"

"Is that your stick up there on that ledge?" Rays of the sun filtered through branches now heavy with leaves. At first all Sam could see was a couple of ravens that appeared to be talking to each other. They would voice a loud, sharp, kraaak and then seem to chuckle, making a sound like you were clicking your tongue. Suddenly Sam's eyes caught a flash like someone signaling with a mirror. In Girl Scouts they'd practiced how to use something shiny to call for help. The glimmer was coming from an outcropping of rock about twenty feet above her head.

"How could it get up there?"

"Tinga, that's not nice. Come down here with Wind's Talking Stick," called Wisdom Keeper.

Sam stared at the sheer craggy wall and saw nothing except the sparkle of the stones on her stick.

"No, you can't keep it, Tinga. It's Playful Autumn Wind's stick. She's worked hard to make it her own."

Sam continued to stare and finally saw something wavy. It looked like the phenomenon she'd seen last summer on an Arizona highway. The road up ahead had looked like it was shimmering and her mother had said it was actually heat rising from the pavement."

"I don't see anything, Grandmother. What are you looking at?"

"Ahhh, see those ravens. I think they are telling you to get out of your head, Wind and rely on those psychic powers of yours."

"Sam narrowed her eyes to slits and the waviness began to take shape. There was a small figure that appeared to be lying on its stomach, arms hanging loosely over the ledge. Sam couldn't tell if it was male or female. Pointy ears stuck out of red curly hair that was just a little lighter than Chloe's. It was the color of red that her mom would have said was *not natural.* The figure waved at her as it giggled and then tossed Sam's stick to her left. Sam gasped, fearful that it was going to drop. But another hand reached out and grasped it. Drawing her vision back to see the whole wall, Sam noticed two other tiny figures perched in the rocks.

"Okay, I'm seeing things," said Sam standing, but still refusing to believe her eyes.

"Tinga, Luna, Gideon. Come on down here and meet Playful Autumn Wind and bring her stick."

Sam heard a murmuring like wind in the trees and watched as the three figures conversed. She realized the sounds she'd heard before much have been them talking. Two of them finally began the descent down the rocky wall while the third stood, pushed off from her perch and floated like a beautiful butterfly to the ground.

"Sam, this is Luna."

Luna appeared to be the most human looking of the three except for her height and pale pink, iridescent wings. Sam was close to five feet tall and Luna came about to her waist. Watching Sam scrutinize her, Luna performed a little pirouette. She flapped her wings and the movement actually took her off the ground a couple of inches. She had on tight leggings that were very similar to a pair that Sam owned. Her shoes were bright green with long, pointed, turned-up toes. A vest of white feathers covered a vibrant pink top and her hair was short and blond. When she stopped twirling Sam got a look at her eyes. They sparkled like sapphires.

The other two tiny people leapt the last couple of feet onto the beach.

"You three have been up to no good today," said Grandmother with a voice that held scolding, but her eyes danced with laughter.

With closer scrutiny Sam figured that Tinga must be a girl too. From this distance she could see that her skin was the pale green of early spring leaves and shimmered and her eyes were the darker color of summer grass. She had high, prominent cheekbones and looked exactly how Sam had always pictured an elf would look.

"Wind, I want you to meet Tinga and Gideon."

Tinga smiled and did a whimsical curtsy when Wisdom Keeper said her name. "I've already kind of met Samantha. We both like to play soccer."

"How did you know I like to play soccer? You mentioned me playing soccer yesterday too, Grandmother."

"And, I am Gideon," the gnome reluctantly handed her the stick.

Sam looked a little confused, not getting an answer to her soccer question, but she focused her attention on the second little person as she took the stick from his hand.

"Uhhh, thank you."

This one was definitely a boy or man. He could have been the model for Yoda in *Star Wars*. He was shorter than both Luna and Tinga and his wrinkled skin was a dark gray-green color. He wore a white wraparound martial arts gi outfit like Tyler had when he was taking karate classes.

"Well, she deserved it," chuckled Gideon. "She said we didn't exist."

"I guess so," Grandmother laughed, "but I think you have changed her mind."

It didn't appear that she was in any danger and Sam's curiosity began to get the best of her. "What... what... who are you?"

"I'm a faery," said Luna and then pointing, she said, "Tinga is an elf."

"She already knew that, Luna."

"How do you know that, Tinga?"

"I heard her think it. She thinks I look exactly like an elf should look."

"Whatever. Gideon is a gnome."

Sam dropped to the blanket, speechless, which made her almost the same height as the standing little people. Wisdom Keeper sat down on the other end.

"You really made a nice Talking Stick," said Tinga. "I'm sorry I took it. I just wanted to see it up close. Will you tell us about it?"

Sam stared at the stick in her hand, almost like she was wondering where it had come from. It was obvious she was still a little dazed. Luna chuckled, and Sam tried to center her thoughts. "Well, I wanted to add something from every member of my family, even my brother. My dad was throwing away a pair of loafers that had tassels and I got them, unwound 'em, and wrapped the fringe right here and here. Then I added these feathers that my mom had in a jar. She said they were from a Cardinal and a Blue Jay. I used this rainbow yarn from our craft box to hold them on." She turned the stick and continued, "Tyler had a keychain with this silver arrowhead on it from when he was in Cub Scouts and he said he didn't want it anymore, so I attached it with this leather shoelace." Sam was pretty relaxed now and she pointed at a large, multi-faceted, clear quartz crystal. My granny in Montana sent me this and I glued it to the top and wrapped more leather around it to hold it. I just thought these turquoise and red stones were pretty and glued them in these knotholes. That's it."

"It's really neat," said Gideon.

"I bet Wind doesn't realize that her Talking Stick has something from each of the children of Grandmother Earth," said Wisdom Keeper.

"Yeah, you're right," chimed in Luna.

Sam pulled her eyebrows together, "The Earth has *children*?"

"Well, Sam, when the Great Mystery created our world, we say that her children were born. We consider the rocks, stones and crystals to be one of her children and you have turquoise, coral, and the silver arrowhead. Those are minerals. The second child was the plants, the grasses, herbs, fruits, flowers and the trees. The stick itself represents those children."

"I can see that."

"Next came the sacred animals, the swimmers, crawlers, four-leggeds, winged ones, and even the mythological animals, like the unicorn. You have leather and feathers, to represent them."

"Unicorns?"

61

Wisdom Keeper ignored her, "Last are the sacred humans and when …"

"Let me guess. When I hold the stick, I represent the humans," beamed Sam.

"You're right, Grandmother," said Luna, "She is a quick learner."

"And, very pretty too," crooned Gideon.

Note: If you would like more information on how to make a Talking Stick, see Appendix C.

Chapter 9
Seeing is Believing

Sunday afternoon they'd packed up her mom's van and the RAV4 and headed back to Kansas City. Sam had gone to bed around 9:30, but now all of a sudden she was wide awake. She'd been dreaming about little people, but the dream was already fading. It was still dark outside. She looked over at her alarm clock. The numbers flashed, indicating 2:00 AM. She lay there recounting the events of the previous afternoon. Had she really seen *little people*? Could a bear really be her friend?

"Wind. Samantha."

"Wisdom Keeper?"

"Yes, Sam. I'm right over here. Turn on your lamp."

Sam fumbled for the light on her nightstand and found the switch. The old woman was sitting at her desk. Just like the night of her birthday party, somehow Grandmother just appeared.

"You were dreaming, Wind."

"Yeah, but how did you know?"

"Well, I've had many winters to become wise. I just know these things."

Sam looked doubtful, but dismissed it. "I was wondering if I had been dreaming yesterday afternoon too."

"Ahhh, you don't believe your own eyes."

"Well, it's just that everything I've been told indicates that little people can't possibly exist. It's kind of like believing in Santa Claus, the Easter Bunny or the Tooth Faery... or ghosts."

Wisdom Keeper raised her eyebrows. "You mean to tell me you don't believe in Santa Clause?"

"Grandmother. I'm twelve years old. I haven't believed in Santa Claus since I was five."

"I don't think age has anything to do with it. Let me think..." She took hold of her necklace and played with the silver feathers for a minute. "Your scientists today are just discovering what ancient peoples have known for millennia. They call it the science of quantum physics. Have you heard of quantum physics?"

"Yeah, my dad was watching something about it on the Science Channel one time and Chloe's brother says he is going to study it in college."

"Good. I know it sounds very strange, but your science of quantum physics says that all material things around you, your dresser," she pointed across the room, "your desk, the bed you are laying on, are not really real until you focus on them. It takes your conscious mind focusing on something to make it real."

"You've lost me," said Sam. "How can this bed not be real?"

"There is a story about Columbus' voyage to what he called the New World. He came as part of three ships."

"Yeah, the Niña, Piñata, and Santa Maria," chimed in Chloe. "We learned that in school."

"Well, when Columbus arrived, the native shaman saw waves coming to shore like he'd never seen before. For a long time he studied the horizon and was finally able to make out the ships. At first they just looked like that wavy energy you think looks like heat coming off the pavement," she winked.

"I don't remember saying…"

"Ahhh, well, he pointed them out to the people, but they couldn't see them. After he described them several times, they were finally able to see."

"How could they not see them?"

"Because they had never seen anything like them before and had no *frame of reference*. Your mind can only see *what it has been told it can see*. The reason you know that you are sitting on a bed is because when you were very little, your mother and father told you that it was a bed. Your quantum physics says that *the material world around you is not real until you make it real*. Atoms, which you have been taught in school make up everything, are not really *matter*, solid things. They are only *tendencies and possibilities of consciousness*. I know that is hard to understand, but we actually create our own reality with our thoughts, words and emotions."

"So, you're telling me that the only reason I could see Tinga, Luna and Gideon yesterday was because you told me they existed?"

"I helped you create a frame of reference. When you were a child your parents told you about Santa Claus and they very much wanted you to believe, so you did. Then as you grew up you saw a

Santa at the mall with a fake beard and your science teacher at school talked about the Earth and how big it was, and you began doubting whether one man and a bunch of reindeer could really travel all over the globe in one night. You finally asked your mom and dad and they admitted that they had made it up, because they just wanted you to learn about the spirit of giving to others. You quit believing."

"Well, Santa Claus, really…"

Wisdom Keeper could tell that Sam still didn't believe.

"This is what happens to so many young people in your Western society. When they are small they can see all the entities in the Universe. Many lonely young children will conjure a friend, someone they can talk to. The friend has a name and the child has no problem seeing and talking to them."

"You mean like Tinga or Luna?"

"It could be, but it doesn't have to be a faery or gnome. It could be someone like me. But, then one day the child overhears their mom or dad talking about Billy's or Susie's *imaginary* friend. Billy or Susie see their parents laughing and believe *they* are being laughed at. Sometimes parents take it so seriously they actually sit the child down and tell him or her that the friend does not exist and that it isn't healthy for them to continue their behavior. More than anything the child wants love and approval from his or her parents, so over time they give up their friend. Do you remember when we talked about becoming an actor in a play? They become someone that can't see the friend and they grow up believing that the friend never existed."

"But they really did?"

"Yes. Animals can see entities too. I once had a lot of fun watching a kitten the first time he saw one of the little people. I was at a friend's house and was giving a group teaching. My friend had a little six-week old kitten and while we were talking the kitten scampered into the room. I had seen Dogan sitting underneath a chair, but no one else had. I don't think you've met Dogan yet, but you will. Dogan is a troll."

"Trolls exist too?"

Wisdom Keeper nodded, "When the kitten walked by, Dogan reached out to grab him and the kitten jumped back. Everyone saw the kitten jump and they wondered what was going on. The kitten crept closer to Dogan again and he made a scary face this time and the kitten jumped again. Soon everyone was straining to see what the kitten was seeing. They thought at first it was a bug. But there was no bug under the chair. When I told them that a troll was sitting under the chair, they didn't believe me, but after a while they could begin to see a wavy energy. Finally they were all able to see Dogan. But, the kitten had seen Dogan from the beginning, because no one had ever told him that little people didn't exist."

"I bet that was funny."

"It was. My mother never told me that told me what I was seeing as a child wasn't real, so I grew up believing. Sam, when I did your naming ceremony, what did you see?"

"Ahhh, well, I saw... I saw a white light that you pulled out of the sky. You moved it with your hand and it went into the Earth. I think that is what I saw anyway. And, I think I saw your aura too."

"You did see it. I thought so. You have great gifts, Sam. You are like the shaman in the Columbus story. You have the ability to see things others cannot until they are trained. We call this training *remembering what you already know*, because like I said, everyone had these abilities at their birth. When you show and tell others what you see, they will be able to see also. People see based on their frame of reference, and the entities of the Universe will appear to them based on their belief system."

"What do you mean by that?"

"Well, some people might not be able to see faeries and elves, but they can see angels."

"Angels?"

"Absolutely. What do you see over by the door?"

Sam squinted and suddenly saw a beautiful figure in a flowing white gown. She had golden, wavy hair and large silvery wings. She smiled and waved.

"Is that an angel?" Sam glanced back at the figure, but his time saw Luna standing there. "Where did the angel go?"

"She didn't go anywhere, Wind. She appeared to you as an angel because you were thinking about angels. Someone with a strong Christian background will always see angels, if they believe they can. With your frame of reference, you are probably always going to see Luna or Tinga."

Chapter 10
Independence Day

This year the 4th of July fell on a Friday creating a three-day Independence Day holiday, so Sam and her family took off for the cabin on Thursday evening as soon as her dad got home from work. Tyler brought two of his friends, Josh and Matt, and Sam asked Chloe to come along.

The boys got up early on Friday to ride the Jet Ski in the calm water before the rest of the world was out boating and skiing. Sam's dad was doing what her mom called *futzing* with the Evinrude motor of the ski boat. As Sam washed the breakfast dishes, she looked out the kitchen window. She saw Josh ride the Jet Ski up beside the dock and cut the engine. After buckling his lifejacket Matt did a cannonball into the water and swam over for his turn. Sam was swishing suds over another plate when she saw movement in the big oak tree that stood over the dock's catwalk. She blinked twice and then realized she was seeing Gideon, Luna, and Tinga. Gideon seemed fascinated watching her father and Luna and Tinga were laughing and pointing at the boys.

"What's up?" asked Chloe as she dried a glass, "Looks like you just saw a ghost."

"No, no. I uhhh, I thought Matt was going to hit his head on the dock. I guess he's okay."

Chloe leaned over and looked out the window. Matt had turned the ski to head out of the cove and was pulling himself up by the handlebars as he accelerated. "He looks fine. Since when do you care what Matt does? He and Tyler pick on you all the time."

"I don't." Sam tossed the last of the silverware into the dish drainer. "Let's go swimming."

Sam grabbed a towel and walked out onto the large stone front porch while Chloe ran upstairs to find her suntan lotion. The screen door banged behind Sam and Tinga turned and waved. The branch she was sitting on bounced up and down. Her bright red hair really stood out among the branches of green leaves. Sam glanced around carefully to see if anyone was watching and then she gave a little wave back. The door banged again as Chloe came out and at the same moment Gideon and Luna yelled, "Hi, Playful Autumn Wind."

Sam waited for Chloe's reaction, but there was none.

"Come on. I thought you were going down to the dock," said Chloe.

"I am."

They walked down the winding concrete path directly under the tree. Sam glanced up to see smiling faces. "Are you going to ride that Jet Ski, Sam?" asked Tinga. "It looks like it would be as much fun as Luna's flying."

Sam froze on the path and Chloe ran into her back. "What are you doing? You're acting so strange."

"I thought I heard something. Did you hear something? Maybe Mom was calling me."

"Couldn't have been." Sam's dad looked up from where he was sitting in the rear of the boat. "Your mom went into town to grab a few things at the grocery store."

"Oh, yeah." Sam kept going, but looked over her shoulder. Her fan club continued chattering away. *How was it possible that her dad and Chloe didn't hear the little people, couldn't see them? It was like the natives not being able to see the ships.* The three continued laughing, getting a big kick out of Sam's nervousness.

The girls chose the west side of the u-shaped dock, leaving the east for the boys. Chloe tossed an air mattress into the water and jumped in trying to land on top of it before it floated away. With one more glance at the tree, Sam followed. She squinted over at the oak several times in the next hour, but didn't see anything. If the little people were gone, she hoped she hadn't offended them. No telling what they might decide to steal this time.

Late in the afternoon, Sam's dad got out the bottle rockets and Tyler set up the launch pad, which consisted of a number of short pipe pieces stuck in the ground a couple of inches and then leaned against the rock seawall facing out into the cove. For the next couple of hours the guys had a great time setting off the series. "Launch one, launch two! Thar' she blows! Cowabunga! Look that one went off under water." A couple of gross later, they were ready for roman candles, fountains, flying repeaters, and aerial avalanches, and Sam's dad moved in to supervise.

After dark Sam's mom, Kari, and Chloe setup chase lounge chairs on the dock and reclined to watch the sky. Sam sat in the boat and honked the horn in judgment of each display. Her rating system was two blasts for *pretty good*, three for *really cool* and four for *absolutely fantastic*. She was saving her highest award, five blasts, for the finale, a Screamin' Meemie.

Right after a three blast parachute launch, Sam noticed her friends were back. One minute the hammock was empty and the next there were four tiny people leaning back, arms folded under their heads. The hammock was strung between two posts that supported the cover over the well of the dock where the boat was tied. Luckily it was opposite the side where Sam's mom and Chloe were lounging.

"Hey, Sam. Can you give us a push?" asked Gideon.

Sam shook her head *no* and then glanced over her shoulder at her mom.

"Oh, come on."

"No," whispered Sam, timing her response with a burst of pops and booms. All she could really see of the gnome was two yellowish eyes and his two huge ears sticking out from the sides of his head.

"Well, you're no fun, but these fireworks are great," said Tinga. "Oh, by the way, this is Abril. She's a friend of Luna's. She likes to play soccer too."

Soccer? She wanted to ask what all the talk about soccer was, but of course, she couldn't in this company. Sam could see a silhouette of a petite figure with long flowing hair. Abril evidently had wings like Luna, and Sam marveled at the way they sparkled every time embers fell from the sky. During the next blast, Sam did a small wave using just her hand and wrist and murmured, "Hi, Abril."

When the Screamin' Meemie finale had died down, the four visitors tipped the hammock to scoot out. It bounced wildly behind them. About half way up the walk Gideon called back down, "Hey, Sam, are you coming to the river tomorrow? We're having a birthday party for Wisdom Keeper. It sure would be great if you could come."

Her mom was just getting up and Sam caught her staring quizzically at the swinging hammock. Sam hit the horn twice and hoped Gideon would take that as a *yes*. Kari said nothing and headed up the winding path. When she got close to the four little people, they parted to let her pass and then waved a final goodbye.

Lying in bed Sam whispered, "Chlo, Can you keep a secret?"

"Yeah, sure."

"Okay, we're going to a party tomorrow."

Chloe fell asleep immediately after all the day's fun, but Sam lay awake wondering what she could possibly give to Wisdom Keeper for a present. It had to be special. Just before midnight Sam slipped out of bed and crept downstairs to the kitchen. She found just what she was looking for in a bottom drawer, a tub of Plaster of Paris that had been there for years. The last time she'd made something like this was probably when she was in kindergarten, but somehow it seemed appropriate. There was a metal pie plate under the sink and food coloring in the cabinet with the cake mixes. Sam read the plaster directions, measured the water, and added drops of red and brown until the mixture was the same color as her mom's flower pots. She poured her concoction into the pie plate and went to look for some paints. By the time she got back, the plaster had set enough for Sam to create her masterpiece. She spread her fingers out as wide as she could and pressed her palm into the middle of the plate. In the morning it should be dry enough to paint. After wiping up the counter tops, she tiptoed upstairs with her present and hid it under the bed.

Chapter 11
The Birthday Party

Mornings were always interesting at the cabin. Formally, the house only had two bedrooms. One was Sam's parents and the second contained two sets of bunk beds and a double bed. Since Ty had brought two friends, they had claimed the second bedroom and Sam and Chloe had been relegated to what was affectionately called Grand Central Station. It was a very wide hallway on the back of the house that led to the bathroom. It also contained a set of bunk beds and several chairs. The cabin only had one bathroom and to alleviate a little chaos, especially in the mornings, they had a take-a-number contraption just like the one Sam's mother said they had at the pick-up counter at JC Penney's when she was a girl. The bathroom was first-come, first-served and some weekends lower numbers were actually bought and sold out of desperation.

"What are you doing in there Sam," yelled Tyler, as he banged on the door, "washing your hair? You've been in there for an hour."

"Oh, I have not. It's been two minutes."

The bath had a shower and tub, but Sam could never figure out why. Her mom wouldn't let anyone use it. The cabin was on a septic tank and with the number of people that came to the lake, she was afraid it would get stopped up. It didn't much matter since during the summer everyone was in the water most of the time anyway and anyone wanting to wash their hair took the bar of floating Ivory soap, sat on an air mattress and shampooed away.

When Sam opened the door, Grand Central Station looked like a doctor's office waiting room. Even her dad sat holding a number. Sam flitted through the room and stuck her tongue out at her brother. "Mornin' Dad." Her nose told her bacon was cooking and she followed the aroma down the stairs. Chloe was setting the table. "That smells wonderful, Mom. Do you need Chloe and me to do anything special today?"

"I don't guess so," she smiled.

"Cool. Well," she glanced at Chloe, "I thought Chloe and I would take a hike."

"It's going to be hot. Better take some water."

"Okay."

Within an hour Ty and his friends were out water skiing with Sam's dad and her mom was reading a magazine in the shade of the umbrella on the dock.

"Come on. I gotta' finish something," said Sam. She raced upstairs and fished her terracotta plate out from under her bed.

"What's that?" Chloe reached out and touched the outline of Sam's fingers.

"It's a present for someone, but it's not finished yet. I've got to paint something on it."

Sam produced the acrylic paints and began using a small brush to create a circle of bright yellow in the middle of her palm print. As she came around to where the circle began, she went just inside and continued another circle and then another, and another."

"Looks like some kind of symbol."

"It's a spiral and in Indian it means *infinity*, going on forever and ever." She touched up the edges and then wrote the word *love* across the top of her fingers and *you* below her hand.

"Love you forever? Who are you going to love forever?" asked Chloe.

"You'll see."

"Where are we going? You're acting strange again." said Chloe as they began to cross the meadow.

"It's a secret. You promised you could keep a secret, right?"

"Yeah," said Chloe rather insulted.

Sam had her gift in her backpack along with two bottles of water and she led the way. She picked up her skirt and stepped gingerly around a thorn bush to keep it from snagging. She had on a flowered, tiered skirt and purple t-shirt. She'd wanted to look special for the party. She noticed movement and saw two hawks soaring above. The grass had grown so much since spring that it waved and rippled, looking almost like golden ocean waves now. The Moon of Strong Sun had matured the grasses and their tops carried the seeds that guaranteed another bountiful year. The bloodroot and jack-in-the-pulpit flowers that Sam had seen a couple of months ago had been replaced with daisies, sunflowers and tall purple thistles.

They jumped the creek, which was barely a trickle this time of year and took the cliff trail around toward the river. Sam now claimed this as her special place. Rounding the bend, she stopped dead in her tracks. She'd had no expectations about the party and this was amazing. The grandmother sat on her blanket and was surrounded by little people and animals. The first thing Sam saw was Griz. His eyes twinkled when he saw her and he let out a growly-roar.

"Hi, Griz."

Gideon waved and flashed a huge smile, "There she is."

Chloe grabbed her arm, eyes riveted on the bear.

Sam focused on Gideon and realized he had been petting or talking with a red fox. Standing within a few feet of him was a white-tail buck with antlers still in velvet, bent over nuzzling a rabbit. Luna called down from a perch on the cliff and Sam saw that she sat beside a Red-tailed hawk. The raptor nodded a greeting as it had in the meadow. Another faery on the other side of the hawk was evidently Abril, Sam's fourth guest for the fireworks. Sam hadn't been able to get a good look at her in the dark and now saw that she was beautiful. Her long black hair fluttered in the breeze. A bright yellow tube top was a great contrast to her dark chocolaty skin. She appeared to be about the same size and age as Luna. Tinga was brushing and braiding Wisdom Keeper's long white hair and she called, "The party's already started, Sam. Where have you been?"

Suddenly Gideon appeared by Sam's side and took her hand. Looking up into her sea-green eyes, he said, "You sure look beautiful today, Wind. That's a very pretty skirt."

"Thank you, Gideon. You look nice too." He had on a red tunic today and looked like he had also dressed up for the occasion.

"Who's your friend, Wind?" asked Grandmother looking over.

"Uhhh, oh, sorry. Grandmother, all of you guys, this is Chloe."

There were five or six other small people sitting or playing in the clearing. A fellow that looked like a troll doll extended his hand and in a deep voice said, "Hi, my name is Dogan." He wore an animal skin as clothing and his dark, frizzy hair stuck out in all directions.

Without thinking, Sam extended her hand to shake his and Chloe's fingernails dug into her arm.

"Ouch."

Sam turned to see Chloe's eyes as big as saucers. Well, that answered one question that Sam had had yesterday. Her friends *were* real, but Chloe just hadn't had the right *frame of reference*, as Grandmother called it.

"Come on, Chlo," said Sam trying to pry loose the nails that were promising to draw blood any minute. "I want you to meet my friends."

An older elf-like person jumped up and held his hand out to Chloe, "I'm Dash. Join the party." Dash had a white beard and moustache and wore a green striped shirt. His eyes laughed and it was obvious that he was thoroughly enjoying himself. Tight lavender leggings covered his short, stocky legs and on his feet were purple shoes. His belly hung over a brown belt and jiggled like Jell-O.

Chloe still held back and even inched around behind Sam refusing to shake Dash's hand.

Wisdom Keeper held out her arms, "There's nothing to be afraid of Chloe. Come here Playful Autumn Wind and give me a birthday hug. I'm celebrating my sixty-sixth year today."

Sam went forward, "This is amazing."

"Unbelievable," mumbled Chloe, still almost attached to Sam's side, her wide eyes taking in everything around her.

After receiving her hug, Wisdom Keeper patted the blanket next to hers and gestured for Sam and Chloe to sit. Hesitantly, Chloe came forward as she watched an enormous bald eagle land in the huge trees that hung over the river.

"I thought *my* birthday party was great, but it has nothing on this one." Sam slipped off the straps of her backpack and fished inside. "Here, Grandmother, I brought you a present."

"Oh, this is beautiful, Wind. Did you make it?"

"Yeah, I used the infinity sign. See? It was hard to come up with something on such short notice."

"Wow, that's better than my present," pouted Dogan.

Wisdom Keeper added the plate to a number of other things on the blanket in front of her. There were several feathers, a crystal, a nugget of turquoise, a bouquet of sunflowers, a bowl of raspberries, a woven leather bracelet, and a few other things.

"Dogan, I love your gift of tobacco. I'm going to use it in my sacred *chanunpa*, my pipe, while I say prayers for all of you."

Chloe watched Tinga put the last touches on Grandmother's long braid and then she tucked a daisy behind her ear. "How did you...

how… where did you meet all these people… and animals?" whispered Chloe, eyeing Griz again.

Before Sam could answer a black shadow crossed overhead and they heard raucous cries. Everyone turned to see a raven land near the river. He proudly waddled between the other guests and deposited a shiny silver dime on Wisdom Keeper's blanket.

"Oh, *wadoh*, Raven. Thank you so much. I am glad you could come help me celebrate."

"Ya always have to make an entrance, don't ya, Raven," said Dash.

Raven cocked his head, beady eyes sparkling, and made it a point to ignore Dash. "Hi, Sam," he said and then lifted off and flew to the cottonwood, where he and the eagle exchanged nods.

"Ppsssttt. Did that bird just talk to you?" murmured Chloe, astonished.

Sam shrugged and then giggled.

"Let me answer," said Wisdom Keeper. "I have known since before Samantha was born that she would one day find me. She is becoming a young woman now and learning to take her own power. I am going to help her find the magickal mysterious character that is deep inside of her and I believe that one day she will take my place as the Wisdom Keeper. But, of course that is many winters away."

"This is just plain weird," replied Chloe eying everyone around her. Then she glanced at Wisdom Keeper fearing that she might have hurt her feelings.

Grandmother smiled. "Wind is learning many of the ways of my people. In our ways, it won't be long before her body and yours too, Chloe, flower with the first signs that you are becoming women. Young men also experience signs and this is a time to celebrate. In the old days, it was the first time a young man would be allowed to go with the rest of the men on a buffalo hunt and one of his Clan Uncles would monitor him on his first vision quest. Rites of passage are very important and the beginning of some very important teachings. When the time is right, I hope that Sam will enter into her Becoming Woman ceremony with pride."

Chloe was taking it all in and thought she understood what the grandmother was implying. But, it was hard for her to imagine wanting to celebrate something like that.

With a sweeping hand, Wisdom Keeper indicated everyone in the gathering, "The little people and many of the animals around here have agreed to help me with Sam's teachings. They have great wisdom. Anyone can see and hear the messages they have if they will just listen."

Chloe thought for a minute, then said, "Do I have a magickal mysterious character inside of me?"

"Of course, we all do."

Chapter 12
The Crystal Dig

"Let's go over the list again," said Kari. "You've got bug spray, right and suntan lotion? How about your rain poncho and hiking boots?"

"It's not going to rain, Mom, but, *yes*, I put it in."

"I know, I know, but it's on the list. I wish I was going with you. This sounds like so much fun."

Kari was petite, barely 5'2" tall, but had a strength that Sam didn't really appreciate yet. She had a master's degree in social work and had worked her way up to vice-president of a non-profit company called JCCFC, Johnson County Cares for Families and Children. The organization handled a number of situations concerning the children of Johnson County, Kansas.

It was Wednesday night and eight members of Sam's Girl Scout troop were leaving in the morning to go on a *crystal dig* near Hot Springs, Arkansas. Sam had never heard of digging crystals when the troop first talked about going, so she got onto the Internet and did some research. According to geologists Arkansas and Brazil have the best quality quartz crystals in the world. When Sam saw a picture of a crystal wand she couldn't believe it had come directly out of the earth. It was a perfectly shaped, six-sided prism terminating with six small triangles on one end that formed a pyramid shape and it was so clear you could see right through it. Apparently, there were numerous crystal mines near the Ouachita River, where Sam's troop was staying. Each girl would pay a small amount and be able to dig for her own crystals. The web site said that Sam could easily find small crystal points, finger-sized wands, and some crystals could even be larger.

The six-hour trip went fast with the girls playing their Game Boys and listening to their I-Pods, but they were definitely ready to get outside and run and play by the time they got to the resort. They fell in love with their cabin immediately. It rested on top of a large hill that overlooked the river. After claiming beds and unloading the van, they took off to explore.

The lazy river was about forty yards across in front of the resort and the owners had mowed the grass and manicured a length of about three football fields along the shore. Huge trees with picnic tables beneath were scattered along the way. There was one huge area with a single old oak tree right in the middle. A hundred yards up the river an old sycamore hung over the river and some kids were already there using a rope and old tire to swing out over a calm eddy and drop into the cool water. Sam and her friends ran to change into swimsuits and joined them. After several hours of the fun, they were exhausted and made their way back to the cabin. Mike, Jennifer's dad, had built a fire in a large ring of stones and the girls roasted hotdogs for dinner.

The owner of the resort, simply called Ol' Tom, stopped by bringing hand drums and gourd rattles just as the sun was setting and soon Sam, Chloe, Jennifer and the others were fascinated by his stories of the Indians who used to live in the area. Tom was old. Sam figured about the same age as Grandmother Wisdom Keeper. He told them he was half Cherokee and half Irish and had lived in the area all his life. His hair was long and pulled back and he wore denim overalls without a shirt, and beaded moccasins. Around his neck was a four-strand choker of long white bone tubes separated by turquoise beads. Suspended in the very center was a large claw of some kind.

As the fire flickered, Tom's eyes glistened and he settled on a stump to tell his tales. An owl hoot-hoot-hoooed somewhere in the distance and was answered by another close by. "For thousands of years, this magnificent site was the gathering place of many nations. Tribal leaders and spiritual elders made pilgrimages to the *Great Manataka Mountain* to sit in council with other tribes and to heal themselves in the medicinal waters of the springs. Manataka means *Place of Peace* and this area was decreed sacred by the Great Mystery. When people entered, they prayed and made peace offerings to the Creator, the mountain, and to each other. Gifts were given to the caretakers of the mountain, the Tula Indians of Tanico, and others who lived in the around here, the Caddo, Quapaw, Osage, Tunica, Shawnee and Pawnee. All were at peace here, even if they were enemies somewhere else. They also brought gifts for the animals, fish, birds, plants, stones, winds, and the water and fire spirits of the land. They came from far away. Today, historians say the Maya Indians were only found in Mexico, but a large Maya Calendar Stone was found very near here and the Grandfathers say that the Lady of the Rainbow, referred to as *Ixchel* by the Maya, presided over the valley. Dressed in all white buckskin and holding one eagle feather in each hand, she stood on the mountain overseeing the peace. If anyone brought a weapon into the *Valley of the Vapors* or entered without goodness in his or her heart, a vision of the Rainbow Woman would be seen at twilight rising from the mists as a warning to the offending person. If the guilty one did not listen to this warning, the Lady of the Rainbow dropped one feather at his feet, which meant it would be wiser to *fly away* than to disturb the peace again. If this warning was not heeded, she dropped the second feather as a sign to his family and others to remove the offender from the valley by whatever means was necessary."

Mike approached with sticks and marshmallows, "Can you girls cook these and still listen to Tom?"

"Yeah."

"Sure."

"Okay, I'm putting the graham crackers and Hershey bars over here."

The girls jumped up to grab different ingredients and then all eyes were back on the old man. As the sweet white puffs turned golden, he continued, "My Grandfathers saw dense green forests and steam rose from abundant hot springs on the sides of the mysterious mountain. The valley was shrouded in misty vapors that curled upward through the tall trees. Sometimes the vapors joined low clouds and floated away in the pink and purple evening sky and other times they hugged the ground like a soft white blanket. Manataka was a place of strange, mystical beauty. Everywhere the sound of trickling water made sensual music as it bathed the faces of the cliffs and splashed into creeks that flowed on south. Where the steaming waters poured forth from the rock, exotic mosses in shades of red and orange painted the stones. Particles of silica sparkled in the sun like millions of diamonds while pyrite fragments seemed to catch fire and glow. But the most magnificent sight to behold could be seen for miles in any direction before visitors even reached the valley. Do you know what that was?"

"No," said Jen as she blew on a flaming marshmallow trying to put it out.

"Was there a big gate or something?" asked another one of the girls.

"You've got the right idea, but not exactly. Approaching visitors would say, *We know when we are there when the sign appears in the sky.* The sign was an enormous rainbow that stretched across the whole valley."

"That must be where *Ixchel* got her name."

"Maybe," laughed Tom. "The rainbows of Manataka didn't just disappear after a few moments of glory like other rainbows. Manataka rainbows would build and build in size and become more brilliant throughout the day because of the constantly running hot and cold springs. Rainbows have special meaning to native peoples, a sacred purpose. They are signs of the Creator's Great Blessings and Manataka has always been blessed." He stared off looking at something in the beautiful starry sky. "It is said that there were seven holy caves on the great mountain and in each one was a magnificent shining crystal encoded with secret messages from the Star Nation people. Some called the messages *shields* and others say that the wisdom of the Star Nation people was brought in the form of thirteen life-size crystal skulls and that one of them was actually here in the valley. Whether it was shields or skulls is a story for another night, but everyone agrees that the messages brought great wisdom that helped us live lives full of abundance."

"What are Star Nation people?"

"Ahhh. It is believed by the Cherokee and many other indigenous tribes that their ancestors came from the stars, especially the constellation of Pleiades. If you look close you can see The Seven Sisters, that's another name for the constellation, right up there. See that small cluster."

"I can see it."

"Wow, you can see so many more stars down here than you can in Kansas City."

"Cool."

"Well, many of the gifts that were brought by the visitors to the valley were placed in certain caves, but no one ever approached the most sacred crystal cave. It is said to have been the working place of the Star People and the resting place of the spirits. That may be where the crystal skull was kept. After the Civil War, many workmen came to try and capture the sacred waters of *Nówâsalon*, the *breath of healing* that spewed from the sides of the mountains creating dozens of crystal clear pools. They built ornate bath houses for the rich and the native peoples were no longer allowed in. Since that time it seems that the sacred caves have disappeared. Some say they were destroyed by the invaders, but what I like to believe is that they are still here, but hidden by supernatural forces. Maybe they are protected by the *little people* who live around here. You know the faeries and elementals," Tom chuckled.

Both Sam and Chloe turned to stare at Ol' Tom and then at each other, eyes wide.

"Well, I have been going on and on. When the tribes gathered, they danced and sang around huge campfires just like this one. I brought drums. Would you like to learn a song and then dance?"

Chloe whispered to Sam, "Yeah, maybe Dogan and Tinga will join us. Ha ha."

The chant they had learned the night before was still in Sam's mind as she woke. It seemed appropriate. It was the *Cherokee Morning Song, Wendeyah*. She hummed as she showered and combed the tangles out of her long hair.

Wendey yah ho, Wendey yah ho
Wendey yah, Wendey yah
Oh oh oh oh, Heya ho heya ho, Yah yah yah

The vans were packed with lunch, sodas, and snacks by 9:00 AM and everyone piled in for the trip to the crystal mine. Sam figured a crystal mine would look like a cave and she was surprised when they approached a huge flat area surrounded by mountains of dirt. A bulldozer was just dumping a load in the middle and several people rushed over to attack the new pile. There were probably ten other groups of four or five individuals digging in other mounds. She grabbed her bucket, gloves, and spade and followed Jennifer's dad. He'd been crystal digging before and had promised to show them what to look for and the best places to dig. They selected a spot close to a family with three kids and then Mike had them crawl to the top of one of the piles on the perimeter. He pointed to a location far below and Sam saw the bulldozer, looking very tiny from such a long distance, scooping up another load from an open-pit. Mike explained that for safety reasons diggers were not allowed in the actual mine, so after the dozers uncovered a quartz vein they brought out the dirt containing the crystals.

Sam heard some cheering and saw the oldest boy of the group near them holding up a crystal.

"Let's go see," exclaimed Chloe.

What the boy had wasn't just one crystal, but five or six attached at the bottom forming one piece that was about the size of his palm. Two tips were slightly broken, but the others were perfect. The cluster wasn't shiny though like the one Sam had seen on the Internet. The boy explained that when he got home he would soak his crystals in oxalic acid for a few days to remove the clay, iron and other mineral stains. He assured her that after a short while in the acid her crystals would be as beautiful as the ones she'd seen on the Internet.

Someone else hollered across the way signaling they'd found something and the girls rushed back to their buckets and scoops to get started. The huge pile of clay was a good texture and brushed off their clothing, but if it had been muddy… well, Sam realized why they had been told to wear *very old* clothes and tennis shoes. The morning wore on with most everyone finding points and a few small wands. Then right before lunch, Sam heard Chloe shout, "Oh my gosh. Come look at this you guys."

She had a large crystal, nearly two inches in diameter and about six inches long. One of the triangles that formed the point was wider than the five surrounding it.

"Ahhh, let me see. This one is actually called a *take out* crystal by indigenous healers," said Mike, "If it was polished up a bit and the bottom rounded it would fit in your hand like this." He placed the bottom of the wand in the palm of his left hand and extended his fingers and thumb upward to hold it in place. "This flat triangle part would be rubbed over different parts of the body to draw negative energy to the surface. Then it could be whisked away."

"That's beautiful, Chloe. Now, I'm going to find the next really big crystal," said Sam already moving back to grab her claw digger. She looked around. Just like Ol' Tom had described in his story last night, millions of tiny pieces of crystal or silica embedded in the clay reflected the sun. The whole landscape glistened like diamonds. Sam searched for a spot that might be shaded some from the sun, but close to its zenith, none could be found. She pulled a baseball cap from her backpack and then smeared more suntan lotion on her nose and bare arms.

By lunch time several of the girls had found more crystals, but none as large as Chloe's and Sam hadn't found anything that she considered special. On the way to the picnic area, Mike noticed the mine's gift shop was open.

"Oh, you're going to want to see this. Before we eat, I'm going to give you a half hour to browse in here."

Just inside the door was the largest crystal cluster you could imagine. Some of the hundreds of points were actually a foot tall and the whole piece measured about three feet by four feet. A clerk saw the girls enter and walked over. "You know the owner of this mine was offered a million dollars for this crystal at a rock and gem show in Tucson, Arizona last year and he turned it down."

"A million dollars?"

"Yep, a million dollars."

"It's amazing."

The other girls wandered off after a few minutes, but for some reason Sam seemed to be drawn into the brilliant spires. A sign said, *Do Not Touch*, so Sam extended her hand palm down and moved it slowly back and forth about six inches above the piece. Something strange tickled her hand and then actually ran up her arm. She jerked back, but then out of curiosity extended her hand again. An image suddenly popped into her mind. She was seeing the Manataka Mountain the way it must have looked hundreds of years ago. She could see the rainbow stretching all the way across the horizon, just like Ol' Tom had described it. She heard giggling behind her and turned, but no other scouts were near. She finally joined the others to examine different crystals and stones on numerous glass shelves.

By 3:00, everyone's energy was fading and Mike announced that they would have another half hour to dig before heading back to the cabins. Sam studied the bottom of her bucket. She had about twenty crystals, but was disappointed that she hadn't found anything out of the ordinary. She closed her eyes and pictured the crystal she hoped to find. Suddenly she felt tapping on her shoulder and opened her eyes to see Gideon standing beside her. The gnome pointed to a pile of clay that had just been brought up by the bulldozer. When Sam turned back, Gideon was gone. No one else seemed to have seen the apparition except her.

"I'm feeling lucky. I'm going to dig in that new pile. Anyone want to come?" asked Sam.

The sun was getting lower in the sky, but the temperature was still around ninety degrees on the flat clay mesa. The other scouts were drooping like wilted flowers.

"I'll go," said Jennifer.

"Me too," said Chloe.

As they headed over to the new pile, Sam pulled Chloe back for a second and whispered, "Gideon told me to come over here."

"Gideon?"

"Yeah, he was here one second and gone the next."

"Well, let's see if he knows what he's talking about."

Several others from another group were working the edges, so Sam climbed to the top. She immediately found a couple of small crystals and then she heard metal scraping on stone. Carefully, she worked around the edges of a large piece with her digger. When the clay was pulled away, she knew she had a cluster. The bed of about eight inches by four inches connected twelve beautiful finger-sized points ranging from and inch to two inches tall.

"I did it," shouted Sam. "Look, look what I found."

The normal cheer went up and a group formed around Sam to check out her crystal. Chloe reached out and touched a couple of the points, "I'll never doubt a gnome again."

Chapter 13
The Eagle Dance

When they got back to the camp, forty to fifty more cars, trucks, and vans were in the parking lot. Ol' Tom was directing traffic.

Mike yelled out the window, "What's going on?"

Tom came walking over. "Oh, I guess I didn't mention that we were hosting an Eagle Dance this weekend for one of the local tribes. They're going to be dancing down by the river."

Pizzas were just coming out of the oven as they arrived and after devouring several slices the scouts went to see what was going on. A huge circle of stones surrounded the oak tree that Sam had seen in the meadow and four large saplings with forked tops marked north, south, east and west. About twenty other forked poles marked spaces in between and round leather shields were being hung on one of the branches on each one. They weren't close enough to see what was painted on them, but they could tell that each one was different. An encampment of tents and several actual tipis had been erected around the area. Men and women moved in and out setting up tables and canopies with chairs underneath. About a dozen young kids raced in and out in a game of tag. A group of men were building a dome-like structure off to one side. They saw Ol' Tom surveying the event and ran to join him.

"What do you think?" he smiled. "You're going to get to experience an actual Eagle ceremony." He handed Sam a flyer. Here, this explains what is going to happen. Everything is being set up tonight and the Dance will begin at sunrise and last till sunrise on Sunday morning. See that lodge being constructed over there?" He pointed to the partially domed structure where two men were working. "That will be a sweat lodge and the dancers will purify themselves tonight in preparation for the celebration. The drummers are getting set up over there." He pointed to the northeast direction.

Sam glanced down at the paper in her hand and read: *As the ancestral drums come alive and merge with the heartbeat of Grandmother Earth, voices echo songs that have been sung since creation. Dancers in bright-colored ceremonial attire feel the call, take their own power, and rhythmically emerge from all eight directions of the medicine-wheel arbor. The Eagle's piercing call resonates as the participants ride the hypnotic beat, praying and moving toward the incredible essence of the Tree of Life. The arbor is alive. It pulsates, inhaling and exhaling as the ceremony progresses. Prayers soar on the wings of the Eagle to the Great Mystery and answers spiral back to the Dancers. The energy ebbs and flows as the day and night wear on, but the pulse never weakens. Finally, at the break of dawn on the second day the Dance Chief announces, This Dance is finished in Beauty.*

Chloe had been reading over Sam's shoulder, "Wow, that gives me goose bumps."

"Yeah," said Sam.

Someone called to Tom and he started to move away.

"Is it okay for us to walk around?" asked Jennifer.

"Sure. See you later."

Sam, Jennifer and Chloe went over to watch the sweat lodge being built. From what they could see the dome was constructed of sixteen small, flexible, stripped willow trees whose ends were being placed in holes that had been dug in a circle. The men were gently bending them over and then tying them with jute string to form the dome shape. The north poles were connected to the south ones and the east ones to the west and all the way around. Sam glanced at the setting sun and noted the door to the lodge would be facing the opposite direction, east. Just outside the door was a circular mound of dirt with a large buffalo skull in the middle. Two short forked poles had been set in the ground before the skull and a bar that had been painted in rainbow colors rested in the cradle of the forks. In a straight line continuing on east was a large fire ring that already contained a bunch of stones resting on a small log platform. Two boys that looked like seventh or eighth graders were placing logs and branches around the stones in a tipi shape. They were dressed in shorts and t-shirts and didn't look any different than kids in the girl's school, except for their facial features, long black hair and darker skin tone. Sam noticed that their faces seemed rounder, like Grandmother Wisdom Keeper's. They had high cheek bones and very dark eyes.

"What's your name?" asked Chloe as one of the boys approached.

"I'm Maichin Little Bear and that's John Two Crows," he said pointing to the other boy who was depositing a large bundle of logs in a pile by the ring.

"I'm Chloe and this is Sam and Jen."

"I have a medicine name and it's Playful Autumn Wind," said Sam looking up into Little Bear's eyes. They were as black as coal and had a twinkle that said he was just looking for adventure. Wow! He sure was cute. "What are they going to do next?" She indicated the sweat lodge structure, but didn't really take her eyes off Little Bear.

"When they have the frame done, my uncles will cover the lodge with canvas tarps and then with blankets. We'll be starting the fire to heat the Grandfather stones at sundown. Two Crows and I will be tending the fire and running the rocks for the Fire Chief," he said proudly. "And then it's our job to keep the fire going all day tomorrow and until the Dance ends on Sunday."

"That's neat."

"What's *running rocks* mean?"

Two Crows came over and smiled at Chloe, "It means that when the Lodge Chief calls for rocks, we dig them out of the hot coals with a pitchfork and take them into the lodge. Inside, the Lodge Chief pours water on them and that creates steam that purifies the dancers who will be praying. It gets really hot. There's some other stuff going on too, but..."

"Wow, what are they doing now?" asked Jen. She had turned and was watching a man and woman secure a long string of tiny colorful bundles between one of the forked poles on the circumference of the arbor to the center tree. Several other long strings were already draped and it reminded her of a May Pole.

"That's Elsie and she's a dancer. Her husband is helping her with her prayer ties. There are four-hundred and five ties on that string and each one is filled with a pinch of tobacco. When Elsie tied the bundles, she put a prayer in each one," said Little Bear. "Are you guys staying here?"

"Yeah, over there in the cabin on the hill. We went crystal digging today and I found a really neat cluster," said Sam.

"That's neat. I'd like to see it. You'll have to come over and watch tomorrow. That's when things really get going. About an hour before sunrise, Chief Running Deer will walk through camp playing his flute to get everyone up and then the drummers and dancers will get into position. The drummers and singers sit over there under that tent and drum the whole twenty-four hours. You'll like it. The dancers will all be wearing their regalia too."

"That means fancy outfits," laughed Two Crows. "I get to dance in two years when I am sixteen."

"There's my dad waving. I guess we better go," said Jennifer.

Little Bear watched as the man walked their way. "I hope you will come back tomorrow, Sam, uhhh, Playful Autumn Wind," he said, with his eyes twinkling again.

Something inside Sam did a little flip flop as he looked down at her. "I want to, but I think we have to go over to Hot Springs tomorrow or something."

"You'll have fun. Come after. We'll be here."

As they walked back to the cabin, Jennifer asked, "What's a medicine name and where did you get one?"

"Oh, Sam has an Indian friend that gave it to her and I hope to get one soon," said Chloe.

Sam shot her a warning glance, "Yeah, uhhh, I see her around sometimes."

"What about me? I want one," chimed Jen.

When Sam woke there was just a glimmer of daylight on the horizon and she thought she could hear the sound of a flute in the distance. "Ppsssttt," she called to Chloe as she climbed down from the top bunk.

"Yeah, I can hear it too," whispered Chloe. "Are you coming, Jen?"

There was nothing but a groan from the other bed, so Chloe and Sam grabbed shorts and t-shirts and slipped out the door. The clock in the kitchen read 6:00 AM. The night before the leaders had agreed to get up at 8:00, so the girls figured they could watch the beginning of the dance and then get back before breakfast.

The dew on the grass made the hill slippery as they headed toward the meadow, but the slightly damp earth smelled wonderful. Song birds were just greeting the day. The bird's voices mingled with the beautiful melody of the Native American flute and the rushing sound of the river. As they got closer they could see that the whole area was buzzing with preparations. A man and a woman hurried past talking seriously. At least Sam thought it was a man and women. They were both wearing colorful skirts with fridge on the bottom. The woman had bells on her ankles and the man had something on that clacked mysteriously as he walked and sounded more like wood. Ribbons, the color of the rainbow fanned from the yoke of his shirt. The woman's top looked like a peasant blouse that Sam's mom wore on occasion. It too had colorful ribbons. Both had on lots of jewelry and wore an Indian patterned blanket across their right shoulders.

Sam and Chloe found a spot where they could see the route Little Bear had said the dancers would take to enter the circle. Even more strings of prayer ties had been put up and an arch had been placed in the east direction. It was flanked with two large painted skulls. One had antlers and one horns. Everything was quite beautiful and festive. Two men hurried by with an enormous drum. It was almost as wide as both of Sam's arms outstretched. They placed it in the drummer's tent and Sam could see at least two other big drums already there. Suddenly there was a loud screeching noise behind Sam and she and Chloe nearly jumped out of their skins. They turned to see Little Bear. It looked like he had a mouthful of feathers.

"Oh, man, you nearly scared me to death. What's that?" asked Sam.

"It's an eagle whistle. You'll be hearing them all day. It's how we honor the eagle and ask him to take our prayers to Great Mystery. See, this part is actually a short eagle bone. It's decorated with eagle feather fluff and you tie it around your neck with a leather strap so your hands are free."

Their attention was drawn to the tent of drummers and singers as they began an interesting chant.

"They're ready to start," said Little Bear. "The dancers will march all the way around the arbor two times clockwise on the outside and then the drummers will change songs and the dancers will go inside and walk around there two times and then they drop off at their own dance place. Each dancer has a lane that they will dance in. It's kind of like a piece of a big pie. They go back and forth to the Tree of Life and never turn their back on it."

"I can't believe they are going to dance all day and all night," said Chloe.

"This dance is only twenty-four hours. At a Sun Dance, they dance for four days," said Bear.

The tempo changed, just as Little Bear said it would, and they watched as the long train of dancers veered through the east gate into the circle. When everyone was in their place a man stepped forward and began a ceremony that looked similar to what Grandmother had done when she'd asked for Sam's medicine name. Sam guessed he was Chief Running Deer. He raised a pipe with a long stem to the heavens and said something that Sam couldn't understand and then lit it and smoked to the directions. When he was done, he exited through the east arch and placed the pipe on a small altar. That seemed to signal the beginning of the dancing and the drummers changed to a driving beat and the ebb and flow of to the tree began just as the paper had said.

"This is really neat, but Chloe and I need to get back. Maybe we'll see you again tonight."

"I'll be waiting," Bear said with a big smile.

Walking back to the cabin, they could hear the eagles calling to the Great Mystery and the drum beating the cadence of the Earth's heartbeat.

The scouts spent the day in Hot Springs beginning with the scenic, twisting drive to the top of Hot Springs Mountain, the one that Ol' Tom had called Manataka. The mountain was crowned with a tower and high speed elevator. Looking out from the top the girls were able to see nearly forty miles in every direction and the view looking down on the historic old town was spectacular. The other girls thoroughly enjoyed themselves, but it brought a tinge of sadness to Sam's heart to think it had changed so much.

Mike and the other leaders drove the vans down, while the girls hiked and navigated the twisting trails to the bottom. Next they visited one of the many thermal pools that were part of Bathhouse Row and went for a swim. Instead of being cool like the Ouachita River, the girls discovered that the baths were naturally heated by the various thermal springs that had been capped by the National Park system. They jumped from pool to pool enjoying the different warm temperatures. It was lots of fun, but once again the thought that the springs no longer ran free down the mountain creating the beautiful moss covered rocks dampened Sam's spirit.

The rest of the afternoon was spent on a hayride through the beautiful Ouachita Mountains. The rack was pulled by beautiful Belgian horses and halfway through they stopped on a huge bluff that overlooked a sparking lake. The sun was low in the sky and clouds in the west had turned peach and orange, the edges trimmed with silver. Dinner was being cooked over an open fire on a huge steel grill when they arrived. Cheeseburgers, home fries and pasta salad was topped off with homemade chocolate ice cream. The girl's caravan rolled home and they got back to the resort around 9:00 PM. The troop was exhausted for the second day in a row.

Sam fell asleep almost immediately, but around 4:00 AM a gentle nudge brought her wide awake.

She scrambled out of bed. "Chlo, want to go see what's happening at the Dance?"

"Uhhh, yeah, I guess so. Think we'll get in trouble."

"Nah, come on."

They tiptoed out the back door and could hear faint drumming coming from the river. There wasn't a cloud in the sky and millions of stars looked like small fires in the ebony canopy. The dancers looked entirely different in the silvery light of an almost full moon. A candle had been lit at the rear of each dancer's lane under their shield. They passed the drummer's tent that was lit with several torches and headed toward the fire by the sweat lodge. Two Crows saw them coming and waved. Little Bear asked about their trip to Hot Springs and they made small talk while he added more wood to the fire. Suddenly Sam's attention was drawn to the south side of the circle. She blinked twice, but was positive it was Wisdom Keeper who stood watching the dancers.

"Hey, I'll be back in a few minutes."

Chloe watched her go wondering what she could be doing.

"Grandmother?" she asked, approaching the woman. Her dress tonight was absolutely beautiful. It was almost completely covered with amazing bead and quillwork. Tall moccasins, almost up to her knees, matched the outfit and eagle feathers were anchored in her hair and trailed down her back.

"What a wonderful night for a dance, don't you think, Wind?" Wisdom Keeper swayed and kept time to the music doing her own dance.

"Yeah, beautiful." Sam heard giggling above her in a tree and looked up to see several small figures.

"They should be doing the blessing shortly. I hope you will and Chloe will meet the dancers with me." Wisdom Keeper waved across the wheel and Sam realized that Chloe was staring at them.

"Blessing, what kind of blessing? Is that you up there Tinga?"

"Yeah, and me too," chimed in Abril.

"Can people see you?"

"Tinga and Abril have promised to stay invisible," said Grandmother with a note of scolding in her voice."

"We promise. No mischief tonight," giggled Abril.

"Oh, uhhh." Sam wasn't too sure from the tone in Abril's voice.

Before she could say anything more, Sam saw Chief Running Deer approach the drummer's tent. The heartbeat became softer for a moment or two while he announced the Blessing Ceremony and then the singing began again with a lively, swinging beat that made the dancer's fringe and ribbons fly. A number of people began to line up at the east gate. One by one they entered, stopping at each of the dancers who were now standing at the back of their lanes in candle light welcoming the visitors.

"Why don't we go over by your friends, Wind?"

"Okay, but I'm not sure what I will say."

"Just tell them I am your teacher."

They made their way around the arbor toward the fire, but before Sam could say anything, Little Bear acknowledged their approach. "Grandmother Wisdom Keeper, I'm glad you joined us again this year. How do you know the Grandmother, Sam?"

"She's… she's my teacher."

"Oh, wow!" He was evidently impressed.

"Hello, Chloe. Are you enjoying your experience," asked Grandmother.

"It's amazing," said Chloe swinging with the beat of the drums.

It was impossible to stand still while they were playing. Two Crows threw a log on the fire and then came around. "This is a new friend of ours…" Chloe began.

"Grandmother, we are honored to have you at our Eagle Dance," said Two Crows.

"It is my honor to be here, Two Crows. Chloe, I was asking Sam if she wanted to go through the Blessing Ceremony. Would you like to join us?"

"Sure, I guess. That's amazing that you all know each other." They started back toward the east and Chloe whispered, "Did I see Tinga over there? Someone else was in that tree too."

"Yeah, Tinga and Abril. It's just hard to see Abril with her dark skin. Both have promised to stay invisible. I guess the others can't see them. Just you and me."

Chloe turned and stared at Sam, "Really? They can't even see Tinga? She's as brilliant as the moon with her diamond-green skin. Okay. Whatever you say."

At the entrance to the large circle, they paused to let a man in buckskins pass and then Grandmother entered staying to the left. The first dancer bowed slightly as they approached and the girls heard Wisdom Keeper say, "You have danced a powerful dance, Willow Woman. I ask for your blessing."

Willow Woman nodded and then said something close to Grandmother's ear. They both turned and looked at Sam and Chloe, and Grandmother nodded again.

"Welcome, Playful Autumn Wind and I understand you are Chloe," said Willow Woman, turning to the girls.

"It is my honor to be here." Sam tried to mimic Wisdom Keeper.

"Same here," said Chloe.

The dancer smiled and took a pinch of a blue powder from a terra cotta bowl and sprinkled it on Wisdom Keeper's bowed head. Sam and Chloe glanced down and received their blessings too and then moved on sun-wise. It seemed to be the same with each dancer all the way around the circle. Everyone seemed to know who Sam was. She proceeded, receiving the blessings, but had no idea what to say.

Chapter 14
The Test and the Teaching

School started and Sam quickly adjusted to life at Santa Fe Trail Junior High. She and Chloe were ecstatic when they learned they shared the same homeroom. They began each day chattering away as they walked the few blocks to school. Sam loved the grown-up freedom of moving between classes and even liked all her teachers. Chloe had not fared as well and was having a problem with her math teacher, Mr. McDonald.

The first couple of weeks had been spent in review, but now the students were getting their first taste of algebra. Chloe's older brother had been tutoring his sister, but even with the extra help Chloe was having a hard time.

Sam waited for Chloe outside the gym after school as she always did and was surprised to see her friend exit in tears. "What's the matter?"

"I got caught cheating on a test."

"Your math test?"

"Yeah, I wrote the formulas on my arm and Mr. McDonald caught me when I pulled up my sleeve."

"Oh, man. Why did you cheat? I'm sure you would have passed."

"I don't know. I just don't get it," she sobbed.

They had just gotten to the street when Chloe crumpled on the curb, head on her knees. "Everyone in class knows what I did," she choked out. "I'm so embarrassed. I'm not going to school tomorrow or ever again."

"You know you can't quit school," said Sam, squatting down so she was on the same level. Chloe's wet face was so red that it matched her hair and her freckles didn't even show. "Come on. Let's go to my house. Do your parents know yet?"

"Yeah, I had to go to the principal's office and Mrs. Preston called Mom. I don't think I'm ever going home again either!"

This brought another outburst and Sam helped her to her feet. Several other kids were staring.

"Let's go. We're going to my house. This is Tuesday, Dad won't be home for at least an hour and Ty's got football practice."

Arriving at Sam's, they grabbed granola bars and headed to Sam's room. Opening the door they both stood astonished. Wisdom Keeper sat on the bed.

"Wha... you did it again, Grandmother?" stumbled Sam, not believing her eyes. "How did you get in here? I unlocked the front door when we came home."

Wisdom Keeper ignored the question. "I thought that both of you needed a teaching."

Chloe remained rigid and just stared while Sam went over to give Grandmother a hug. Releasing her she asked, "A teaching?"

"Yes," said Wisdom Keeper. "You've had a tough day, Chloe."

"You know that too?" Chloe began crying again, hiding her face in her hands. "Does everybody in the world know I'm a cheater?"

Wisdom Keeper in a simple tan doeskin dress rose and approached Chloe. At first she pulled back, but then melted into the grandmother's arms and welcomed the embrace.

"Let's sit over here." Grandmother motioned toward the bed and both girls crawled on and sat cross-legged.

"Here. Use this." Chloe's face was still wet with tears and Sam handed her a t-shirt that hadn't made it to the laundry basket.

Wisdom Keeper turned Sam's desk chair around and sat down facing the bed. "Your room is beautiful Sam." She glanced around as if seeing it for the first time. "I love the colors."

Reluctantly, Sam's mother had allowed her to paint one wall a soft purple and another pink, her two favorite colors. The other walls were white and the room contained a dresser, chest of drawers, bookcase and Sam's desk. Posters adorned the walls. Among them was one from the vampire series *The Twilight Saga* and showed Bella and Edward in a warm embrace. The other was a picture of a huge amethyst crystal cluster. The bedspread was purple, with yellow and white flowers.

"Thanks. I'll never figure out how you just show up when I need you," laughed Sam. "I was thinking that I needed your advice while we walked home."

Wisdom Keeper smiled and wove her fingers together grasping her knee in the now familiar position Sam had seen so often. She began to rock back and forth.

Chloe sniffled, "I guess you already know what happened today. I bet you think I am horrible."

Wisdom Keeper did not respond to the statement. "I don't think I have told you our complete Creation Story. Sam, I hinted at it when we talked about your Talking Stick, but there is more.

"Creation story? You mean like in the Bible?"

"Yes. I think you will see the similarities. After all, there is only one Creator and every culture has myths, stories and legends of how life began. In the ways of my people it is written in the records of the sacred kivas… Are you ready?"

Sam propped up pillows and leaned back against the headboard of her bed. She wasn't sure Chloe was listening. She still looked miserable.

"In the beginning since always, the Everything, Wakan Tanka, the Great Mystery, what you may think of as God, was created within the void from a pure energy force called *chuluaquai*. It is, in essence, the spark of life that allows all things within the Everything to take on their particular substance form. Wakan Tanka inhaled deeply and in so doing discovered its female being. This creative, receptive force became the egg and womb of all creation and is known as Great Grandmother, Wahkawhuan. She is the total blackness of the Universe, the blackness that you see between the stars. Then Wakan Tanka exhaled explosively and in so doing discovered its male side, the active, conceptive force of creation, our Great Grandfather Sskawhuan, the galaxies and stars. Sskawhuan knew he was the seed and spark of the Universe.

"Soon, Great Spirit became lonely and realized in its pure formless state that it could never know itself and it longed to discover its full potential. So from this sacred womb space and with a small pinch of its own life-force energy, Great Spirit created the Earth and gave her the first world as a child, the Mineral World; the sands and soils, rocks and stones, gems and crystals. Wakan Tanka could see that the Earth was beautiful and marveled at the formations of mountains, canyons, oceans and rivers. Looking deeply into the Earth's body, Great Spirit saw the wondrous colors of the gems and crystals and knew that it had created something wonderful. But as time went on, the loneliness was not quenched and grew. This had not been the answer, there had to be more.

"So Great Spirit created the Sacred Plants and the grasses and grains became waves on the prairie, the shrubs held the earth in place, the herbs grew knowing they had healing powers, and the fruits and flowers began to bloom bringing great nourishment and beauty. The trees grew tall and strong and using their branches brought the sacred energy of the As Above into their trunks and roots, and into the So Below of the Grandmother. And it was good."

Sam looked over at Chloe and realized she was hanging on every word now.

"But again, Great Spirit only grew more lonely. Wakan Tanka then created the Sacred Animals. The swimmers began to enjoy the oceans and streams. The crawlers languished on the Grandmother's skin loving the feel of the different textures. Four-leggeds began to roam about in the forests and on the prairies, and the winged ones, the birds of the air, took flight and found the currents of the sacred winds. Everything was in harmony, but the Great Mystery knew something was still missing.

"Just like itself, Great Spirit had created masculine and feminine in all things of the Universe, but still longed to know more about its own feminine and masculine sides and the possibilities of the sacred union. Taking two more pinches of its own chuluaquai life-force energy, Great Spirit created First Woman and First Man. They were given the powers of the four directions and told they had dominion over the other children or worlds of the Earth… they were to be responsible for the safety of those worlds and for keeping all in harmony. As First Man and First Woman ate from the Tree of Knowledge they began to understand that they alone on this planet had freewill. They discovered the power of conscious creation and how to determine from a place of Spirit and with passion and lust for life. They saw how beautiful life could be when they were in balance within the sacred union, but Great Spirit urged them to never lose their own individual, autonomous freedom.

As First Man and First Woman walked the Earth and interacted with all of creation… you might say experienced life, Wakan Tanka finally began to understand what it had created and all possibilities. The Great Mystery was experiencing itself through humankind. First Man and First Woman learned they had power to create their own lives as they chose, but that only through co-creation with Spirit would they retain their connection to the source of the Everything. Great Spirit looked down on all that had been created, and it was good.

"And thus was the creation of the Four Worlds of Grandmother Earth as it was told," said Wisdom Keeper. "What do you think?"

"That's a great story. So God isn't really a he?"

"Not in our way of thinking. The essence of the Great Mystery contains both masculine and feminine for balance, just as you do." Sam cocked her head. "Ahhh, but that is a story for another day. I know I keep telling you that, Wind, but we are going to have many years together. Right now, remember that everyone is standing in a different direction on the wheel. They may have different beliefs about whether the Creator is a he or a she."

"Yeah. I like that nobody's right and nobody's wrong."

"There are many teachings that come out of this story, but I want to talk about freewill," said Wisdom Keeper. "Wind, you and I have talked about this a little before. My people believe in reincarnation. Do you know what reincarnation is?"

"Like if you have been a bad person and die, you might come back as a rat or snake," said Chloe.

Wisdom Keeper chuckled. "Not quite. We believe that animals, plants, rocks, the wind… have spirits, but not souls. Only humans have souls and therefore they are the only ones that reincarnate. We believe we have all lived many lives before and will live many more before we achieve enlightenment. Before we are born, while we are still formless and before we have taken on a physical body again, we choose what lessons we want to learn.

"The higher powers that help us make our life choices are called the Chuluamadah-hey." She laughed and her dark brown eyes twinkled. "I have always pictured the Chuluamadah-hey as someone that looked kind of like Gideon. He would be seated, holding a clipboard with a list of lessons, and would ask each of us what we wanted for this next lifetime. There's unconditional love, humility, and a number of other things on the list. When we choose he puts a big check mark beside it and it is written into our Books of Life. Can you picture that?" she laughed again.

"Yeah, but it's not really Gideon, is it?" asked Chloe.

"No, that's just the way I imagine it. At birth, the elders say we go through the *forgetting process* and we don't remember why we have even come here; we just start living life. But our highest-selves or our Hokkshideh haven't forgotten and they present different situations from time to time to help us remember. Chloe, I think you were presented with one of those scenarios today."

"Really?" Her eyes grew wide and a little fearful.

"Now, it's kind of a paradox. Do you know what a paradox is?"

Both girls shook their heads *no*.

"Well, a paradox is something that is kind of hard to understand. What happened to you today just seems terrible right now, but if it helps you to learn a lesson, then it was actually good."

"Good? Yeah, that's really a paradox. I can't see how it could be good."

"Well, the Great Mystery gave all humans *freewill*. Freewill means that we get to make choices. Humans are the only living things on Earth that were granted this gift. All the other children of Grandmother Earth, the stones, the plants, the animals, are all living within their instincts. They just react to what happens around them. A tree just grows the way it always has and a female eagle intuitively knows when it is time for her babies to fly and she gently pushes them from the nest. She doesn't wonder if it is the right time or not, she just knows. Only humans reason and make choices. We get to decide which way we want to go. We get to decide if we want to learn a lesson or not. Life will continue on no matter what, but there is a saying that if you don't learn the lessons, they get harder and harder. Your Hokkshideh will keep giving you another chance to learn, but the next time the situation will be more difficult and have more consequences. What do you think will happen if you keep cheating on tests?"

Chloe smudged her face with the t-shirt again, but didn't answer.

"Have I had any of these chances to learn lessons?" asked Sam.

"Certainly you have and you will have many more. Now, this is going to sound very strange to you girls, but I don't actually believe in right and wrong." She paused for their reaction. "I don't believe there is right and wrong, only lessons to be learned, and there are always consequences to every action we take."

"You mean if someone kills someone, that's not wrong?" exclaimed Chloe.

"There is Sacred Law, Chloe, and killing someone breaks Sacred Law. Right now I want you to see certain situations just as you would the blow-up doll or the driftwood in the middle of your circle. Sam, I believe you have told Chloe about Walking Around the Wheel, right?"

Chloe indicated she knew.

"There is always a different view from the other side and none of us know what someone else has written in their Book of Life; what lessons they have come to learn. Does that make sense?"

"Yeah. Kind of," said Sam.

"So, I'm supposed to learn a lesson and I have to deal with the consequences, right?" asked Chloe.

"Yes."

"But, what kind of a lesson could this teach me?"

"Well, as I said, I have no idea what you have written in your Book, but the first thing that comes to my mind, is that you did not trust in yourself. Now, here is your second teaching for the day. Ready? You both, actually every human, is consciously creating every minute of every day. Your day is going to be shaped by your thoughts, feelings and emotions. What you need to know is that *likes attract likes*. That means that if you are sad or mad, or if you doubt yourself, then you are putting out negative energy and you will attract more negative energy. If you are happy and believe in yourself and feel loving towards everyone, then you are putting out positive energy and will manifest more positive things into your life. What happens to you is what you focus on.

"Chloe, you need to hear this," Grandmother continued, "If you fear that you won't pass your algebra test that is what you are focusing on. As long as you believe you can't learn algebra, then you can't. When you start believing that you have the potential to do anything you choose in life, then you will start passing tests with A's."

"That would be great," said Chloe, without much conviction. "But, I already cheated on my test. My mom and dad are going to kill me. How am I going to tell them that I was just learning a lesson?"

"I'm not going to judge what you did as right or wrong, but many others will. You need to keep in mind how much your parent's love you and that they believe they are acting in your best interest. You probably need to tell them that you won't ever cheat on a test again and that you have learned from what happened. You don't necessarily need to tell them what lesson you have learned. That can be between you, Sam and me. But, every action has consequences and you will need to accept that."

"I'm going to be grounded for a month."

"Maybe, maybe not. Have no regrets. Don't keep beating yourself up about what you did. It is in the past now and cannot be changed. Just take the consequences and go on. Know that you are a better person for this having happened, because you learned the lesson. Remember, if you focus on the fact that you are going to be grounded, then you probably will be."

"And, if I focus on the fact that Mom and Dad are going to understand, then … This just keeps going around and around, doesn't it?"

"Yes. I believe you really have learned the lesson."

Chapter 15
Ol' Man Coyote

Sam stared out her bedroom window daydreaming until a fat gray squirrel ran down a limb that nearly touched her windowsill. The branch bobbled up and down, leaves shaking, and the critter, whose bushy tail jerked back and forth keeping him in balance, stared straight back at Sam. His cheeks bulged with acorns and he paused a moment in fear and then seemed to realize that the human was on the other side of glass and he went on about his business, which was to leap to another branch that would take him onto the roof.

Sam's parents had had problems several years before with squirrels that had tucked nuts under the edges of the shingles. Knowing the roof could be damaged, her father had gotten up on a ladder and pried out the seeds and filled in the holes with brown caulking. Right after the first snow they noticed shingle pieces on the ground and realized the roof was actually being torn apart as the little beasts searched for their harvest bounty. Part of the roof had to be repaired and her dad had hired a tree service to get all branches trimmed away from the house, but evidently the summer's growth had brought the branches near again. Sam watched a couple of other squirrels scurrying about and had much more empathy for their plight this year knowing they were just preparing for the weather to come.

Fall had always been Sam's favorite time of the year. She loved the colors of fall and a few of the trees were already turning. She'd seen one recently that was brilliant yellow against its still green neighbors. Her mind roamed back to the spring when Wisdom Keeper had done the ceremony for her medicine name and she'd been asked to visualize the pile of leaves being whipped around by the wind. It wouldn't be long before there would be piles in her front yard for real.

So much had happened since that ceremony. Sam was getting used to Grandmother being able to read her mind and show up when she was needed, and she wasn't surprised any more when Tinga, Abril, Luna, Gideon or Dogan appeared. Evidently, no one else could see them except Chloe and her, so it was actually kind of fun. She'd found Abril and Luna sitting on her dresser just a couple of nights ago as she'd gone up to bed. Luna was combing Abril's long dark hair with Sam's brush as Abril smoothed generous mounts of Sam's favorite body lotion on her cocoa skin. When Sam quizzed them about their visit they had just shrugged their shoulders and replied that they had been in the neighborhood.

Sam was wondering what her mother would say if she knew about her relationship with Wisdom Keeper when Kari paused in the open door of her room and said, "Doesn't look like you're studying for your history test."

"I have been. Want to quiz me?"

"I need to get something out for dinner right now, but I will before you go to bed."

She started on down the hall. "Hey, Mom." Kari's head popped back around the corner. "It looks like we have squirrels on the roof again."

"I'll tell your dad."

"Mom, tell Dad to go easy on them this year. You know they are only following their instincts. They don't have freewill to make their own choices."

Kari looked confused, like she couldn't imagine where that comment had come from. "Ahhh, okay, I'll tell him." She disappeared down the hall.

Friday came and the family headed for the Ozarks in the late afternoon. Then early Saturday morning Sam took off to find her friends. As she ran through the meadow she stopped and picked several of the long stalks of what her mother called Wild Rye grass. The seeds were golden and ripe. Waving several over her head she turned to continue and was surprised to see a coyote sitting in the middle of the trail ahead. At first she was fearful and then something strange happened. She was positive she heard him say, "Follow me."

His pelt was a gray-brown turning into a buff colored throat and underbelly. His muzzle and forelegs hinted at rusty-red. He turned to continue down the path himself and then waited, looking over his shoulder. "Are you coming?" The coyote's mouth had not moved, but Sam was sure now that he was talking to her. When she got to where he had stopped, she heard, "What took you so long?" Being this close she noticed a dark stripe down his back created by longer black-tipped guard hairs and she saw that the tip of his tail was black too.

"Who are you? Did Grandmother send you?"

"You don't know who I am? I'm Coyote. Wisdom Keeper said you were smart, but I'm holding judgment," he chuckled.

He began to trot down the trail again. Sam ran to keep up.

"You don't have to be rude. I just wanted to know your name."

"Spunky, hummm, I like that. Have you ever heard of a *heyoke*?

"No."

He stopped at the edge of the woods and sat down, "Well, I don't have the best reputation. I admit that. In fact, I am kind of proud of it. A heyoke is generally a little contrary. I enjoy teasing people and having fun with them. When humans are having trouble learning lessons, it's my job to point this out to them. I usually do it by showing them something they didn't really want to see about themselves. It's not my fault that some people take themselves way too seriously."

Sam thought of Chloe cheating on her test and hoped she really had learned her lesson and wouldn't have to deal with Coyote.

"Hey, now. I can assure you that I am a very nice guy."

"So Wisdom Keeper did send you?"

He started into the woods, this time walking so Sam could keep up. "Yeah, she asked me to introduce you to a couple of your allies before they take off for the winter."

"You mean my animal totems? Cool!"

"I think I am going to like you Playful Autumn Wind. By the way, I love your hair. I always wanted to be blond."

"Ahhh, thank you."

Around the next bend, Coyote paused again. "Hey, Flicker. Do you know Playful Autumn Wind?"

Sam tried to follow his gaze and finally saw a huge woodpecker high up in an old dead willow. Instead of the way most birds sat on a branch, the woodpecker was gripping the bark of the main trunk and holding on vertically.

"I don't have time for one of your pranks today, Coyote. I'm getting ready to migrate, you know. Going south for the winter. I don't know why all the other woodpeckers around here don't follow me, but they don't."

"I don't get any respect! Grandmother Wisdom Keeper sent me."

With that comment, the Flicker soared to the ground showing beautiful reddish coral color underneath her wings. She began walking over. "Well, in that case, I can make time."

Coyote rolled his eyes.

The woodpecker spied several crawling insects and gulped them up. She was just over a foot tall and larger than she looked in the tree. Her back and wings were grayish with black horizontal bars and her belly was tawny colored with a necklace-like black patch on her breast. The rest of her body contained black spots that even continued down her legs. She stared at Sam for a few seconds and then bent over and plucked several ants off the ground. As she did, Sam could see her very white rump beneath her shiny black tail.

"Ahhh, ants, my favorite," she said. "So you are a friend of our Wisdom Keeper. I bet you have come to see what teachings I might have for you."

"Well, yes. Grandmother says that each of my totems have a message."

"What is my sitting place on your medicine wheel, my dear?"

"I beg your pardon?"

"When Wisdom Keeper drew your wheel of allies, in which direction did she place me?"

"Oh, yeah, ahhh, southwest."

"The place of dreams," said Coyote.

Another large Flicker flew in and landed close. The coloring was similar, but this one had coral-red at the nape of its neck and under its chin, kind of like a mustache.

"Wind, this is my mate," said the first Flicker.

He seemed more interested in finding ants than talking, so Sam turned her attention back on the female.

"It's important to know where I am on your wheel. I may sit in another direction on someone else's wheel and then I would have a different message for them."

Sam shook her head, "I know it was southwest."

"Well, I am an expert drummer." There was an old piece of board lying against the tree trunk. She hopped over to it and began drumming out a rhythmic beat with her beak. "If you hear me tapping outside your window, you will know that the rhythms of your life are about to change and you need to be alert and ready. Since I sit in your southwest, you can count on the fact that I will be alerting you to opportunities for pursuing your dreams, as Coyote said. When you hear me, if you know you have been resisting change for some reason, my tapping may loosen you up a bit and allow you to see the opportunity and not fear the unknown. Finally, ants are one of the most abundant insects on Earth and they are my favorite food. I know great abundance and will help you find abundance in all aspects of your life as well. These are my gifts to you, Wind."

"Wow! Those are great gifts. I'm so glad to have met you."

"Take care and I'll be seeing you around too, Ol' Man." With a two hop take off, she flew back up to the side of the old willow and ducked inside a hole that was about four inches in diameter.

"That went well," said Coyote. "Let's see who else we can find."

"Ol' Man? Why did she call you that?"

"Well, some folks call me Ol' Man Coyote. Some call me the Trickster. I've been around for a long, long time." They started off on the trail again and Sam fell into step beside him.

"I was here at the time of creation, you know. I am the one who saved the sun."

"The sun, as in Grandfather Sun?" Sam asked incredulously, pointing to the huge yellow orb peering at them from above.

"Yeah. It's a long story, but the sun was about to be stolen and… well, without me there would be complete darkness. How do you think I singed my tail?" Coyote said flipping it around so Sam could see the black tip.

"I don't know."

"Well, when I was putting the sun back up in the sky, I got too close and it burned the end of my tail. That's why it's black today."

"I heard that raven saved the sun," said Sam.

"He tries to take credit, but…."

"Huuummmph." The noise came from somewhere in the weeds off to their left and was followed by a sound like someone shaking a gourd rattle filled with seeds. Then there was a voice. "That's not the way I heard the story either, Wind."

"What's that?" whispered Sam nervously, "Not being able to see where the voice was coming from.

"Not what, but who. I am Snake." A long sinewy rattlesnake slithered onto the path before them. A series of large light-bordered dark diamonds were quite evident on his brown back.

Sam jumped back hiding behind Coyote.

"The way I heard the story was that you were trying to *steal* the sun when you almost set yourself on fire," laughed the serpent.

"Like I said, I don't get no respect," pouted Coyote.

"Don't be afraid, Playful Autumn Wind," hissed the rattler. "I'm one of your allies, in fact a very important one. I sit in your northwest, the working place of your self-esteem, which sits across the wheel in the southeast. I'm the one who influences the rules and laws that you create for yourself to live by."

"Nothing wrong with this guy's ego," came a voice from above.

Sam glanced up to see Luna hovering above, tiny pink wings undulating to keep her stationery. Sam waved and then moved out from behind Coyote, losing some of her anxiety.

"Ha! Now *you* ain't getting any respect, you scaly serpent," chortled Coyote.

"Boys, boys, behave now," said Dash. The smallish elf was sitting on a limb in a nearby oak. "I don't think you want the wrath of us *little people* to come down on you. You are supposed to be showing Sam the gifts her animals have for her, not fighting."

Looking up from below and in his sitting position, Dash's large belly took up his whole lap and his huge green shoes completely hid his short, stocky legs. But, Sam could see his eyes twinkle between his large green hat and his moustache. "Morning, Wind."

"Morning, Dash."

Snake rattled the bony appendage at the end of his tail again to get their attention. "Like I was saying," he smiled at Coyote through his two long hollow fangs and Sam noticed that he had coiled himself into a tight knot, "because I shed my skin, sometimes as many as four times a year, I will be around to remind you, Wind, of the milestones in your life. I show people that something must die before something can be reborn; that you may have to let something go in order to move on and grow." The rattler was on a roll now. "If you see me wound into a spiral like I am now, you need to look at what Wisdom Keeper calls the *karmic patterns* in your life."

"She'd talked to me about karma, but what are karmic patterns?" asked Sam, sitting down cross-legged on the path facing Snake.

"Ahhh, well karma is like those lessons that you wrote into your Book of Life and karmic patterns are spirals that get out of hand when you don't learn the lessons. Those rules that I mentioned are the things that you have decided you *should* always do, or that you *shouldn't* ever do. It may even be when you decide you just *can't* do something, when you know you have the potential to do anything you ever choose. Sometimes your *should's* and *shouldn'ts* are good, but other times you have just created them out of fear."

"Yeah, that makes sense."

"Well, dear Wind, your allies will always be here for you. I will share more with you as time goes on. Where are you heading now Coyote?"

The large canine had lain down in the weeds and was nearly asleep.

"Cooyyote!," Snake hissed.

"Oh, ahhh, the grandmother asked me to find Snow Goose." He got to his feet. "Ready, Sam? I'm going to need another nap soon."

Sam bade the rattler goodbye and thanked him for his gifts and once again began to follow the coyote.

Dash jumped down and took up the journey behind Sam and the faery flitted along above. "Goose spent last winter down by the creek," said Dash. "We should probably start down there."

Even before they reached the marshy wetland they heard the familiar chorus of honking and saw several geese peal off from a large irregular *V* high in the sky that contained probably a hundred or more geese. They landed in an eddy of smooth water that was oblivious to the rushing current a few feet away. It was obvious that this was a family and Sam remembered reading in her totem book that not only do geese mate for life, but goslings generally stay with the parents for up to a year.

"Coyote, who are your friends," honked the large gander. At first he appeared to be completely white with a mustard-colored bill, but fringes of the black wing tips appeared as he waddled closer. His mate came ashore with a loud nasal *whouk*.

"This is Sam and Dash and... well there is a faery around here somewhere. When did you fly in?"

"We left the Arctic Circle several weeks ago and have been heading south. Your summer has created a great bounty. It appears we've chosen a great location for our winter season."

"Welcome back," waved Dash. "Do you remember Grandmother Wisdom Keeper?"

"Of course."

"Well, Sam Playful Autumn Wind is just learning about her animal allies. Your guidance is her gift in the southeast of her wheel."

"Ahhh. I see. Well, Sam, I will be happy to work with you. The first teaching I have for you is teamwork. Have you noticed the way a flock of geese fly?"

"Sure in a *V* shape.

Coyote looked bored and Sam saw him creep away probably looking for a place to snooze.

"Just don't start snoring," called Goose. "Yes, Wind, we fly that way for a number of reasons. The *V* shape allows each of us to see around the one in front and that way no one's vision is ever impaired. Even working as a team it is important for everyone to have a clear idea of where they are going. We also fly this way to help each other save energy and this allows us to fly longer distances. Humans that have studied our habits call it the *drafting effect* and many of your cyclists now race using the same techniques. The lead goose breaks the wind and begins the process of creating currents that each of us use to our advantage. The wind current created by the goose in front of us pulls us along and that makes it easier. From time to time the leader breaks away and another in the team takes over."

"Wow! That really is teamwork."

"This is a cozy group," said Wisdom Keeper, looking down at the bank of the river from a slight rise. "Have you had a good day Sam? By the way, where is that lazy coyote?"

"There is so much to learn, Grandmother."

"There is, and now you know that your totems will always be there to guide you."

A loud snorting caused the branches of a nearby bush to quiver.

"What is that noise?" asked Wisdom Keeper.

Dash was trying hard to hold back his laughter and then he heard Luna tittering above and he could no longer contain himself. His belly began shaking and soon he was bent over hooting.

"Oh, Coyote. Doesn't look like he's ever going to change," said Grandmother.

"If he did, he just wouldn't be our Trickster," laughed Luna.

Chapter 16
Ghosts and Goblins...
and, faeries, elves, gnomes, and trolls.

"Sam, this is the second time I've gathered up our brushes and combs to wash and found long black hairs. Where are they coming from?" asked Kari.

"Ahhh." Sam knew they had to be Abril's. She had to think fast. She grabbed a grocery bag that Jennifer had left sitting by her desk and pulled out a silky black wig. "This, ahhh, I was brushing Jen's wig. I borrowed it. Ahhh, I was thinking of being a faery on Halloween."

"Oh, well that explains it. I'll be glad to help you get your costume together. Do you actually know what a faery looks like or do we need to find some pictures?"

"Ahhh, I pretty much know what they look like."

"Okay. Make sure you get some breakfast."

Sam relaxed a little as she pulled her sweater over her head. That was a close one.

When she walked into the kitchen Tyler was spooning dry Honey Bunches of Oats into his mouth. Sam never could understand how he could eat cereal without any milk, but he did.

"Dad, where does Grandma live in California?" asked Sam.

"Big Bear Lake, Sam, duhhh, how can you be so stupid. You've even been there," chimed in Tyler.

"I'm not stupid."

"Yes, you are."

"I am not, you are. Stay out of this, I asked Dad, not you."

"That's enough you two," said Jack, as he poured coffee into a "ToGo" cup.

Ty got up from the table on his way to the computer and as he passed Sam, he flipped some of her hair into her face. "Duhhh."

"Tyler!!!"

"Ty are you ready for school?" asked Kari coming down the stairs. She turned and glanced back at the table. "Ty, you didn't put your bowl in the dishwasher."

Ty continued to sign on to the Internet.

"Any time I say anything, he says I'm stupid," whined Sam.

"Yeah, that's because you're stupid," laughed Tyler.

113

"Ty you don't have your shoes on and your dad's going to be ready to leave in a couple of minutes. You should have checked your email earlier. Get going or you'll be walking to school in the rain."

"Dad, can we pick up Chloe on the way?"

"Sure. Give her a call and tell her to be ready."

Tyler got up from the computer, disgruntled, just as Sam picked up the phone. He intentionally ran into her on his way to get his bowl and nearly knocked her down.

"Tyler, what the…" There was a click on the line. "Hey, Chlo, want a ride to school? Yeah. How long Dad?"

"Ten minutes."

"Did you hear that, Chlo? Okay, see ya." Sam hung up. "Tyler, why did you run into me?"

"Cause you're stupid."

"School bus is leaving in five minutes. You two better be ready."

Jack backed the electric RAV4 out of the garage and hit the remote button to lower the door. "What's with you two? All you do is fight any more."

Tyler looked around the headrest and sneered at Sam. She sneered back and a minute later the SUV pulled into Chloe's drive. She ran out the front door and jumped in the passenger side of the vehicle.

"Thanks, Mr. McLaughlin."

"Dad, will you pick us up if it's still raining this afternoon?" asked Sam.

"Nobody ever melted in the rain, Sam. It wouldn't hurt you to get wet," said Tyler turning in the front seat to look at the two girls.

"Tyler, I wasn't even talking to you."

"Who cares."

"Honey, I've got a meeting at 2:00. If I can get there, I will. If I don't make it, you will have to walk. Ty's right, no one ever melted in the rain. Just get home and get warmed up if you get wet. There's hot chocolate in the pantry."

There was a long line of cars dropping kids by the canopy that led to the school's front door.

"We're going to play a game while we wait," said Jack, eyeing Tyler and then Sam. "Take a minute to think, then, I want both of you to say something nice about the other. Do you understand?"

Both kids looked bewildered.

"Are you ready? Sam you go first."

"Ty, you sure do fart a lot."

Chloe burst out laughing and Tyler gave her a dirty look.

"That's not exactly what I had in mind," said Jack, putting his hand up to his mouth and trying not to laugh himself. "Sam, try again."

"Well, Tyler, you are very good at video games," she said more seriously. "And, you are a great third baseman."

"Okay, that's pretty good," Jack nodded, impressed that this might be going somewhere. "Now you, Ty."

He thought for a minute more. "Sam, you are very good at taking care of Bailey." Bailey was the kid's three and a half year old niece.

"Good, good. That's a start." They were now next in line. "Have a great day. I'm going to quiz you tonight about something you learned today, so be ready."

The doors opened and the kids poured out. Just inside the building, Ty acted like he was stumbling and bumped into Sam again and then ran off to meet some other eighth graders.

Her books went flying to the floor. "Tyler, what the…"

The group of boys now surrounding Tyler bent over in gales of laughter. Sam gathered her books and headed toward her locker hiding her face.

When the 3:15 bell rang, Sam was very ready for the day to be over. It had not been a good day. Something horrible had happened in nearly every class. In her math class she'd been called to the board to do a problem and when she got there, she'd drawn a complete blank and had to sit down embarrassed. In English, she'd gotten reprimanded for talking when it was Jennifer that was whispering to her and not the other way around. Chad had decided to sit across from her at lunch, which didn't make her happy at all and when she'd gotten up to change seats, she spilled chocolate milk all over her shirt. It seemed the dreary skies outside had followed her inside.

She exited the building glad to see the dark clouds were clearing. Chloe's mom was waiting to take her to a dentist's appointment, so Sam waved goodbye and started home. She tried to jump a large puddle at the curb, missed by several inches, and splashed water all over the back of her jeans. When she reached her driveway, she wasn't ready to go in. Maybe going to the park would cheer her up. It always worked when she was younger. She wasn't surprised when she saw Grandmother sitting on a swing.

Luna flitted over, "Having a bad day, Sam?"

"It can't get any worse."

"Come swing with me, Wind," called Wisdom Keeper. "It hasn't been easy, but I've been saving this seat just for you."

Sam smiled. There was no one else but Luna and Grandmother in the park.

"Tell me about your day."

"I don't know. Tyler started picking on me this morning and then things got worse when I got to school. The whole day's been awful."

"Sam, first, when Tyler picks on you, you can't take it personally. He is dealing with his own insecurities and you just happen to be there. He knows exactly what pushes your buttons and getting a reaction from you somehow makes him feel superior."

"Making me feel bad, makes him feel good?"

"It is always your choice to decide how you feel. You know you're not stupid. It's your choice if you decide to believe him. Do you remember when we talked about freewill?"

"Yeah, you talked about freewill when you told the Creation Story and Chloe got caught cheating."

"Well, today I want to talk about conscious creation. One of the things that First Man and First Woman learned was that the gift of freewill allowed them to consciously create their lives. You have the ability to make choices and you make those choices every second of every day. Like whether to pay attention in class or look out the window and daydream…"

"Yeah. You know I don't really think I'm stupid."

"But, you created a perfectly horrible day for yourself based on the feelings you allowed Tyler to create in you."

"You mean because Tyler said I was stupid then I *was* stupid today?"

"No, I mean that because you *believed* what Tyler said, because you *felt* stupid, then you manifested a number of negative scenarios today. There's a big difference. Your thoughts and feelings are what manifest in your reality. *Nothing is real until you make it real.* What you focus on happens. It is your choice to manifest what you fear as Chloe did with her math test by creating a situation that caused her to get an F. Or, you can consciously create something beautiful."

"But how can I get Tyler to quit calling me stupid?"

"Ahhh, you can't. No one can change someone else. But that doesn't matter. You don't have to change something; you have to *quit focusing on it.* The next time Tyler starts in, just ignore him completely. Act like you didn't hear him. When you react to what he says, it gives him *power.* When you don't react in the same way you have in the past, it will throw him off and you will retain *your* power. Eventually he will give up and quit picking on you, because he isn't getting what he wants. Does that make sense?"

"Yeah, it does, but it's so hard. He makes me so mad."

"It is hard to change old patterns, but I know you can do it."

"You know, I think I feel better already. I'm going home. I've got to get my Halloween costume together. Hey, Luna, where are you?" Sam shielded her eyes from the sun as it popped out from behind the clouds and she finally saw Luna sitting on the top bar of the swing set. "Guess what. I told my mom that I was going to be a faery for Halloween and she asked me if I knew what one looked like. Ha!"

"That's funny," giggled Luna. "Are you going to dress like me?"

"Well, I got a black wig from my friend, so I'll probably look more like Abril."

Luna feigned a pout.

"I'll see you later."

"Wind, one more thing before you go. You've seen several occurrences where you or Chloe manifested something negative because that's what you were focusing on. Now, I want you to work on manifesting something wonderful into your life. Tonight before you go to bed, I want you to decide what it is you want. Then I want you to begin focusing on it. It may not happen immediately, but it will happen if you really want it to. Look into the future and see it as if it has already happened, like you already have it or are doing it. Then I want you to get so excited about having it or doing it, that you actually fall in love with it. Can you do that?"

"I'll have to think about what I want. Do you think I can really make something like that happen?"

"Of course, Wind. It's a law of the Universe. It's kind of like the Great Mystery is just waiting to see what you will do with your life. Focus on the negative and you will get negative back. Focus on the positive and you will get positive back."

Sam jumped off the swing and threw her arms around Wisdom Keeper. "Thank you Grandmother. I'm so glad you are in my life."

"Me too, Playful Autumn Wind."

Jack pulled in the drive a few minutes after Sam got home and she raced out to meet him. "Dad do we have some wire around here? Kind of like coat hangers, but longer."

"I think so. What for?"

"I need to make myself some wings. I'm going to dress up like a faery for Halloween."

"Aren't you a little old to be trick or treating. That's for babies," said Tyler coming up behind her.

Sam started to defend herself and then remembered Grandmother's words. Without turning she said, "Yeah, I could use your help, Dad. I was thinking I could make four big circles out of wire, two for each side, and then connect them in the middle and figure out a way to attach them to my back."

"I can see that," said Jack. "Help me unload the car and then I will help you look."

"Geee, Sam. What are you going to do steal candy from all the little kids?" said Tyler, trying again.

"Remember all that pink netting that mom had left over from Aunt Missy's wedding?" asked Sam, still not turning around to face her brother. Jack looked at her a little quizzically and tried to hide a smirk, realizing what she was doing.

"I think it's downstairs in the basement."

"Well, I'm going to drape it over the wire to make my wings."

Sam got an armful of files from the back of the RAV4 and they walked toward the kitchen.

"Oh, hi, son. How was your day?" asked Jack.

While Sam was doing her homework that night, her mother called up to say she had a phone call. She ran to the kitchen and picked up. It was Chad. He couldn't leave well enough alone.

"I was thinking about how stupid you looked today with all that chocolate milk down your front," were the first words out of his mouth. "And, I heard that you can't even remember how to do algebra. Ha!"

She tried to think of a nasty comeback, but then realized that Chad was no different than Tyler.

"And, you called me up just to tell me this, Chad?"

"Yeah, I was just sitting here thinking about how uncoordinated you are."

"Well, you have too much time on your hands. Sweet dreams, Chad. Good night."

When she crawled into bed, she began thinking about how immature Chad was. In fact all the boys at school seemed to be immature. She glanced up at her wall and saw the poster of Edward and Bella from the *Twilight* movie. They were so romantic. Edward was very mature. Of course he was a vampire and he was over a hundred years old, but he'd been frozen in time at seventeen. Surely there were some boys at school that were more mature than Chad. She fell asleep thinking about Bella and Edward being in love and could almost feel Edward's arms around her.

A week later, dressed in pink tights and one of Kari's peasant-style blouses, Sam pulled on her wings. Pieces of elastic had been attached to the center of the gossamer appendages and when she pulled them over her shoulders the wings were held snug against her back. Sam had added sequins and glitter hoping to make them sparkle like Luna's and Abril's. After braiding her long blond hair and then coiling it on top of her head, she donned the black wig and then added a flowery halo-type headpiece with long ribbons that spilled down between her wings. She looked at her feet wishing she had green slippers with turned-up toes, but her tennis shoes were going to have to do.

"Who ever saw a faery with black hair? You would have made a better witch, Sam," said Tyler.

Sam bent over to look at her niece who was dressed as Sleeping Beauty in a pink gown, tiara, and tiny pink slippers with about one-inch heels. She had a magic wand and had been running around the house *casting spells* on everyone. She would place the wand on your head and say *poof*. She was adorable. "What do you think, Bailey? Am I a good faery?"

The three and a half year old wasn't quite sure what to think of her cousin who was suddenly wearing black hair. But, the voice was familiar so she didn't protest.

"I'm Sleeping Beauty," she said for the umpteenth time.

Sam heard a knock at the front door and when she opened it she saw Chloe dressed as an Indian maiden. Her mom had made her a long tan dress that looked very much like one that Wisdom Keeper had, minus the fancy beading. And, of course, hers wasn't real doeskin. She had a red woven band around her head and had stuck a fake eagle feather in the back.

"You look great," exclaimed Sam.

Tyler flipped on the TV. "I still think you two should have gone as goblins or ghouls. That would have been more realistic."

Chloe looked like she was going to return the spiteful remark and Sam grabbed her arm and shook her head. "Ignore him," she whispered.

Chloe looked surprised, but kept quiet.

"Okay you girls. Have fun," said Kari. "Make sure you hold Bailey's hand and go up to every house with her. And, don't eat any candy until your dad or I have had a chance to look it over. And, stay together. When you get back, I will take you to your party."

"Okay, Mom."

They started up the street and were suddenly surrounded by what looked like a bunch of kids with amazing costumes. Then the girls recognized Tinga, Luna, Abril, Gideon and Dogan.

"Great costume, Sam," said Abril, fluffing out her own black locks.

"Thanks. Are you guys going trick or treating with us?" asked Chloe.

"Sure. This is the one night of the year that we don't have to be invisible."

Chapter 17
Bear Heart

Sam pulled the mail out of the mailbox and flipped through it. When she saw the postmark from Kalispell, Montana, she ran for the kitchen. "Hey, Mom, we got a letter today from Granny. Can I open it?"

"Sure. What does it say?"

Sam scanned the neat print on the bright marigold-colored paper. "Well, ahhh, she just finished crocheting over fifty hats and scarves for homeless women. What do you think? My bet is we will all get a hat and scarf for Christmas. Ha!"

"You're probably right."

"She got a perfect bill of health from the doctor last week, and, oh, wow, she's coming down for Christmas. That'll be cool. I haven't seen her for about two years."

"That will be wonderful."

"It says she will be here for a week, ahhh, arriving on December 20th.

Between classes on Monday, Sam walked past the principal's office and saw a boy standing with his back to her talking to one of the secretaries. For some reason he looked very familiar. When he turned she knew why. It was the cute guy she'd met at the Eagle Dance.

"Little Bear, is that you?"

"Playful Autumn Wind?

"Yeah, it's me. But, up here everyone calls me Sam. What are you doing here? I thought you lived in Hot Springs."

"Uhhh, well I did until last week. I moved up here and am going to be going to Santa Fe."

Sam felt an uneasiness and thought she saw a look of sadness in his eyes. The twinkle she'd seen before was definitely not there. "That's cool. What grade are you in?" He was even cuter than she remembered. He seemed to have filled out and had more muscles.

"Eighth. What grade are you in?"

"I'm only in seventh. My brother, Tyler, is in eighth. You may have some classes with him. Be on the look out. Hey, the bell is about to ring. Maybe I will see you later."

"Yeah, I hope so."

Sam ran down the hall knowing she hadn't imagined the sadness, but at the same time his words, *I hope so*, echoed in her ears. She couldn't contain a smile as she scooted into her seat in Language Arts.

After school, waiting for Chloe, she saw Little Bear coming out the side door of the building.

"Little Bear." She waved and he joined her on the sidewalk. "How was your first day?"

"Okay. I got all the classes that I wanted."

"Saaammm, who's your new friend?" It was Chad. The tone of his voice was mocking.

"Chad, this is Little Bear. I met him when crystal digging this summer. Little Bear, this is Chad Thompson."

"Little Bear? What kind of name is that?" he said with a snicker.

"I'm Maichin Begaye. My father is Navajo and my mother was Irish. Maichin means *son of the bear* in Irish. My dad kind of looks like a bear," he ignored Chad's sneer and laughed. "Most of my friends call me Little Bear."

"Well, that's a stupid name," replied Chad.

"Chad, get out of here. Who asked you to come over anyway?"

"I'm going. See ya round, Litttttttle Bear."

"Don't mind him. He's an idiot."

"You know he likes you, Sam," said Little Bear, looking for her reaction.

"Likes me? That's crazy. He constantly picks on me. I think he likes to make me miserable."

"He likes you, Sam."

"Whatever. Did I hear you say your mother *was* Irish?"

Little Bear suddenly dropped his eyes and seemed to go away to another place.

Sam hesitated for a moment and then said, "Did I say something wrong?"

Still looking away, Bear replied. "No, you didn't say anything wrong. It's just that… she died two weeks ago. She had cancer."

"Oh, my gosh, I am so sorry." Her words rushed out, horrified that she had made such a blunder. "I don't know what to say. Is that why you moved up here? I'm sorry. I shouldn't have asked. I am so sorry."

He finally looked back up and met her eyes for a second. "Yeah, my dad travels all the time, so I'm going to have to live with my aunt." He gritted his teeth to help control his emotions, but tears brimmed in his eyes. He looked back down at the ground and she saw one tear fall.

Sam had never known anyone who had lost a parent before. She suddenly flashed to what it would be like to lose her own mom or dad, but couldn't imagine it. It would be too awful. Before she could think what to say, Chloe appeared.

"Hey, you guys... uhhh, Little Bear?"

"Hi, Chloe. I remember you," he said, but he kind of turned away and didn't really look at her face.

"Hey, Chlo, mind walking home by yourself today? Little Bear and I were..."

"No, guess I don't mind." She immediately picked up on Bear's uneasiness. It was obvious that she'd interrupted something. "I've got tons of homework. Call me later?"

"Yeah, sure." She turned back to Little Bear who hadn't said goodbye. "Uhhh, there's a park near here. Want to talk? Looks like you might need a friend."

He brightened a little, "Yeah, and you are the only person I know."

They walked down Sam's street without talking. Passing her house, she pointed it out to him and he commented that he was living two streets over. They continued on to the end of Sam's street and the park. Sam zipped up her sweatshirt. The sun was shining, but it was still a cool afternoon. Leaves with amazing colors covered the ground and had been blown into piles around several large trees. Sam motioned to the swings that she now considered hers and Grandmother's. Glancing around, she looked for Wisdom Keeper or the faeries. She didn't see anyone.

"Was she sick a long time?"

"No, she just found out she had it a couple of months ago. I guess she'd been feeling bad for some time, but she hadn't said anything. We didn't have any insurance. The doctors said they couldn't do anything for her. I don't really want to talk about this. Can we talk about something else?"

"Sure."

There was silence for a couple of minutes. Finally he said, "Since I've seen you, I've done my first vision quest."

"What's a vision quest?" She remembered Grandmother saying something about a vision quest at her birthday party. It was some kind of rite of passage for a man.

"Well, when a boy becomes a man…" Now that he had started this, he wasn't sure how to proceed.

He looked terribly embarrassed and turned redder underneath his already dark complexion. Sam thought about a recent health class when they'd talked about the physical changes a boy goes through when he starts to become a man and she was sure that was what he was talking about. To help him out, she said, "Well, Grandmother told me a little about vision quests, but not much."

He relaxed a little. "Well, about two weeks after the Eagle Dance, I found a neat spot in the mountains and was sent out by Ol' Tom, that guy at the cabins. Do you remember him?" Sam nodded. He was starting to recover. "He was my monitor. That means he kept watch over me. The only thing you get to take with you is a blanket and you build a medicine wheel and you can have a small fire. You know what a medicine wheel is, right?" He glanced at her for recognition and she nodded again. "You stay inside the circle for three days. You're supposed to get a vision."

"Did Ol' Tom bring you any food?"

"No, on a vision quest you have to fast, no food or water."

"That must have been tough. Didn't you get thirsty?"

He sat up straighter looking proud. "At first, but that goes away the first day. You don't mind after that."

"Did you have a vision?" Before he could answer, Sam caught movement overhead and looked up to see Gideon sitting on the top bar. He was swinging his feet and looking amused. When he saw her turn, he waved.

"On the first day and most of the second, all I saw was a lot of animals. There was a hawk that sat in a tree close by almost the whole time and I saw a bald eagle a bunch of times. There was deer, but the neatest thing was an elk. I know it was an elk and not a deer. I see deer all the time. He was enormous with a full rack and all the skin was starting to fall off his antlers. He was only about twenty feet away and he looked directly into my eyes."

Sam wanted to ask if he'd talked to him, but wasn't sure what Little Bear would say, so instead she said, "I don't think I've ever seen an elk. I'll have to look up elk medicine in a book I have. Wisdom Keeper talks to me about animals and their messages for us all the time."

"That's cool. Uhhh, well, during the night of my second day is when I had my first vision. I saw my mom dying. I knew she was going to die, Sam. The only person I've ever told this to is Ol' Tom and now you." This time there were no tears, he just stared at her.

"Oh, that must have been awful."

"It was. I think I cried most all night, but as the sun was coming up, I saw something else."

"What."

"Coming through the trees, I saw a beautiful girl. She wore a doeskin dress like Wisdom Keepers. It had beading all over it like hers. She just stood there with the sun behind her and I couldn't see her face."

"Wow! What else happened? Think I can do a vision quest?"

"You'll have to ask Wisdom Keeper. Long ago only the men did vision quests, but I think they let girls do them now too. What I was going to tell you was that later in the afternoon is when I saw the elk. He told me that my name is now Bear Heart."

"Bear Heart. That's cool. Is that what you want me to call you?

"Yeah. Little Bear seems kind of childish."

"Then from now on you are, Bear Heart." She threw her arms out in a kind of welcoming gesture and then glanced up again to see if any other little people had arrived. They hadn't.

"Sam, I know who she was now."

"Who?"

"The girl in the woods. It was you."

Gideon made a disgusted harrumph noise.

Chapter 18
Thanksgiving

They got into a routine where Bear Heart would arrive on Sam's door step at 7:30 AM and if it was too cold to walk to school, Jack would pick up Chloe and take all the kids in the RAV4. Most afternoons it was still warm enough to walk home and Sam, Bear Heart and Chloe would walk together. It turned out the only class that Bear Heart and Tyler had together was P.E, but they had become pretty good friends.

"Two more days before Thanksgiving break," said Chloe. "And, I've got a huge math test on Wednesday. Why do they do this to us right before a holiday?"

"So you don't have to clog your memory up with all those facts while you are on vacation," laughed Sam. "What are you doing on Thanksgiving, Bear Heart?"

"My aunt is having what she calls an *orphan's dinner*. She has everyone over that doesn't have close family and would have to spend Thanksgiving alone. My dad is coming in tonight, but he has to leave on Friday morning."

"That's cool what your aunt does. I would hate to eat turkey alone. We are going down to our cabin at the Ozarks on Friday to close it up for the winter. I'll ask my mom and dad if you can come along, if you want."

"Yeah, that would be great. I'll ask Aunt Nina."

"It's too bad that Bear Heart's dad isn't going to get to spend the whole weekend with him," said Jack. "I'm sure he feels kind of abandoned. It's all right with me if he goes to the lake with us, if it's all right with you, Kari."

"Fine with me. I'll talk to his aunt and tell her it is fine with us. Tyler, you and Bear Heart can take the bunk beds in Grand Central Station."

Jack had to work on Friday, so they didn't get away till late. On Saturday morning, Sam asked her mom if it was okay to take Bear Heart out and show him around, since Tyler and her dad were going to be winterizing the boat and Jet Ski and putting them under the house.

Kari said it was okay, but that she would need Sam's help on Sunday to strip the beds and do some cleaning.

"Where are we going?" asked Bear.

"I want to show you my secret place. No one knows about it except me and Grandmother Wisdom Keeper. Well, Chloe too, but almost no one else." She didn't elaborate about the little people.

Rounding the bend by the river, Sam heard giggling in the trees and knew they weren't alone. Wisdom Keeper sat on her familiar log, a picking basket by her side.

"Hi Wind, Bear Heart. I hoped that you would visit me today."

Abril giggled and then said, "She looks like she's in love."

"May be," laughed Luna.

"She's too young to be in love," exclaimed Gideon.

The two faeries looked at each other, puzzled over the gnome's outburst.

Sam could see everyone and had heard everything. She glanced at Bear Heart. It was obvious he'd heard voices and was looking around to make a connection.

Wisdom Keeper glanced at the little people in the trees. "Be gone, all of you. I have something I want to talk to Wind and Bear about."

"But, we have birthday gifts," whined Tinga.

"Okay, but then you have to leave us alone."

As the little people floated out of the trees and climbed down from the cliff, Bear Heart saw them for the first time. He stared unbelieving.

"Are you little people? I've heard of you, but never seen you before. I didn't think you really existed."

"Better not say that," laughed Sam. "If you don't believe in them, they steal things from you. Right, Tinga."

"Only once, Sam, and we gave it back," she chuckled.

Gideon approached to shake Bear Heart's hand, but he didn't look too happy. "May the best man win, Bear Heart."

"Gideon, you be good," scolded Wisdom Keeper.

"Well, if he thinks I'm not going to put up a fight for Playful Autumn Wind's hand, then he is crazy."

Bear glanced at Sam and then almost laughed, but he held it in.

"Giddeeon!" The little gnome moved back, but not too far. A look of resolve on his face. "Bear Heart, I understand you have a birthday in a few days."

"How did you know that, Grandmother," questioned Bear Heart, getting his second surprise in just a couple of minutes.

"You never mentioned your birthday. When is it?" exclaimed Sam.

"It's the 28th."

"Well, we have presents today," said Luna, hovering closer. She floated to the ground and presented him a beautiful red hawk wingtip feather. It was nearly a foot long.

"And, I have a raven feather," said Tinga, manifesting right beside him. She placed it in his hand and then did a little curtsy.

Abril was next and handed him a stick of bound up sage. "You may need to burn this smudge stick to get rid of Gideon's negative energy," she laughed.

"Thank you all. I never expected…"

"I bring you elk medicine, my son," said Grandmother. "A friend of mine shed this antler last spring. I thought it would be the perfect gift." She reached over and picked up a huge antler nearly three feet wide and with four points on each side.

"Elk? Do you know about my vision quest too?"

"No, I didn't, but I'm guessing you had a visit while on your quest. Do you know why an elk may have come to you?"

"No, he just showed up and told me that I had a new medicine name. I wasn't Little Bear any more. I was now Bear Heart."

"Ahhh, well, elk is your main animal ally. He will bring you many gifts over the years."

"You mean like mine is the Red-tail hawk?" asked Sam, surprised.

"Yes, Wind. I'm going to let you explain to Bear about his animal totems. It will be good practice for you." She turned to the little people. "Now you scoot along. You promised."

As they waved goodbye, Wisdom Keeper motioned for Bear Heart and Sam to join her on the log.

"Thank you for the gifts," Bear called after them.

When the three were settled on the fallen tree, the grandmother began, "I understand you have had a recent loss, Bear Heart."

Bear looked shocked and then turned his eyes to the ground. "Yes, my mother crossed over about a month ago."

Sam watched as he tried to hold in the emotions that suddenly flooded him. She reached over and took his hand and he returned the gesture with a small smile and then looked away again embarrassed.

"Bear, I am very sorry for your loss. I hope to share some wisdom with you today that will help you feel better." She waited a minute till he seemed more at ease. "I cannot be sure why your mother decided to cross over at this particular time, but I do know that she would not have done so unless she was complete with the lessons she'd agreed to learn. This may not make her absence any easier, but I know it was very hard for her to leave you. Did you know that I visited with her a few days before she died?"

"I didn't know that." He swiped at his eyes with his sleeve.

"Yes, and she asked me to look after you because she knew that your father would have to continue to be gone much of the time. Of course, I agreed. But, just like Wind, I have known for a long time that I would be working with you for many years to come. Ol' Tom and I have agreed to work together to provide your training and one day you are destined to become a respected elder and help to pass on the teachings of our people to the next seven generations."

Sam didn't say a word, but her mind darted back to the day of her naming ceremony when Grandmother had indicated that her destiny was also to help pass along the sacred teachings.

"One of the reasons your mother may have entrusted your care to your father's sister, whether she realized it or not, is because your father may not approve of your *sacred dream*, this destiny of yours. Your father tries very hard to forget that he is Indian. Sometimes I think he is ashamed. Your father loves you very much in his own way, but you are a reminder to him of his lineage."

Bear Heart stood and stared off across the river and a tear ran down his brown cheek.

"What do you think of what I have told you, Bear?"

"My mother told me before she left that I was to share her passion of the teachings of the Red Road with others. How is it that an Irish woman can feel that way, when my own father can't?" He turned in anger to face the log.

"Ahhh, the marriage of your mother and father is an interesting one. She was drawn to him originally because of his bloodline and she hoped that he would teach her the ways of his people. They spoke to her heart. He was drawn to her because of her Irish roots and his desire to forget that he is a red man. They loved each other very much, but a wall was built between them when your mother realized your father couldn't give her what she desired, and your father realized that she was not going to help him forget."

"But, I used to hear them arguing over me. Mom wanted me to participate in sweats and pow wows and Eagle Dances and he would get mad and stomp out of the room."

"He may not have agreed, but he respected her feminine intuition, Bear. Even though he refuses to practice what he was taught as a child, he still honors the teachings. They are a part of him and always will be. You have to understand that he is perfect for where he is in his soul's evolutionary journey. Every one of us is. We have all written something different into our Books of Life. And, we are all trying to learn different lessons. Your father's lessons are very different from yours, but in the end we all will learn. It is the way of our Hokkshideh, our highest self."

"Playful Autumn Wind, what do you think of what I have said?' Sam had sat quiet for so long that Wisdom Keeper's words startled her.

"I, ahhh, I don't know. It's kind of sad."

"Well, Bear Heart chose his parents before he was born, just as you did. You both chose them because they would give you the best environment for learning your lessons. You even chose that you would have a brother, Sam. The ways of our souls are a mystery. But, in time we see that the choices we made are for our highest good."

"I chose Tyler to be my brother? No way," she said, astonished.

"Yes, and you have already learned a great lesson when you discovered a way to get him to quit teasing you so much."

Sam sat with such an incredulous look on her face that everyone laughed and it relieved some of the tension. She had been finding her own truth in almost everything that Grandmother taught her, but having chosen Tyler as a brother... That was too much.

"Bear, Ol' Tom has agreed to teach you about the changes that you have recently experienced in your body and in time I will work with you and Sam, so that you understand the power of a woman. All is as it should be."

Chapter 19
Granny

When Sam left the river with Bear Heart, she already knew what she wanted to get him for his birthday. On Monday, she got her mother to take her to Border's and she immediately found the book that Chloe had given her for her birthday. But, then a number of other books in the same section caught her attention. She finally made the decision to buy one called *Animal Speaks* by a man named Ted Andrews. She especially liked what it said about elk.

Bear Heart seemed to be more content at Sam's house than at his aunt's and it was fine with everyone. The only thing that Tyler just couldn't figure out was what on earth Bear saw in his sister.

Sam had gotten very comfortable going over to Bear's aunt's house too. She'd discovered much about her new friend that he was not open to sharing. Bear's aunt's Navajo name was Niyol, which means *wind* in the Diné language. She learned that the word Navajo was actually a Pueblo word that means *the enemy*. The Spanish started using it, not understanding that it was actually an insult to the people who called themselves Diné. In their language Diné means *The People*.

Bear's father's Indian name was Ahiga, which means *he fights*. Nina laughed when she told Sam that their mother claimed her son had come out fighting and never quit. Ahiga had changed his name to Bill during his first year of school and now in business used the surname of Johnson. But, for some reason he had never forced Bear to shun his heritage.

Somehow over the years Niyal's name became Nina, not because she felt she had secrets, but just because it was easier for people to spell. She encouraged Sam to call her Aunt Nina, just as Bear Heart did. She was a short, round woman and had the same dark eyes as Bear. Sam never saw her without a smile on her face and a twinkle in her eye. She wore her dark hair long and always had it pulled back from her face with brightly beaded barrettes.

Nina told the story of Bear's great, great grandfather, Gaagii, who was a powerful Diné medicine man. His name meant Raven's Magick. Upon hearing of the wondrous Manataka Mountain, he and his wife traveled all the way from Arizona to Arkansas to see for themselves. Their plans were to only stay a season and then go back, but Gaagii became crippled and the Hot Springs area became a permanent home. The generations since had stayed, except for her. She had never married and was a nurse at a hospital close by.

She and Ahiga had been brought up catholic and today her beliefs stretched between Catholicism and the *old ways*. Sam marveled at her Navajo nativity scene which Nina produced one day while decorating for the upcoming holidays. It had several more animals than just cows and sheep. An eagle perched above the manger and there was a bison, a mountain lion, and even a snake. Nina found Sam studying the crèche, which was actually a six-sided terracotta Hogán, a traditional Navajo home, and explained that the four additional animals were her power animals. A wild looking Kachina dancer and a Santa viewed the scene from the sides, creating an interesting paradox. True Kachina's are spirit beings, like archangels, but in ceremony members of the tribe impersonate the entities for flair and to bring the stories to life.

The Saturday following Thanksgiving, Nina had a party for Bear. Ol' Tom, drove up from Hot Springs and brought Two Crows. Early in the afternoon Bear, Two Crows, Tyler and Josh had gone to play paintball. It had been mostly Tyler's idea and the admission to get into the Lone Wolf Paintball field was Ty's gift to Bear Heart. Bear hadn't been too sure he was going to enjoy getting blasted with pellets of paint that might be coming at him at three-hundred feet per second, but once they were outfitted with goggles and chest protectors he felt a little more comfortable. His rented marker or gun looked like a futuristic terrorist weapon. Staff at the field gave them a few pointers on bunker running tactics and they ended up having a fantastic time dodging around the huge inflated objects. Everyone came home with a few bruises, but by the end of the day all the boys were hooked.

At 7:00 that evening Sam and her parents went over to Nina's for dinner. Chloe joined them after receiving a special invitation from Bear that Sam found out later was mostly Two Crows' idea. Since Bear's dad had been in for a few days at Thanksgiving he didn't make it back for the party. Nina served a venison stew flavored with tomatoes, beans, corn, squash and piñon nuts and Sam got her first taste of authentic Navajo fry bread with honey.

Sam gave the *Animal Speaks* book to Bear after dinner and he immediately turned to check out elk medicine. Sam read over his shoulder and they learned that the Shawnee Indians had called the huge animal wapiti. Bear read – *elk is an animal of great power, strength and stamina – its primary defense is outrunning its predators and if healthy usually has no problem outrunning a mountain lion, grizzly or pack of wolves or coyotes – if elk has come into your life it may mean that you are about to hit your stride.* They also read that other than during the fall rutting season, most elk remain in small herds of their same gender. They take four to five years to mature and the adults are fierce protectors of their young defending them with sharp hooves. Elk don't migrate long distances and their thick coats are well suited to protect them against harsh winters and severe cold. Finally putting the book aside to rejoin the others, Sam was sure Bear was standing a little straighter and puffing out his chest as elk do during the rutting season.

The month of December was so busy with getting ready for the holidays that Sam and Bear Heart didn't talk much more about his encounter with Grandmother at Thanksgiving. Tyler and Bear hauled all the boxes of Christmas ornaments up from the basement and together with Sam's father's guidance, they decorated for the season. A lacy band of white crystal ice cycles swept across the front of the house attached to the guttering. A wooden cutout of Santa Claus normally adorned the front yard, but the energetic boys toted him up onto the roof and secured him by the chimney. The large sleigh with Santa Snoopy at the reigns and Charly Brown and Woodstock hanging on for dear life also went up on the roof. Sam and her mom erected the large Christmas tree in the living room and placed red lights around the edge of the picture window to frame it from the outside, while the tired guys drank hot chocolate and gave strong recommendations as to where certain ornaments should be hung.

By the 20th when Granny was to arrive, the area around the Christmas tree in front of the window was brimming with colorfully wrapped packages with beautiful bows. Sam wondered where her grandma's presents would fit. She knew she would come loaded. Granny took Christmas very seriously.

On Saturday, they all piled into Kari's van, including Bear, and headed to the Kansas City airport. They'd gotten their first snow of the year the night before and the landscape was a glistening white carpet. The resting, bare branches of the trees looked like they were covered with marshmallow fluff. Holiday songs played on the radio and they sang along. The only way the day could have been better, in Sam's opinion, was if they had been going to get her grandma in a one-horse open sleigh.

Granny was inundated with hugs at the gate and surprised to see Bear.

"Granny, this is my friend Bear Heart, Bear this is my Granny," said Sam.

"So nice to meet you, Bear Heart. That's an unusual name. I'm guessing that you are Native American."

"Yes, my father is Diné."

"That's interesting, Kalispell is up in Blackfeet territory, but my side of the family was Cheyenne."

Sam jerked her head up. She'd never heard anything about Indian blood in her family. "You mean I'm an Indian," she exclaimed.

"Well, you have a little Indian blood," laughed Granny. "Let's see. It was my grandmother who was Cheyenne, so she would have been your great, great grandmother."

"I haven't thought about that for years," said Kari. "Let's get Mom's luggage and head to the car. She can finish her story then."

The carousels seemed to take forever and Sam's mom and dad kept talking about different subjects. But, when they were settled in the car, Granny continued. "So Sam, your great, great grandmother was raised Cheyenne after she was rescued as a child. There had been a raid on her village and most everyone had been left for dead. Several Cheyenne hunters found her still alive. I believe she was three or four. I remember visiting her when I was little and she was pretty old then. They never had much, but she was still one of the happiest people I've ever met. She used to make the most wonderful soups and stews and I always thought it was neat because they were made with *real* buffalo and venison, you know, deer meat. After she died, I still visited some cousins from time to time."

Both Sam and Bear Heart were on the edge of their seats leaning forward to the middle row so they could hear.

"She was actually the medicine woman of the tribe. People brought their sick and wounded and she did her magick. Some had to be sent on to hospitals, but many were helped. I remember some gatherings where they did ancient rituals too. Of course, it had to be kept very quiet. In those days native people were not allowed to celebrate their own religion. In fact, if they were caught they were treated as criminals. It wasn't until August 11, 1978 that the Native American Religious Freedom Act was passed. Before that all ceremony had to be kept strictly secret. Do you remember the Longest Walk in 1978, Kari? Let's see, you would have been about seven or eight years old."

"What's a Longest Walk?" asked Sam, so excited she was ready to pop out of her skin.

"Sam, Granny is going to be here for a week. Let her get her breath. Maybe she will tell you more at dinner," said Jack, looking in the rearview mirror. Seeing that Bear was just as interested, he added, "If its okay with your aunt, you are welcome to join is Bear."

The rest of the trip home covered logistics. Sam had agreed to sleep on the couch in the family room, more than willing to give up her bedroom to her grandma. And, they'd planned to do several other fun things for entertainment. It was a family tradition to go see *A Christmas Carol* at the Missouri Repertory Theatre on the Sunday before Christmas. Kari bought tickets in July so they'd be assured of sitting on the front row to watch Scrooge's dilemma with the Ghosts of Christmas Past, Present and Future. One evening they planned to tour the Plaza to see the lights. Since 1929, the area called the Country Club Plaza in Kansas City had been lit with literally miles of twinkling lights from Thanksgiving through New Years. The Plaza boasted that it was the first shopping center in the world designed to accommodate shoppers arriving by automobile. The buildings had been architecturally designed by the J.C. Nichols Company to represent those in Seville, Spain and today every intricate detail of the ornate structures was outlined with holiday lights. The store windows displayed fun, animated holiday scenes that could be viewed by visitors bundled up in the backs of elaborate horse-drawn carriages. Kari and Jack hadn't completely agreed, but Sam hoped their evening on the Plaza would end at the Cheesecake Factory and a piece of the delicious creamy pie.

The dining room table had been extended and everyone had a hearty bowl of chili before them when Granny began her story.

"You all know that almost every treaty made with native people was broken at some time," she began. Everyone nodded. "Well, in 1978, eleven bills were introduced into Congress that would have destroyed the final treaties protecting native sovereignty. Some one had to stand up to the government and President Jimmy Carter. So, the native people decided to take a walk all the way across America to make people aware. The walk was a peaceful, spiritual effort to educate the public about native rights and native ways of life."

Sam glanced over and realized that Wisdom Keeper was sitting on the steps that led upstairs. She nearly had a heart attack and kicked Bear under the table. He saw what she was seeing, but Tyler looked directly at the stairs and they could tell he saw nothing unusual, so she relaxed a little and tried to listen.

"It started in San Francisco and went all the way to Washington, DC. Some of the Indians walked the whole way, 3,600 miles. It took months and months and they finally arrived in Washington on July 15th. Along the way people opened up there homes and provided food for the walkers and they accepted donations. Some people just watched from street corners and cheered the procession along and others joined in. There weren't just Indians; there were people from all walks of life. You saw blacks, whites, and people from Asia. I particularly remember one family with turbans on their heads. On some stretches of the route there were actually several thousand walkers at one time. Sam, Tyler. Your mother and I caught up with the group in Sacramento, California at the State Capitol and we walked about twenty miles with them and camped out one night. Your grandpa picked us up when we couldn't take any more."

"I'm remembering more now, Mom. I rode part of the way with a family in a station wagon that had a girl about my age," said Kari.

Sam stared. It was unbelievable that her mother had actually been a part of something so important.

"Yes, yes, very nice people," said Granny laughing. "Your little legs just couldn't keep up with the pace of the adults. Where was I, oh, yeah. On that last lap into Washington, the group really grew and I believe there was something like a hundred thousand people who gathered on the mall in Washington. Some famous people joined in too. Senator Ted Kennedy, Muhammad Ali, and even the famous actor Marlin Brando. And, it worked. Congress voted two days later and every one of the bills was voted down. Finally, after hundreds of years, native people earned the right to religious freedom."

"That's cool," said Sam.

"Yeah," chimed in Bear. "I think I remember my dad saying that my grandfather was one of the people in Washington."

Sam glanced back at the stairs and Wisdom Keeper was gone. She hadn't seen her get up.

"Well, that's not the end of my story. The first walk was for religious rights and in 2008 they did it again. To honor the 30-year anniversary of the first walk another group walked all the way across the country. I even heard that some of the kids who walked the first time, walked in this second event. This time it was to remind everyone that we need to take better care of the Earth."

"Wow, that wasn't very long ago. That's a great story Granny."

"You know, I was just thinking about something else," Granny paused a minute, "One of the rituals that I used to participate in when I went to visit my grandmother on the reservation was a Winter Solstice ceremony. And, tomorrow is the Winter Solstice. Would you like to do a ceremony right here after we come home from the theatre?"

"Yeah," said Sam and Bear at the same time. Sam started to say something else and stopped.

"What, Sam?"

"Uhhh, I was thinking that a friend of mine might like to come."

"Who, Sam? Did you want to invite Chloe?" asked Kari.

"Uhhh, just a friend. You don't know her." She glanced at Bear. "I think I can get hold of her."

"Well, that's fine with us," said Jack. "Anyone you want to invite."

As Sam gathered her pillow and blankets and headed to bed in the family room, she wondered how on earth Wisdom Keeper had appeared earlier and now that she was gone, how was she going to invite her to the Solstice ceremony. She brushed her teeth in the downstairs bath and when she came out, she had the answer.

"Do you want me to turn the lights out, Sam?" asked Abril. "I think I can reach the switch."

"Hey, Sam, are we invited to the ceremony tomorrow night?"

Sam glanced up and saw Luna perched on the blades of the ceiling fan. For a minute she thought she was seeing double. Both faeries were dressed exactly alike.

"What are you guys doing? You look like twins."

"Oh, we were bored today. Can we come?" repeated Luna.

"Well, you can come if you do two things for me."

"Here it comes," said Abril.

Sam ignored the faery. "You can come if you will tell Grandmother Wisdom Keeper about the ceremony and ask her to come. She was here earlier, but she vanished."

"And the second thing?" questioned Abril.

"You have to promise that you will stay invisible."

"I knew that was coming," said Luna. "Okay, I guess we can do that... for you, Wind."

"Oh, and one last thing," said Sam. "Please, tell Grandmother to knock on the front door this time."

Chapter 20
Winter Solstice

Sam lay awake for a long time after Abril and Luna were gone. Now that she had invited Wisdom Keeper to the ceremony, she was going to have to tell her parents how she knew Grandmother and that they had been working together since spring. She'd wanted to do it for a long time and now that she had Bear Heart's support and had heard Granny's story, it seemed the right time.

But, would they think she was crazy if she told them she was destined to become the next Wisdom Keeper when she was Grandmother's age? She knew they would think she was nuts if she told them about the little people and that animals came to birthday parties and actually talked to her. Better take this in stages.

She relaxed into the feeling that everything was going to work out and then was again filled with dread. If she told her parents, Tyler was going to find out too. Oh, man. He'd probably find something new to bug her about.

When Sam woke, her mom and Granny were fixing waffles in the kitchen. They were the big thick kind that soaked up lots of butter and syrup. She couldn't wait. She grabbed some plates and silverware and began setting the table.

"So, did you get hold of your friend last night, Sam?" asked her mom.

"Yeah, I think so."

"You think so?"

"Uhhh, she's going to call me back."

"Is this someone you know from school?" asked Granny.

"Well, not really... Hey, you know I need to get out of these pajamas and get dressed before breakfast. Be back in a jiffy."

Kari glanced at her mother. "Did you get all that? Something fishy is going on."

By the time Sam got back downstairs, she was glad to see that Tyler and her dad were up and that the conversation had turned to the play at the Rep.

At 6:15 Sam and Tyler were cleaning off the dining room table and putting away the leftovers from dinner when the doorbell rang. Peeking through the curtains, Sam could see Bear Heart, Aunt Nina and Grandmother Wisdom Keeper. She didn't see any faeries.

"Hi, come on in. I'm glad you could come, Aunt Nina." Sam turned and realized her mom and dad were standing behind her. "Mom, Dad, I would like you to meet a friend of mine. This is Grandmother Wisdom Keeper. Uhhh, Grandmother these are my parents, oh, and this is my brother, Tyler, and my Granny from Montana."

To Sam's surprise, Grandmother had on a very nice navy blue dress that could have been purchased at any Kohl's department store. She wore flats, instead of moccasins, and a brown leather coat. The only thing that resembled *the Wisdom Keeper* that Sam knew was her long white braid and the amazing turquoise necklace.

"So nice to meet you," said Wisdom Keeper. "You know you have an incredible daughter, but I don't have to tell you that."

"Uhhh, nice to meet you too," said Jack. "Somehow I, uhhh, I thought Sam was inviting one of her classmates. But, you are certainly welcome. Come in. Tyler, would you take, uhhh… Wisdom Keeper is it?" Grandmother nodded. "… take Wisdom Keeper's and Nina's coats, please."

Sam rolled her eyes at Bear and then caught sight of Granny eyeing Wisdom Keeper with a slight smirk on her face.

When they were all seated in the family room, Kari asked, "So, Wisdom Keeper, how do you know our daughter?"

"Oh, Samantha and I met last summer down at the Lake of the Ozarks. I don't live too far from your cabin, and, well, she and I were both picking wildflowers in a meadow. We struck up a conversation and have been friends ever since."

Kari and Jack glanced at each other. "Sam, why didn't you ever mention your friend?" asked her dad.

Suddenly, Granny broke in. "Grandmother, you look like you might be American Indian. Am I right?"

"Yes, I'm Maya and Cherokee."

"Well then, Sam's probably told you that I used to go to my Cheyenne grandmother's ceremonies when I was young and somehow

I've found myself promising to do a Winter Solstice ceremony for everyone tonight. I'm wondering, would you be willing to help me?"

"It would be my honor."

"Oookay, let's go out in the backyard for a few minutes. I want to show you what I've set up and see how we might work together. Are you all okay in here for a few minutes? Promise to behave while we're gone?" she laughed.

"Okay, Mom," said Kari, hesitantly, and once again looked to her husband for his reaction.

Granny was acting very strange.

As the two women left the room, Sam noticed Bear smiling. He knew something she didn't.

"How was the play this afternoon?" asked Nina. "I've heard it is a winner year after year. Bear and I will have to get tickets for next Christmas."

"Oh, it was great," chimed in Sam, thankful for the diversion. "You should have seen the Ghost of Christmas Future this year. He came right out of the stage. He was about eight feet tall. It was amazing. Mom what was your favorite part?"

After Granny and Wisdom Keeper slipped through the sliding glass doors to the patio, Granny took hold of the other woman's arm. "Are you *the* Wisdom Keeper?"

"Yes."

"And, my granddaughter?"

"She is destined to be the next Wisdom Keeper far in the future."

"I knew it as soon as I saw you. My grandmother told me I would be meeting the Wisdom Keeper one day. For a time I thought I was to be the next Wisdom Keeper and then I thought that it might be my daughter, Kari. Now, I know who she was talking about." Her voice trailed off.

Grandmother smiled and the two women's eyes locked for several seconds.

"And, how does Bear Heart fit into this?"

"They will receive teachings and be working together."

"Well, this is a wonderful evening, Wisdom Keeper. Don't worry about my daughter and her husband. I will take care of everything."

When the two grandmothers returned they were smiling and Granny looked over at Sam and winked. "I think we are ready," she said. "Sam, can you get me seven sheets of paper and seven envelopes?"

"Yeah, sure." She got up and headed to the kitchen.

"In just a minute, Wisdom Keeper is going to start by explaining a little about the beliefs of indigenous people surrounding the Equinoxes and Solstices and then she is going to call in the energies that are needed for the ceremony. After that we are all going out in the backyard and sit around a fire for a few minutes. Okay? But, first we need to *smudge* ourselves. I think I can handle this part," she laughed.

Sam returned in a couple of minutes, just as Granny was lighting something in a large seashell. "This is called smudge, and it is the way most ceremonies are begun. It is used to banish any negative energy that anyone has brought to the circle. I hope I've remembered the lessons from my grandmother. I created a mixture of white sage to banish negative energy, sweetgrass for blessing, lavender for beauty, and cedar for balance." She glanced at Wisdom Keeper and the woman nodded. "I want each of you to stand up and I am going to fan this smoke over you. I wish I had known I was going to do this; my grandmother left me a beautiful hawk's wing that would have been perfect for a fan, but... oh well. Wisdom Keeper, will you go first?"

Wisdom Keeper stood with both of her hands outstretched at about waste level, palms up, while Granny used her hand to fan the billows. Sam was pretty sure Wisdom Keeper could have pulled a hawk's wing out of thin air, but she didn't say anything. After a second or two, Grandmother turned around, allowing Granny to do her back.

"Some people like to smudge their hands and even their feet. Who's next?" asked Granny.

Sam got up next and they went around the room. Tyler was last and he allowed his grandmother to do his front, but before he turned, he started clowning around and fanned some of the smoke under his arm pits.

When everyone quit laughing, Wisdom Keeper rose and went to stand by the fireplace. Bear Heart got Sam's attention and grinned as he discretely pointed to the fan above. Luna and Abril waved. Abril was leaning way back like she was thinking of flapping her golden wings to make the blades go around.

Wisdom Keeper frowned at the tiny figures. Abril sat up straight, looking a little guilty. Wisdom Keeper began. "Indigenous people honor the cycles of life. We see these cycles all around us, in the days, months, seasons, years, and even in our lifetimes. The calendar of my Mayan ancestors has tracked these cycles for millennia, for at least 5,000 years. But, that is a teaching for another day.

"Native people especially honored the seasons because they played a huge role in our survival. The people needed to know when to plant, when to harvest, when the animals would migrate, and when to prepare for the long winters. Tonight marks the end of the Big Snows Moon and the beginning of the Earth Renewal Moon and this is the midpoint in the season of winter. It is the shortest period of light and the longest darkness for the year. I know that Western society considers this the beginning of winter, but that is not what the ancient's believed. They celebrated the final harvest around your time of Halloween and then watched the tree nation drop their leaves and prepare for their resting time. They knew it was the beginning of winter. Now six weeks later it is the middle of season and six weeks from now we will celebrate the beginning of spring during the first part of February."

"I like that," laughed Nina, her round face beaming. "I never liked waiting till the end of March for spring to start."

"Before my people began tracking time, many were afraid that the sun would go away forever because it dipped so low in the sky and each year they would plead with the energies of the Universe to bring back Grandfather Sun. The ancient's ritual usually consisted of building a huge bonfire in recognition of the light and warmth of the Sun. It was lit three days before the Solstice and kept burning for three days after. If the fire ever went out it was a very bad sign that the Grandfather might not return.

"Your Granny and I have started a fire in your backyard fire circle. It is certainly not going to be a huge bonfire, but will serve our intent. We will go outside to complete our ceremony, but right now I will begin our celebration by calling to the powers of the directions to be with us and then Granny will give you some additional instructions."

No one's eyes had strayed during her comments.

"Are you ready?" Everyone nodded.

Sam watched as Wisdom Keeper did basically the same ritual she had done before. When she saw the flowing white energy follow the grandmother's hand across her chest and down, she glanced at Bear Heart. He and Aunt Nina seemed very interested, but not surprised. Tyler looked bored. Both her parents watched, fascinated, but didn't appear to be seeing the magick. Granny was a different story. She squinched up her eyes like Sam did when she wanted to see auras and Sam knew she could see the energy movement. Suddenly, Granny looked in her direction, like she'd known Sam had been watching her. She flashed a warm smile and then pointed at the fan above, chuckling quietly. *Oh, my gosh*. Granny could see the faeries too. Abril and Luna held up their hands to show innocence and to indicate they hadn't been up to any mischief. Sam wrinkled her brow and glared at them anyway and then glanced at her mom. Kari had a quizzical look on her face and was studying the ceiling, searching for what her daughter had been looking at. Sam gave her a bright smile and nervously shifted back to Grandmother.

Wisdom Keeper turned to the south and called the powers, then to the west, then the north and finally to the east. Then she did something that Sam hadn't seen before. Uttering words that Sam couldn't understand she did a quick spiral down and then immediately back up and ended with *Awanestica*. Sam did remember that awanestica meant *I have spoken*.

Complete, Grandmother turned once again to include the whole room. "Well, we now have a sacred space to work in." She held out her hand, palm up to Granny, and Granny rose and took her place at the end of the room.

"When I was a girl," began Granny, "my ol' Cheyenne grandma told me that we all deserve to have everything we want in life and the only reason we didn't have it was because we hadn't *dreamt it in*. When I would ask for something she would say *dream it in*. When I would complain about something I didn't have, she would say *dream it in*. She told me I would never have something in my life that I wanted if I didn't first *dream it in*."

Sam was now forgotten and Kari's attention was riveted back on her mother, seeing a side of her that she'd never seen before.

"Sam, if you give everyone a piece of paper and an envelope, oh, and we will need some pens." Sam jumped to retrieve the items. "I want you to dream what you would like to have happen in the next three months. Assume there are no restrictions of money or time. You have all the resources you need to achieve whatever it is you want, even though you may not realize it. Where do you want to go? What would you like to have, or do, or become? I don't want you to worry about how any of this is going to be accomplished, because if you do you probably won't write anything down."

"So, Granny, this is kind of like manifesting?" asked Sam.

"Yes, that's a very good word for it."

Sam stared at Grandmother and the old woman smiled.

Tyler immediately started scribbling on his paper. Jack looked over at Kari and shrugged his shoulders and then turned pen to paper. Kari took a long time and finally began.

"When you are done," said Granny. "Place your page in the envelope, seal it, and write your name on the outside."

Sam looked over at Bear Heart and he had his head down, busy writing something. Nina sat with her head back and eyes closed. Sam couldn't think of anything to write.

"Stumped?" asked Abril grinning. The two faeries had appeared, one on each side of her.

"Don't tease her, Abril," scolded Luna. "We're supposed to be helping her. Wind, what do you want more than anything? You know you don't have to speak. Abril and I can read your thoughts."

Sam appeared a little worried, but then tried to focus. *Well, I'd like to get an A on my science project*, she thought.

"Bigger," said Luna.

Hummm, I wouldn't mind Bear giving me a kiss.

"Ahhh, a woman after my own heart," said Abril, "but bigger, Wind."

Sam suddenly knew what she wanted to write. *I want mom and dad to accept me for who I am. I want them to like Grandmother Wisdom Keeper, so I don't have to keep any more secrets.*

"Good, good." Abril flipped her long flowing black hair over her shoulder. "See what she can do with a little coaxing."

"I'm the one who told *you* that, Abril," said Luna, exasperation in her voice.

"It looks like we are all done," broke in Granny, with a grin. "Let's all go out back. Bring your envelopes."

She led the way through the kitchen to the deck and patio. Outside three logs were burning intensely in the large copper bowl. The fire popped and crackled and sent up sparks through the mesh cover spiraling into the night.

When they'd all gathered around, Granny continued, "In the Cheyenne ways that I learned, it is my understanding that messages are sent out to the Great Mystery of the Universe using smoke. I would like all of you to wave your envelopes through the smoke and picture your message being taken skyward. Now this is important. I want you to see the future, see all your wishes as if they have already happened. Back inside we are all going to put our envelopes in the big desk and leave them there till the Vernal Equinox. At that time you will get your paper back and remember what you wrote. It will be interesting to see who was able to *manifest* their dreams, as Sam put it."

"That's cool," said Bear.

"I will probably not be here in Kansas City, but I am sure Grandmother Wisdom Keeper will be glad to facilitate your next ceremony."

Wisdom Keeper nodded.

"Will you close out our ceremony, Grandmother?" asked Granny.

Wisdom Keeper pocketed her own envelope and raised her arms, "Wakan Tanka, sacred entities of the Universe, Grandfather Sun, we ask that you creep higher and higher in the sky as the days go by and shine brightly upon us. Bring your warmth and light into our hearts. Take the dreams of these people and manifest them into the highest good for all. This ceremony is ended in beauty. Awanestica."

Chapter 21
Valentine's Day

Love was in the air for Bear Heart. Though he thought of his mother often, the devastation of feeling abandoned by her had vanished. He had family again. He didn't even seem to mind that his father only came to visit about once a month. Life was good. And… he was very aware of the changes to his body and to the way he felt when Playful Autumn Wind was close. When she tossed her long blond hair and flashed him one of her perfect smiles, his insides melted. A couple of times he was afraid to speak, fearful that he might stutter and stammer.

Sam's body had changed too and looked much more like an hour-glass. When she wore a tight fitting top and leggings, her favorite, it was impossible to not notice her tiny waist and very long legs. Bear found himself holding back at times just to watch her walk up the stairs, pony tail swishing along with her hips. She seemed completely oblivious to the effect she had on him, at least that is what he thought. But, Sam never forgot her wish that one day Bear would want to kiss her.

Bear had no idea what Sam's grandma had said to his aunt or to Sam's parents, but Grandmother Wisdom Keeper came and went fairly frequently now. The little people were still under orders to remain invisible to all the parents, which bothered the heck out of them. Bear accidently overhead a conversation between Wisdom Keeper and Gideon one day.

"Well, that's not fair," exclaimed Gideon. "Bear Heart gets to go over to Wind's house all the time."

"You are a boy, Gideon."

"I know it, and so is Bear Heart."

"You are a boy *gnome*, Gideon. You can't be popping in on Sam like Tinga and Luna. She's becoming a woman. Bear doesn't just appear in her bedroom."

"Grandmother, she is the most beautiful girl I have ever known. And, I'm over a hundred years old." He thought for a minute, "What if I promise to not go near her bedroom?"

"Gideeeon."

"Yeah, yeah."

On the afternoon of February 1ˢᵗ, Bear dropped his school books on the dining room table and began rummaging though the freezer. He popped a barbeque chicken Hot Pocket into the microwave and then was going up to his room when his aunt came around the corner. "There's a call for you on the answering machine. Ol' Tom said he was going to be in town this weekend and wants to talk to you. His number's on the machine."

Bear found the number and returned the call. They agreed to meet at Bear's on Saturday morning.

Nina was at work, so Bear Heart and Tom had the house to themselves. Bear had a cozy fire going in the fireplace, so they got comfortable in the great room.

"Bear Heart, Grandmother Wisdom Keeper has asked me to work with you. She knows about young men, and I certainly remember the time when I was your age. In the *old ways* of our people, after a young man's vision quest, it was time for the training of manhood. Have you ever heard of the Chuluaquai Quodoushka[3] teachings?"

Bear indicated he hadn't.

"Well, long ago, this training was very common among native traditions. Today it is rare, because of the Western mentality that dominates Indian cultures. Instead of going with the flow of the Universe and honoring the normal passionate feelings of young men and women, society tries to ignore and suppress these instincts, which does not work. Trying to force young people to bury these natural impulses only confuses and may cause irreparable damage to the psyche or even the physical body. What works is to teach you to respect and honor your feelings and work with them instead of pretending they don't exist or that they are somehow immoral."

Bear's eyes told him that he knew exactly what feelings the man was referring to.

"Chuluaquai in our language means *life force* energy. Quodoushka means *the merging of the masculine and feminine*. Together the words are interpreted as *sacred sexuality*. Sex between consenting adults is the most beautiful act in the Universe and certainly not something to be

---

[3]For information on conducting your own Rites of Empowerment, see Appendix A/*Wild Women Rites of Empowerment Bible*.

ashamed of. Shame can only come when the act is used to manipulate or violates someone's *children's fire* in some other way. Our children's fire is our spark or spirit. It is actually our humanity.

"I know of your feelings for Playful Autumn Wind and I believe the feelings are mutual."

Bear's head jerked up with this comment and a huge smile lit up his whole face. "Really?"

"Yes. In the future, you and Wind will be receiving many teachings from Wisdom Keeper and it is important to have you be able to interact in a loving, but respectful manner. My training with you will show you how to honor your own impulses, and equally honor hers. It is imperative that you not be influenced by your peers, the other kids at school. You are different than they are. Boys love to boast and many times pressure one another to do things they normally wouldn't do. I know that you already have a strong respect for the feminine, but you need to understand that it is always the woman who makes the choice. Her wishes must always be honored in order to abide by Sacred Law. And, her pleasure should be your utmost goal. It won't be long before Grandmother begins these same teachings with Samantha."

When Ol' Tom left that day, Bear was so excited he cranked up a CD with native drumming and chants and danced like a crazy man around the house for an hour. He hadn't thought life could get any better, but it just had.

Bear knew that the Cheesecake Factory on the Plaza was Sam's favorite restaurant, so he persuaded his aunt to take them there on Valentine's Day. She promised to take a friend along and get a table in another room to give them privacy.

He went to three greeting card stores before he found the perfect card. He already had the perfect gift.

On Valentine's Day evening Nina and her friend Sue, another nurse from the hospital pulled into Sam's drive and Bear jumped out. When Samantha opened the front door, all Bear could do was gawk. He was used to seeing her in sweaters and blue jeans or leggings and thought she was beautiful then. But, tonight she had on a red slinky dress that draped in one direction from her shoulder to her waste and then the skirt reversed the swirls in the other direction. She'd evidently borrowed a pair of long, dangly red-coral and silver earrings from Wisdom Keeper that danced with every movement. Her hair was pulled into a French braid that started high on her head and ran all the way down her back. When he could finally close his mouth, he began the stuttering that he had feared before.

"Uhhh, you look amazing, uhhh, I got you this rose."

"Hey, where are you going, man?" asked Tyler, scooting in beside his sister at the door.

"Uhhh, Cheese, uhhh, Cheesecake Factory."

"That's cool. Want me to come along?"

Sam took the long-stemmed crimson rose, "Thank you, it's beautiful, but didn't you leave me a rose this afternoon?"

He looked puzzled. "No, you got another rose?" He almost panicked wondering who else might have given Sam a rose.

"Yeah, I found one on my bed when I got home. I thought you'd been here."

"Well, it wasn't..."

"I really love the Cheesecake Factory," said Tyler.

"Get real, Tyler. Mom, I'm leaving now."

"Hold on, Sam. I want to get a picture of you and Bear," said her mom.

Sam rolled her eyes, but Bear interrupted. "Yeah, I'd love to have a picture of Sam in that dress." He had stepped inside, but hadn't taken his eyes off Sam.

Bear had on nice dress slacks and a sport coat that looked a little big. Sam couldn't remember seeing it before and wondered if he'd borrowed it. But, it didn't matter, she thought he looked gorgeous. The denim shirt and tie was the perfect touch.

"Okay, you two stand over there by the fireplace."

As Bear walked past, Tyler grabbed his tie and said, "What's this? You're all dressed up for my sister and you bought her a flower?"

"Hey, don't mess with my tie. I like it."

"So do I," said Sam, sounding very mature.

Kari took several pictures and returning to the car, Bear held the back door open for Sam. Nina and her friend had to stifle a laugh from the front seat, as he nearly tripped and fell getting around to the other side.

No one saw the sad look in Gideon's eyes as he leaned against the birdbath in the front yard.

At the restaurant, Bear asked Sam what she wanted and as Ol' Tom had coached him, when the waiter arrived, he ordered for both of them.

"I got you a present, Wind." He scooted the card and a small box toward her.

The cover of the card had a soft focus image of a beautiful Indian maiden and a handsome Indian brave holding hands in a meadow filled with purple flowers. The message inside was signed, Love, Bear. When Sam opened the box, her eyes lit up. Inside was a pink quartz crystal heart about two inches in diameter.

"It's perfect."

Chapter 22
Moon Time

"Hey, want to go play paintball tomorrow?" asked Tyler. "I thought I'd see if Dad would take us."

"Can't tomorrow," answered Bear. "An elder from where I used to live in Hot Springs is coming in and bringing Two Crows. You remember him from my birthday?"

"Yeah."

"Yeah, I guess you met Ol' Tom too. He's going to be giving us some teachings."

"Sounds boring. Wouldn't you rather play paintball? Maybe Two Crows will go too."

"You don't know what we are going to talk about. You might change your mind. I got an idea. Come over tomorrow morning. If you don't like what he is going to teach us, you can leave. No matter what, I will see if Ol' Tom will take us to play paintball tomorrow night. I know Two Crows will really get into the game."

Ol' Tom and Two Crows came into town the last week in February and then again the first weekend in March. Tyler decided to stay for the teachings. Sam asked what they'd been doing after the first weekend, but Bear Heart's answer had been mysterious, so she hadn't pushed.

On Sunday afternoon of the second weekend, Wisdom Keeper came to see Sam. They were sitting in her bedroom when Grandmother said, "I want to tell you a story, Wind."

"Great, I love your stories."

"Well, when I was a little older than you, I got a call from a medicine woman named, Grandmother Leia Thin Sticks. She was the leader of a group of women that had formed a Sisterhood Lodge and she told me she was facilitating a sweat ceremony for a woman named Felicia Jaguar Speaker. Do you remember seeing the sweat lodge at the Eagle Dance?

"Yeah, Bear was helping his uncles build it out of willow branches."

"Right. Well, this ceremony was to take place in a sweat lodge. Thin Sticks needed eight women, counting herself, to do the ritual and one of the women who had been planning to attend called at the last minute and couldn't make it. So, Leia was asking if I would like to join in. I had never had an experience like that, so I quickly agreed.

"At that time of my life, I was really into boys. I always had one or two girlfriends at any one time, but for the most part I saw other girls as competition. If one of my girlfriends and I had a falling out, I saw nothing wrong with going after her boyfriend. Now, you understand this is not something that I am proud of, but it was the way it was. I will explain more about why I believe I did this type of thing at another time, but for now… Well, when I got to Leia's home, I realized I didn't know anyone except her. I learned the reason for the ceremony was because Jaguar Speaker had been raped by some boys in town. This was to be a purification ceremony and to help her put what had happened behind her so she could go on with her life. The actual ceremony is not important here, but what happened inside the lodge is.

"Leia led all of us into the lodge and then she asked two men who had been tending the fire to bring in the hot stones. She poured water on the hot rocks as she called in the directions and then after a couple of chants, she began the first round. In this round we were each asked to place a hand on Jaguar Speaker who was sitting in the middle of the lodge. We were told to remember the love that we had for all sisters and to concentrate our power so that Felicia would be able to use it in her healing. I felt rather awkward. The words *the love that we had for all sisters* was quite foreign to me. I wasn't sure I loved all the women in the lodge, much less all women in general, but I made an effort. When I touched Jaguar Speaker, something magickal happened. I felt warmth come into my heart and then flood out through my whole body, and it wasn't coming from the cleansing steam of the stones. My whole body, down to my finger tips and toes, tingled. Jaguar Speaker was the source. I was supposed to be giving this woman my power and not the other way around. But, I realized that just touching her, I was connected to *all that is feminine* and I had access to the receptive energy of all the sisters in the lodge and probably the Universe at that time. The love poured through me from all those women that I didn't even know.

"I left the lodge knowing that I had a blood bond with all women. There was a connectedness with my sisters that I would never have with a man. Not, that I wasn't still very interested in the male sex you understand," she laughed, "but I realized this was something completely different. I realized it was a gift that I was to cherish the rest of my life. My relationship with all sisters was forever changed from that day forward."

"Wow, I can almost feel the energy you talked about," said Sam, running her hands up and down her arms, which were covered in goose flesh.

"Well, I am telling you this story today, because I feel you are so wrapped up in your feelings for Bear Heart that you are neglecting your girlfriends."

"Gosh. You're right. Chloe and Jennifer have been acting kind of jealous lately. Even though Bear, Chlo and I are back to walking to school every day together, I haven't made a lot of time for her, or Jen."

Just then the phone rang and it was Bear asking if Sam and Wisdom Keeper wanted to go out to a Chinese restaurant for dinner. Two Crows had asked Chloe and Tom was driving. At dinner Sam noticed that Two Crows and Chloe were getting along very well, in spite of Tyler who kept trying to monopolize the conversation. Chloe was glowing from the attention. The spark that seemed to have ignited at Bear's birthday seemed to be turning into a nice little fire. The two were promising to email each other.

During the week, Sam made an effort to call Chloe and Jennifer several times just to chat, and she was really glad when Chloe said she was going to have a sleepover on Saturday. Nothing much else happened during the week, except that early on Saturday morning Sam was sure she heard a woodpecker outside her window. She got up to look for her Flicker. She remembered that Flicker migrated for the winter and she didn't know when she would return. She couldn't see any birds, so she put it out of her mind.

Chloe's mom swung by and picked up Sam on Saturday. Chloe, Jen, Abby, and Sienna were already in the Chevy Tahoe. Sienna had transferred to Santa Fe just before Christmas. Her mother and stepdad had moved from Albuquerque, New Mexico. Her mother was black having come from somewhere in the Caribbean. Sienna had never met her real father. He had been a tourist and gone on his way a week after meeting her mother. Her mother had finally married a wonderful man when Sienna was three and he had adopted her. With her mixed blood, her hair was as dark as Jennifer's, but not straight. Sam had seen her at school with it rather long and full, but today it was done in tiny cornrows with beads interspersed and was beautiful. Sam wondered what her blond hair would look like in cornrows. She might have to try it sometime.

The girls were dropped at the Great Mall of the Great Plains Cinemas and promised to be outside at exactly 5:00 when the movie ended. *New Moon* had been out about two weeks, so the crowds were dying down a little. Several of the girls at school had already seen the movie twice. Sam and her friends had all waited in long lines to see *Twilight*, the first in the *Twilight Saga* vampire series, but had gotten smart this time and bought tickets on-line in advance. In the series two of the main characters, Edward and Jacob vied for beautiful Bella's attention. Edward was a very handsome vampire and Jacob a very handsome Indian werewolf. Bella was human. Sam knew that Chloe's favorite was Edward and Jennifer was rooting for Jacob.

When she'd seen *Twilight*, Sam was undecided who she wanted to win Bella's affection, but now that Bear was in her life she felt compelled to root for the werewolf. It turned out that Abriana and Sienna were both Edward junkies. They all left the theatre two hours later with romantic thoughts in their minds, except Sam's wasn't about vampires or werewolves. She wondered if Chloe was thinking of Two Crows.

Stopping by Papa Johns on the way home, Chloe's mom picked up pizza for everyone.

"There are six boxes here," said Jen. "Have you invited the whole class?"

"No," said Chloe, "my brother's going to be home. He can eat a whole pizza by himself."

"Tyler can eat a whole one during baseball season and I don't think Bear would have a problem either," added Sam.

"How is Bear Heart doing? Chloe tells me you got a crystal heart for Valentine's Day, Sam," teased Abby.

"Yeah, and a red rose, too," chimed in Jen.

"He's fine," blushed Sam.

"He's more than fine," exclaimed Sienna, "That is one fine Indian."

Everyone laughed.

"Well, Two Crows is pretty cute too," said Sam, trying to change the focus.

"Who's that?" asked Sienna, "another Indian?"

"Yeah, he's a friend of Bear's and he thinks Chloe is really cute. I hear she's been getting some pretty regular emails from him and he's got her number for texting," said Sam.

Now it was Chloe's turn to blush.

"How do you meet these guys? How about introducing me to one?" said Sienna.

"I think Chad likes you, Sienna," kidded Jennifer.

"Uuuggg. He's such a show-off and he kind of scares me sometimes. You gotta find me somebody else."

"You have to wait in line. I'm next," exclaimed Jennifer.

The girls played video games, listened to their I-Pods, and giggled up in Chloe's room till about 9:00 PM, then came down to the family room to watch a video. Sienna was the first to crash in her sleeping bag at midnight, but the others continued to chatter away. At 1:00 AM Sam went to the bathroom and came back with a smile on her face. "Guess what?"

"What?" asked Chloe.

"I think I started my period. Well, Grandmother Wisdom Keeper calls it your *moon cycle*."

"How do you feel?" asked Chloe.

"I'm sure she feels fine," said Jennifer. "It's no big deal."

Jennifer had started her cycle several months earlier and now felt she was the expert of the group.

"I can't believe it," said Sam, excitedly. "Grandmother said she wanted to do a blessing way ceremony for me when I started. I can't wait to tell her."

"Who's this Grandmother?" asked Abby, "And, what's a *blessing way*?"

"It's a *rite of passage* ceremony and Native Americans do them all the time," said Chloe. Now she was the expert. "I'm going to see if Wisdom Keeper will do one for me too."

"Well, at least you got a medicine name, Chloe. I still don't have a medicine name," complained Jen.

"You have to ask for it. Grandmother won't do the ceremony for it unless you ask. It would cross your children's fire," smiled Chloe. "Sam's medicine name is Playful Autumn Wind and mine is Laughing Fox."

"What are you guys talking about? Children's fires, medicine names, rites of passage?" asked Abby.

"Sam knows a Native American medicine woman named Grandmother Wisdom Keeper. She works with Bear Heart, too. Sam is going to be the next Wisdom Keeper one day." Chloe was feeling very superior now.

"I kind of knew a medicine man in Albuquerque," said Sienna, from deep in her sleeping bag. "I used to see him around town."

"We thought you were asleep. What was his name?" asked Sam.

"Black Hawk."

"Hummm. Maybe Wisdom Keeper knows him. She seems to know everyone."

"Tell Abby and Sienna the story of your name, Sam," said Jen.

Sam described the leaves spiraling into the air and then falling back to Earth and Grandmother, at first, thinking her name was Playful Autumn Leaf and then realizing that she wasn't a leaf, but the wind.

"That's really neat. What's your story, Chloe?"

"Well," Chloe was going for the drama, "when Grandmother did the ceremony for my name, she saw a vision too. There was a meadow filled with yellow daisies and she was walking through it when she saw a red fox coming down the trail. The fox got right in front of her and began doing a dance." She got up and began twirling around. "When the fox got done with his dance he was laughing. So, Wisdom Keeper knew my name was Laughing Fox."

"You kind of look like a red fox, except I've never seen a curly fox," said Abriana. "Maybe we will all have medicine names someday."

Chapter 23
Estanatlehi

As Sam ran home from Chloe's on Sunday morning, she noticed a couple of hawks soaring overhead. She sure was seeing a lot of hawks lately. Then just as she was about to open the front door, she was sure she hear a woodpecker again. She laughed. The rhythms of her life had changed. She burst through the door to find Wisdom Keeper and her mom enjoying a cup of coffee at the kitchen table. Wisdom Keeper had on a pair of nice slacks and a red sweater with a native geometric print. She always looked strange to Sam with regular clothes on, but so far she'd never warn her native attire when she'd visited Kari or Jack.

"Wow, you're here. I don't know if I will every get used to this," Sam laughed.

Grandmother gave her a knowing smile.

"Used to what, Sam?" asked Kari.

"Oh, nothing. Are Tyler and Dad around?"

"No, it was such a nice day that they went to the batting cages. Baseball season is around the…"

"Good, because I have some news. I started my moon cycle last night."

"Your what, dear?" asked her mom.

"My moon cycle. I started my period, Mom."

"Oh, and I'm guessing that moon cycle is a native term for that."

"Right."

"You are going to have to be patient with me, Sam. It's going to take me a while to pick up this lingo."

Sam went over and gave her mom a big hug. "And, I love you so much for letting me be me."

"Well, I am trying. With your excitement, I'm guessing congratulations are in order. Things were different when I was a girl. I remember my friends called it the *curse*."

"Things haven't changed that much, Mom. It's just that I am able to see things from the other side of the wheel."

Kari stared in disbelief. There were many more changes in her daughter than her just starting her period. She had matured so much in the last year.

Grandmother gave Kari an empathetic smile. "Yes. Sam may no longer be your little girl, but she will always be your daughter, Kari."

Kari nodded, not picking up that Wisdom Keeper had read her thoughts.

"This is exciting, Sam. I guess we have a blessing way ceremony to plan for you. Of course, if it is okay will your mom."

Kari saw the excited look on Sam's face. "Well, I guess I am just along for the ride. I need to go *with the flow of the Universe*, as Sam keeps telling me. What's a blessing way ceremony?"

"If you will get me another cup of coffee, Sam, I will explain."

Wisdom Keeper got comfortable after taking a whiff of the steaming cup in her hands. "I will start with a little history on why our people feel rites of passage are so important."

Sam grabbed a chair and scooted close to her mom. Kari relaxed and put her arm around her daughter.

"Rites of passage, or what I call *rites of empowerment*, have helped people celebrate the natural evolution in their lives for thousands of years. Some ceremonies were designated by chronological age and others by events, such as a woman having a baby or a young brave making his first kill in a buffalo hunt. In Western culture it is normal to celebrate births, birthdays, graduations, marriages, and deaths. In Jewish tradition rites of puberty are still celebrated with bar and bat mitzvahs. In Catholic and Christian circles baptisms and confirmations are celebrated, and some Native Americans are lucky enough to experience blessing way ceremonies and vision quests. You know that Bear Heart was put out on his vision quest by Ol' Tom."

Sam nodded.

"But, most of the current rites of passage gloss over and fall short of addressing the emotional issues that mystify and create havoc in our worlds today, such as calling the beginning of a woman's moon cycle *the curse*. The *child within* can suffer significant, and many times traumatic, internal confusion - physiologically, emotionally, mentally, spiritually, and sexually. Many of your psychologists feel this is what is creating greater and greater stress, sickness, and disease in our lives.

"Indigenous peoples celebrate the natural cycles of change. Remember we did the ceremony at the Winter Solstice to honor the middle of winter and the beginning of the return of Grandfather Sun. Soon it till be time to honor the Vernal Equinox, the day of equal sunshine and darkness, which reminds us to keep a balance of everything in our lives.

"All cycles are measured within the Six Cosmic Laws:

Death brings Life,
Life brings Rebirth,
Rebirth brings Movement,
Movement brings Change,
Change brings Chaos,
Chaos brings Death.

"And, the cycle continues on with Death Brings Life, never ending. It is understood that change is inevitable; in fact, it is the *only thing* that is constant in our world. Second, it is implicit that for our souls to evolve there *must be movement.* Thirdly, we accept that in order for *anything to be reborn, something must die.* Celebrating rites of empowerment promotes the mourning that goes with accepting these *little deaths,* or changes in our lives, and even *death-death,* which is our actual crossing from one life to another. These rites create the feeling of *closure* and heal the wounds of our inner child and spark our *spirit child*; the one who has no fear of dancing on the edge and jumping into the abyss. You'll learn more about your spirit child soon, Wind."

Wisdom Keeper took a long sip of her coffee. "It may sound crazy for someone to *celebrate* a divorce, because many times they are *messy*, as you might say. But, if the separation of marriage is inevitable, the parties need to heal and move on. They need to recognize what was good about the marriage and learn from the issues that caused the separation. Without this healing, an individual may suffer needlessly for years. You remember the story about the girl who had been raped, Sam? That was a healing ceremony, but similar to a rite of passage."

She nodded.

"That actually makes sense," said Kari. "My sister-in-law, Sam's aunt, is still dwelling on issues from her divorce and it's been almost three years. She can't seem to let it go."

"Maybe we can work with her," said Wisdom Keeper.

"I think we should try," said Kari.

"Rites of empowerment celebrate our growth and maturation as individuals as we travel along our *path of heart* toward enlightenment. Rituals balance our masculine and feminine energies and help us regain what our people call the *five Hauquas*, which are health, hope, happiness, harmony, and humor. These are every human's inalienable rights."

"This is fascinating. Can I stop you for a minute Wisdom Keeper?" asked Kari. Grandmother nodded. "If you two haven't had breakfast, I thought I might fix us an omelet. It won't keep me from listening."

"Yeah, I'm starved," said Sam.

"Sounds wonderful, Kari. Wind, I want to tell you a little about the goddess Estanatlehi, which we give credit to for bringing us your Kinaaldá ceremony. If you can't remember that, you can call it your *Becoming Woman* ceremony. I have a book here with some quotes." She mysteriously pulled it out of her bag.

"Okay."

Kari got up and began rummaging through the refrigerator, but made sure she could still hear everything Wisdom Keeper was saying.

"Estanatlehi is most commonly known as Changing Woman, but different tribes have other names for her, such as Turquoise Woman, White-Shell Woman, Painted Woman, Self-Renewing One, Spinning Woman, and Weaver of Cycles. She is a Diné and Apache goddess and there are many myths surrounding her that I think you will find amusing." She glanced at her book. "In the myths, Changing Woman matures very fast. In fact, everyone in these legends grows rapidly. Depending upon the story, she grew to puberty in four, eight, twelve, or fourteen days. Her sons grow to maturity in eight days," she laughed. "And, Changing Woman never grows old. When she sees herself aging, she walks to the east through the seasons and as she does, she becomes younger. You might say she was the first *time traveler*. One myth says she cycles through all ages in one year. In spring she is a child, in summer she becomes a young woman, in fall she is mature, and in winter she prepares for her death so she may rebirth in the spring."

"I kind of like the idea of just walking to the east and getting younger," grinned Kari.

"That would be nice, wouldn't it," smiled Wisdom Keeper, "Estanatlehi describes her birth by saying that *as the flood waters draped over dawn's sky, I was found by First Man as I lay on a bed of flower petals wrapped in a rainbow.* A second legend also includes the great flood, which I think you would call Noah's flood. This time she survives by floating in an abalone shell and she then wanders the lands as the waters recede. In another she is found by Coyote. You remember Coyote, Sam?"

"Yeah, he took me on a journey to see Flicker and Snake."

Kari turned with a quizzical look, but didn't say anything.

"Well, this legend says that *after being born of darkness and dawn on Spruce Mountain, she was covered with a blanket of clouds and rainbows, and secured to her cradleboard by lightning and sunbeams.*

"Lightning and sunbeams. I love this story," cried Sam.

"Here are several descriptions of her blessing way ceremony. One says *I was dressed in jewels, white shells, turquoise, abalone, and jet and blessed with pollen from the dawn and from the twilight.* In another, *My hair was washed with the morning dew and songs were sung in my honor.*

"After her ceremony, she takes Grandfather Sun as her husband and births twin sons, whose names are Monster Slayer and Born-for-Water and it's not long before they have rid the Earth of all monsters except age, poverty, famine, and winter. They take off to build their mother a house made of turquoise, some say crystal, on an island *cradled in the salty waters where Earth and Sky meet.* Here Changing Woman receives the Sun as he comes home each night."

"Yeah, when the sun goes down."

"Quit interrupting Wisdom Keeper, Sam."

"Sorry."

"There's one more myth. She molds first man and woman from cornmeal and covers them with a magickal blanket. In the morning they are alive and breathing. For the next four days, the pair reproduces constantly, forming the four great Diné clans. Now that is definitely fast," she laughed. "Wow, this is so cool. As soon as I eat, I've got to go call Granny and tell her about the ceremony."

Note: For more information on Rites of Empowerment for women, see Appendix A/*Wild Woman Rites of Empowerment Bible.*

Chapter 24
Chuluaquai Quodoushka

"Wind, Grandmother told us about your ceremony. Will you let us make your dress?" asked Tinga.

Luna, Tinga and Abril were sitting on Sam's dresser when Sam's alarm went off the next morning.

She tried to rub the sleep from her eyes, "That sounds great, but I've got to get ready for school right now. Can we talk later?"

"We know, we know. Come on girls, let's get to planning. We've only got about three weeks if Grandmother is going to do the ceremony on Wind's birthday." The trio vaporized right in front of Sam's eyes.

Sam had called her Granny after Wisdom Keeper had gone the day before and she'd been congratulated and then Granny had said what Sam really wanted to hear; she wouldn't miss the event for anything. She'd be back for her birthday.

Every time Sam turned around Tinga and the two faeries were scurrying around doing something. They showed up with a tape measure one day to see how tall Sam was and to take her other measurements. Another day they came with a menu.

"Why do you want to know if I like lasagna?" asked Sam.

"Because we are planning the menu for the feast. I thought lasagna, salad, and garlic bread would be good," said Luna. "But, Tinga thinks you might want burritos because she knows you love Mexican food."

"Can you guys cook?"

"Of course, we can cook," exclaimed Abril, "but lots of times it's easier to just manifest something." Her iridescent golden wings fluttered and she levitated about two feet of the ground and then waved her tiny hand. "Here, would you like some ice cream?" A swirly chocolate cone appeared in her hand that was almost the same color as her creamy brown skin.

"Yeah, thanks," said Sam, smiling.

"So which is it? Lasagna or burritos."

"Lasagna, I think. Mom and Granny really love Italian food."

"Okay." The three little people circled up, everyone talking at once. They completely ignored Sam for the minute.

"Well, there will be thirteen humans and six of us little people."

"Probably need at least three pans to be safe."

"What if someone doesn't like lasagna?"

"What should I put in the salad?"

"Everyone likes lasagna."

"I say four loaves of garlic bread."

"Tomatoes, green onions, croutons."

"Don't forget the Parmesan cheese."

"I don't care what kind it is, I just love cheese."

They sounded like buzzing bumble bees. Suddenly Tinga turned back to Sam, "And, what kind of cake?"

"That's easy. Red velvet with cream cheese icing." Sam licked her ice cream and laughed.

The last weekend in March, Sam's parents decided to go to the lake and open the cabin up for the summer. The very cold weather that would have frozen the water pipes was passed. Sam asked all four of her girlfriends to join her, but Jennifer had to do something with her mom and Abriana was grounded because of poor grades. Neither could make it, but Chloe and Sienna accepted the invitation. Bear and Tyler stayed behind to work with Ol' Tom one last weekend. It was remarkable that Tyler was suddenly interested in native teachings. Nina said it was fine for him to stay over at her house.

The girls took off for the river right after breakfast. No one asked where she was going any more. Sam was excited because it would be the first time that Sienna would meet Wisdom Keeper and the little people. The more she'd gotten to know Sienna, she was sure her new friend would be able to see them.

Abril was the first to see the girls when they rounded the cliff. "Hey, Sam. Hi, Chloe. Been looking forward to meeting you Sienna."

Sam and Chloe waved to the tiny figure as she floated down from above. She looked exotic as usual, sporting her large hoop earrings and gold armbands. They sparkled in the sun, contrasting with her shiny black hair that looked like it had been combed by the wind. Sam had never seen her in a skirt and as she drifted to the ground, it billowed like a pale blue parachute. Sienna had been warned, but her initial response was still priceless. It was obvious that she hadn't truly believed what her friends had promised.

"Wisdom Keeper said she would be along shortly," said Tinga. "We wanted to be here. I think you are going to get another teaching today."

Tinga was wearing a multi-colored tie-dye sweatshirt and dark green leggings that set off her luminous pale green skin to perfection. Her pointy ears stuck through her bright red-orange curls and when she came forward to greet Sienna her smile made her dimples extra noticeable. Luna had been on the ledge above too, but suddenly just materialized beside Sienna. She had on a hot pink t-shirt and leggings and her vest made of white feathers.

"Maybe you better sit down, Sienna," said Chloe, laughing. Sienna looked pale even with her dark skin. "I know I had the same reaction the first time I met these guys." She patted the log beside her.

Before she could sit, a loud growling noise erupted from the woods and a second later a cinnamon-colored bear could be seen moseying toward the clearing. Sienna didn't stop to sit on the log, but leaped behind it and crouched down. Sam ran to give the bear a hug, but Chloe hung back and just waved, "Hi, Griz." She hadn't quite gotten up enough courage to hug the gentle giant yet.

"Griz," your scaring Sienna to death," said Grandmother following behind and seeing the young girl cowering behind the log. "That's not nice. Welcome Sienna, my name is Wisdom Keeper."

"Uhhh. Hi. Nice to meet you." Sienna wasn't ready to come out and remained with the log between herself and the bear until he ambled over to get a drink out of the river and then lay down on the sand. She finally put one leg over the log and straddled it, still ready to make a fast getaway.

Grandmother spread out a blanket and Sam and Chloe plopped down cross-legged in front of her. Abril lay down on her side propping her head up with her forearm and hand. Luna and Tinga settled in on the sand with their backs to the log.

"I'm glad all three of you could come today. I've wanted to talk with Wind about something before her big day and this is really something all of you should hear, including you little people. She glanced at Sienna, but didn't coax her to join them on the blanket. She knew she would when she felt more comfortable.

"Wind, I think you know that Ol' Tom has been working with Bear Heart and Two Crows and now it is time for you to receive the teachings of womanhood. I know all of your mothers have talked to you about your moon cycles and probably sex, but they may not have approached the subject in the way that I will today. Everyone comfortable?"

"Yeah."

"Yeah."

"In times long ago…" Wisdom Keeper spoke for a time about when she had been a girl of thirteen and then began on the beauty of the Chuluaquai Quodoushka teachings. She talked about many of the same things that Tom was discussing with the boys, but then her comments became focused on what every woman should know.

"As a woman you are the Universe, the Great Grandmother Wahkawhuan, and the blackness between the stars. You are also Heyotomah, Grandmother Earth. The feminine is the great womb of creation. You are sacred and all life comes from you. Sam, Chloe, do you remember these words from the Creation Story of our people?"

They nodded. Chloe was hanging on every word and when Griz started snoring, Sienna finally got off the log and came over to sit on the blanket.

"Bear Heart and Two Crows have been taught that they are Sskawhuan, the Great Grandfather, the galaxies and stars and Sohotomah, Grandfather Sun. As the masculine they are the spark of the Universe, they provide the sacred seed of creation."

"That's like the egg and the sperm that we talked about in health class, right?" asked Chloe.

"Yes, but the intent of these teachings is to show you the beauty and power that you possess as women, not to be scientific. Many girls in your Junior High and High School are going to be pressured by boys to have sex. They will actually be looking for love, but will not understand the difference between love and sex. They will want to be accepted and be popular and because of this they may offer themselves. Some will even become pregnant and then have to make some tough decisions. I want you all to learn to respect and love yourselves enough that you understand the difference between love and sex. A boy who tries to talk you into something that you are not ready for does not love you.

"There is nothing wrong or immoral about the feelings your body is expressing. When you come close to a boy or even kiss, you may tingle all the way down to your toes. This is perfectly natural. It is the way it was intended by the Great Mystery. Honor your feelings and work with them instead of trying to suppress or pretend they don't exist as some may ask you to do. Explore and find out what feels good to you. Every woman's body is different. This will teach you control and without these experiences, when you are ready to make love someday you will not be able to share with your partner what brings you pleasure. When the time is right, I want you to experience the perfect bonding of receptive and assertive energies creating a sacred union, what is called *chuluaquai quodoushka*. I will give you many more teachings in the years to come."

"How will you know if it's really love?" asked Sienna. "When my mom met my dad, she thought it was love. He promised to marry her and then he left after a week."

"Ahhh. I am not going to tell you that a commitment of marriage or even the act of marriage means that someone really loves you. Because there are many marriages where love is missing and there are many couples who are deeply in love and for some reason are not married. There are those who believe they can only get what they want through manipulation or lies. They do not feel worthy enough to ask for what they want. Their self-esteem is so low they have forgotten how to be honest with themselves, much less someone else. It is not only young people that do not know the difference between sex and love and some individuals may truly feel they are in love for an instant.

"Your parents may try to keep you from situations where they feel *something could get out of control*. Worrying about when that might happen will drive them and you crazy and it will never work. If you want to be in that situation, you will be and there is nothing they can do about it unless they lock you in your room."

"Isn't that illegal?" asked Abril.

Wisdom Keeper ignored the faery's comment. "What does work is helping you to learn to love yourself enough that you want to take responsibility for your life and your actions. In the end, you, and only you, are responsible for your body."

"That doesn't sound very romantic," sighed Chloe.

"You are absolutely right," chuckled Grandmother. "It doesn't. I don't want to say that romance is overrated, but I will say that romance without true love will always fade. Sienna, to answer your question, when it is true love your heart will know. Your actions will not be frantic and frenzied, but deep and relaxed and focused on your partner's pleasure. Nothing will give you more pleasure than pleasing your lover. And, your lover will feel the same about you. I hope that you will all wait until that time."

Sam had been quiet through most of the discussion. Finally she said, "I am not quite thirteen, but know I am falling in love with Bear Heart."

"Ahhh, I believe you are, Wind. And, that is why it is so important that in the coming years you respect each other and that both of you take responsibility for your actions. You and Bear will have many years to explore sexual love when you are both much older and I have many more teachings for you that will make that time even more beautiful."

"Aaahhhh," sighed Tinga.

"Don't be goofy," said Luna. "Grandmother is serious."

"I know, I'm just dreaming of the perfect elf. Leave me alone."

"Do any of you have any more questions for now?" asked Wisdom Keeper.

No one did.

"Then Sam, if you don't mind I would like to talk with Sienna and Chloe about your ceremony. Why don't you wake up Griz and take a walk."

"You mean I can't stay? Everyone has secrets they are keeping from me."

"You will understand everything soon enough."

"Okay."

"Oh, Sam, tell your mom and dad that I will be stopping by the cabin in the morning to talk to them."

Everyone watched as the two headed down the trail. Griz's rear did a rhythmic dance that you would never see on anything but a bear.

"Both of you will be holding a space on Sam's Becoming Woman medicine wheel. Every direction has a special aspect. Sienna, I'm going to ask that sit in the northeast, so let me tell you a little about the energies of that direction. Northeast is the place where we *design and choreography* our lives. That means it is the place where we make decisions and choices and set our priorities and goals. Each direction on the wheel has a light side and a dark side. You might say, good and bad, but the light really means *a time when we can see* and the dark means *a time when what we need to see is hidden.* The light of the northeast is a beautiful place where we *go with the flow of the Universe* knowing that we are being guided. We don't fight change or resist life. But, in the dark it is the place where we sabotage ourselves."

"What does sabotage mean?"

"In this direction it generally means that we unintentionally mess things up for ourselves. It may be by procrastinating or putting off doing something we know we need to do. Like, well, like waiting until the last minute to study for a test. You didn't intentionally plan to get a bad grade, but you allowed yourself to be distracted by something until it was too late to study. Or, the opposite could be what I call *jumping into the abyss* without thinking. An example might be getting into a car with friends and going joy riding when you know the driver has been drinking alcohol. If you had taken the time to think about it, you would have realized the results could be disastrous and that it wasn't worth it. The light side of the northeast is about finding a balance of your feminine receptive and your masculine assertive energy." Sienna gave her a quizzical look. "Yes, each of us has both male and female tendencies, but sometimes they are not balanced. Some women are more feminine and some are more masculine and there is certainly nothing wrong with that. It is what gives us some of our character. Ahhh, where was I? Oh, yes. Each direction has what we call *Warrior's Attributes.* These are traits that help us to find the balance between the light and the dark of a direction. The attributes for the northeast are *relaxation and focus.* You might say that if we relax and focus we will find equal amounts of time to work and to play."

"I think I've got it."

"Good, what I am asking you to do is create a prayer that reflects your desire to help Wind find that balance in her life. Think about it and if you have trouble, I will be glad to help."

"Okay."

"Chloe, you will be sitting in the west and sharing this space with Bear Heart. His intent will be entirely different than yours and I will be working with him later. I want you to remember two things

173

about the west. It is the place of magick and relationships. By magick, I mean the abilities to see things others can't see, like being able to see Tinga and Luna and hear Griz talk. This is just one aspect of Sam's psychic powers that she is going to need to develop even more if she is going to become the next Wisdom Keeper. The west is the place where she will find her *power and strength*, which are the Warrior's Attributes, to achieve her destiny."

"Power and strength. Got it."

"Second, you are Sam's best friend. I want you to stress how much her friendship means to you and to let her know that you would do anything to support her on her journey."

"That's easy."

"Good. Just like Sienna, you will need to prepare a prayer to Great Spirit showing your intent.

Sam walked with Griz along the river for a long way and she found out much about her power animal. At first he had seemed a little shy, but after a few minutes he was as talkative as Coyote.

"You know, I'm pretty famous," he finally said, "They even named a constellation after me – Ursus Major, the Great Bear. Can you find the Big Dipper in the sky?"

"Sure. When I lay on the dock in the summer, I can see it right over the tops of the trees."

"Well, the last of the three stars that make up the handle is my nose. And, the North Star is actually part of the Ursus Minor, the Little Bear constellation, which appears right above me."

"That's cool. I'll never look up at the night sky again without thinking of you," she laughed.

"I am the biggest of all carnivores, but," he paused a minute and sat back on his haunches and patted his stomach, "as you can see, I will eat almost anything and not just meat. They say I am omnivorous because I also love fruits, nuts and berries. But, do you know what my favorite is?"

"You'll have to tell me."

"Honey. Boy, do I love honey. Just like that Pooh Bear story that your mom probably read you as a kid. It doesn't slow me down though. You don't want to try and outrun me. I may weigh fifteen-hundred pounds, but I can still do thirty-five to forty miles an hour."

He rolled back down onto all fours and started walking again. "I don't really hibernate as a lot of my friends do, but I have learned to slow my breathing way down in the winter when I am in my den, so that I don't use near as much energy and my fat will last a lot longer. One of the things that I will remind you of from time to time is how to go inside yourself and be resourceful; how to awaken your potential. If I was a female grizzly, I would have two or three cubs every four years while I was in my den sleeping. The cubs would only weigh about a pound, but by spring when we were ready to emerge, they would weigh eight or nine pounds and grow to my size in about four years. That's another thing that I will teach you. No dream is too small. All dreams start small and can grow to be as big as I am," he said with a laugh that sounded more like a growl. "Some native tribes say that I am the keeper of dreams."

They'd come to a large tree and Griz suddenly reared up on his hind legs and backed up to the trunk. He rubbed his back on the rough bark for several minutes making loud, contented groaning noises. The tree swayed precariously and for a minute Sam thought he might actually uproot it, but it held.

"Ahhh, that's better. When you've got an itch that has to be scratched... Just like my cousin the polar bear, I don't really have any enemies. My cunning and strength are renown and nobody really wants to mess with me. Since I am your power totem, I sit in the center of your wheel. That means that I can work with all of your other allies and I will lend them my strength when you need it."

On the way back he told her a story about the daughter of the Chief of the Sky, which he said was a Modoc Indian legend. "One day a small girl became lost in the forest and she was found by a grizzly bear. He carried her to his cave and she became part of his family. When she became a young woman she did not understand there was a difference between herself and her siblings. She married the old grizzly's eldest son and they had many babies. They looked almost human and were not nearly as hairy as a bear. As time went on she feared she might never again see the old grizzly that had saved her, so she sent out one of her sons to find him. He did and when they returned, the old grizzly was furious, but then he got to know his grandchildren and learned to love them. He realized they were a new race that had power and strength, fine brains, a love of nature, and a wonderful connection to spirit. They became the first Indian people."

"You don't really believe that, do you?" asked Sam.

"No," growled Griz, "but it is a great story."

Note: For more information on the Star Maiden's Circle and the energy of the directions, see Appendix D.

Chapter 25
Preparations for the Ceremony

On Sunday morning, Wisdom Keeper knocked on the cabin door as promised. Sam didn't have to be told to disappear this time and she, Sienna and Chloe headed down to the dock. She was getting used to the idea that much of her ceremony was supposed to be a secret. Jack and Kari welcomed the grandmother and they gathered on the couch in the living room.

"Jack, many times men are not invited to women's rites of passage ceremonies, but this time I feel it's important for both you *and Sam* that you be there."

"I'm very glad to be included. Is there something you want me to do?"

"I would like to have you escort your daughter into the wheel after everyone is seated. Have you had a chance to meet Two Crows? He's a friend of Bear Heart's?

"He and Bear stopped over one time. I just met him for a second."

"Well, I'm going to ask him to escort Sam as well. So you will both have the honor."

"Fine. You just have to let me know when." He smiled at his wife. At first he hadn't been too sure about this whole thing, but after a long encouraging phone call from his wife's mother in Montana, he was coming around.

"Good. Now Kari, I would like for you to actually sit on the circle in the direction of south. Part of the essence of the south is the child, who we were as children, and no one knew Wind better at that time than you and Jack."

Kari smiled and reached out and took Jack's hand and squeezed it.

"The south is the place of trust and innocence; the place of childlike-wonder. It is natural as we grow older to lose this excitement over discovering new things, this awe over nature and creation. Sam still marvels over these things and it is important that she not lose this quality. I see it when she watches a flower blossom open, when she sees an eagle soar in the sky, and when she receives knowledge that makes sense to her. In the Bible, it says that in order to enter the kingdom of heaven, one must have the innocence of a child, and it is basically the same here. Retaining this ability will be very important for Wind as she enters different aspects of her training in the future."

Kari continued to smile, gazing out the picture window at the pristine lake, gentle waves glistening in the early sun. It was obvious she was remembering special moments she had shared with her daughter when she was small. Finally, with tears brimming in her eyes, she said, "That won't be hard to do at all."

"Good. I would like for you to formulate a prayer asking that she nurture these qualities. The word innocence in the south has a slightly different connotation than you might think. The ancient Latin means *in my own essence*. The potential of the south is the ability to take your own power and dance in the center of your own circle, your own essence, with individual, autonomous freedom."

"That's my little girl, for sure," said Jack. His eyes were misting over as well.

Even though Abriana was grounded, her mother had agreed to bring her over to Jennifer's for a short visit. When Wisdom Keeper knocked on the door, a beautiful Hispanic woman of about thirty-five greeted her. The girls were right behind her.

"Grandmother Wisdom Keeper it is so good to finally meet you. Sam has talked so much about you," exclaimed Jennifer.

"Yeah," said Abby.

Wisdom Keeper knew immediately which girl was Jennifer. She had the same beautiful, dark flashing eyes as her mother and they twinkled with mischief, reminding her of faery eyes. It was obvious that Jennifer was maturing at an early age and Grandmother assumed she had probably already started her cycle. She was very casual wearing an old sweatshirt and jeans with the knees cut out. Abriana was several inches taller and very slim. She had bright blue eyes and light hair and as a second woman stepped from the kitchen, she knew she had to be Abriana's mother. The woman was probably five-foot-ten inches tall. Both mother and daughter were dressed impeccably in high fashion and even though they were both smiling, there was a hint of sadness to their eyes.

"Well, it is wonderful to meet the two of you. I already feel I know you. Is there a place where we can sit and talk?"

"Sure. Mom, we're going downstairs."

When they were seated on an overstuffed sofa full of pillows, Grandmother began. "Jennifer, the southwest is the place of our dreams and that is where I would like for you to sit on Sam's medicine wheel during her ceremony."

"Cool. She's always telling me about her dreams."

"Everything that happens in our lives is first seen in a dream, even if we don't remember dreaming it. Sometimes something we fear is manifested and other times it's something we've wished for very hard, something wonderful. This is called *conscious creation* and we are consciously creating every minute of every day of our lives. So, you see if something isn't going just the way you want it, what needs to be done is for you to change the way you are dreaming."

"That sounds so easy," said Abby.

"Well, it's not that easy because sometimes unconscious thoughts get in the way. For instance, if your self-esteem is poor and you don't feel good about yourself, you may hold back and be very shy because you don't feel worthy of having what you want. On the other hand if you have been told that you can do or be whatever you want in life then you are more likely to *engage with life*. You might call it *going for the gusto*."

"Sam doesn't seem to have any trouble *going for the gusto*," said Jennifer.

"It seems that way," said Grandmother, "but she can still use your prayers. Would you think about a prayer that you might say for her that would help her, what does Nike say…"

"*Just do it.*" Both girls answered at the same time.

"Good. Abriana, I am asking you to hold the space in the east. It is interesting that Jennifer's direction and yours are connected. Well, everything on a medicine wheel is connected, but the east is where we manifest everything that we have dreamed. This is the place of vision and it is important that as we move through the other directions on the wheel that our vision doesn't become clouded. We need to see clearly where we want to go. The part of the east's essence that I want you to stress is the *Warrior's Attributes* of *self-development and speed*. Warrior's Attributes are traits that help us actualize the energetic of a direction. Some people beat themselves up because they don't feel they are learning or *dreaming in* what they want fast enough. Some learn fast and others slow."

"And, you want me to say a prayer that Sam dream things faster?" asked Abby.

"No, not at all. These attributes remind us that everyone is going to learn at their own pace and that we need to honor that speed or that pace. Dreams will manifest when they are supposed to."

"So, I need to pray that she work real hard, but be patient?"

"Very good."

Ol' Tom was just completing his weekend teaching with Bear Heart, Two Crows and Tyler when Grandmother arrived.

Nina answered the door. "Come in Wisdom Keeper. I imagine that you want to talk to the *men*," she laughed. "They're out back. It was such a wonderful day they've been sitting on the deck."

"Well, I actually want to talk to all of you."

"Grandmother, it's great to see you," said Tom, as the women opened the French doors to go outside. "I was just finishing up."

"Good, my timing was perfect then. It must be getting lucky," replied Wisdom Keeper winking at Tom.

Bear jumped up and found two more comfortable chairs for his aunt and Grandmother.

"I've been planning Sam's ceremony and I want to invite all of you and then ask if you will help."

"I've been hoping you'd ask," said Tom, "I know that many of your ceremonies are for women only. We would be honored to be a part of it. At least I would."

"Well, I want you and Bear to sit on the circle and I would like to ask you, Two Crows, if you would be willing to escort Sam into the wheel. I have asked Jack, Wind's father, to help also."

"Yeah, sure."

"What about Tyler?" asked Bear.

Grandmother noticed that his voice had taken on a deeper resonance just since the Eagle Dance. He was definitely becoming a young man.

"Tyler, I know that many times you and Sam don't get along, but I would really like it if you would be part of her ceremony."

"Do I have to do something?"

"Well, I would like for everyone to have a part and I thought that you might agree to smudge everyone when they come in."

For a minute he looked a little embarrassed. "I've been meaning to apologize. I got a little carried away at that other ceremony you did. You know... the armpits and all."

"There's noting wrong with a little humor during a ceremony, Tyler. I think you will know in the future when it is appropriate and when it isn't. So, will you agree to the smudging?

"Yeah, sure."

Sam had told Grandmother that she thought Ty was feeling a little left out with all the commotion about her ritual, but now that he seemed to have a purpose he stood a little straighter. She also figured that the teachings from Tom were helping too. Sam wasn't getting all the attention.

"I have a feeling you want me to be Sam's warrior," grinned Tom.

"Well, no actually, I want you to have a challenge. I would like to ask you to be her *child spirit shield*. I've actually gotten quite fond of calling this essence *the cheerleader*."

"It will be a challenge. It's been years since I was a child, as you all know," he laughed.

"There is much to this shield, but I will go over the things that I feel need to be stressed the most in a Becoming Woman ceremony. First, Bear, Tyler, Two Crows, have you ever felt that you had several voices inside your head, everyone asking you to do something different? One might be telling you that you need to get up and get to school, while another is saying, *hey, it's okay to lay here a while longer*."

"Yeah, that happens to me every morning," laughed Two Crows.

"Well, you don't just have two voices in your head, you actually have five. Every person has a child and an adult shield. Your *adults* are just awakening now with your time of becoming men. Up to this point you may have felt your adult's presence more as a big brother. Your child and adult shields are the same gender that you have chosen for this lifetime; they are masculine. Everyone also has two spirit shields. I'll call one of them the warrior and the other the cheerleader. Their gender is the opposite. So, your warrior and cheerleader are actually female and a woman's are male." The boys eyed at each other and didn't seem to happy about this fact. "This provides a way for us to stay in balance. As an example, a man's nature may be to strike out and become aggressive when he is challenged, but a fistfight is usually not the best answer to settle a dispute. If he will listen to his warrior, she will help him make a better choice to solve the situation. A woman may need to take on a more assertive nature than normal when she is in a crisis so that is why hers are male. Does that make sense?"

"Yeah," said Two Crows. Bear nodded. Tyler still didn't look too sure.

Grandmother ignored his reaction. After all he hadn't had near the teachings or experiences of the other two. She was just glad that he was participating. "Your fifth shield is your elder shield, and this shield could be called your highest-self. It is that wise voice that comes to you and generally helps all the other shields to work together."

"And, we all have five shields?" asked Bear Heart.

"Yes, and Bear, I want you to be Sam's warrior and I will talk to you more about that in a few minutes. Tom as Sam's cheerleader, you are her *little boy spirit*. This shield's primary energy is humor and the total absence of fear. It does not know the words can't, or shouldn't and it constantly encourages a woman to *dance on the edge*. It has deep passionate, inquisitive roots and unlimited imagination. Some women are terrified of this aspect of themselves because it takes them into uncharted territory. I don't see this with Sam, but she will need some nudging from time to time. Nudging generally comes in a *trickster* or heyoke form that will help her *jump into her shadow* to embrace her brilliance. Your cheerleader will never push you to physical harm, but it can make you very uncomfortable at times," she laughed.

"I'm going to enjoy this immensely," chuckled Tom. "So are you asking me to say a prayer like the other women on the circle or something different?"

"You will speak as if you *are* the cheerleader. Become her *spirit child* and tell her how she can call on you and rely on you. Wear a costume if you choose. You can let your own imagination run now."

"Good, good. Now I have some planning to do."

"Nina, I would like for you to sit in the northwest of Sam's wheel. There are several important aspects in this direction, but I want you to focus on only one. This is place of our Books of Life, the story that we wrote even before we were born about the lessons we chose to learn in this life. For a while longer, Sam will still be working through her karmic book. These are the lessons. By the time she reaches the age of twenty-seven, this book will be closed and her dharmic book will open. This is not necessarily true of everyone. Sometimes a dharmic book never opens. But, when a dharmic book does open, it means that the person can begin writing an empowering story for the rest of their life. They no longer *have* to engage with a particular lesson if they choose not to. We say they are *at choice*. While in karma, there is no choice. Sam needs to understand that she will have many challenges in the next few years and that she needs to meet them head on to be able to grow into her true magickal mysterious character.

"Ahhh, okay."

"Now your response during the ceremony will be different than Tom's or Bear's. You need to create a prayer to Creator with your intent from this direction."

"Fascinating. I am more than willing to help."

"Now, Bear, I need you to become Sam's warrior and this may be harder than what Tom has to do. I know that right now you would do almost anything to help Sam if she needed it."

"I'm your man," he laughed.

"Even it meant losing her?" His laughter was cut short and he stared hard at Wisdom Keeper with almost panic in his eyes. "Sam's *warrior* is an energy that always has her highest good at heart. Sam's spirit warrior loves her so much that he is willing to do whatever it takes to help her soul evolve, even if that means he loses her as a friend, a lover, or a partner. I am not saying that this would happen. I am just saying that her warrior loves her that much. Her warrior will bring discipline, commitment and follow-through, power and strength, and help her actualize her dreams. This shield's energy is what helps a woman find the strength to lift a car off of her child if necessary or to stand up to an abusive spouse. When this shield is active a woman will *never* give away her power and will *always* embrace change in her life."

"Wow!" It was easy to see that Bear Heart was having a hard time taking all of this in. He finally said, "I'm still your man."

As Grandmother left Bear's, she wasn't surprised to see Gideon on the porch.

"If he's not your man, then I am," was his greeting.

"Gideon, you know it needs to be Bear who sits in the warrior space."

"But, I *really am* a warrior." He proudly pointed with both hands at his white gi marshal arts attire. "I know I can do a good job."

"I know you would too, but I have something very important for you to do."

"What?" he sounded skeptical.

"I need you to use your creative genius and make a container to hold all the prayers that will be offered for Wind during her ceremony. You know what I'm talking about, don't you?"

He brightened a little. "Yeah. I get to use my imagination, huh? It will be my gift to her?"

"Absolutely. And, I know it will be very special if you put your heart into it."

"I'm old enough to know when I'm being patronized, but this is a good idea too. I'll see you around."

"Not if I see you first."

"Hey, that should be my line." The little gnome turned with a grin.

Grandmother only had one other person to contact and her preparation would be complete.

"I've been waiting to hear from you," said Granny.

"How's the weather in Montana?"

"Still pretty cold and there's snow in my yard. I'm waiting anxiously for the Budding Trees Moon to show her face around here."

"The Big Winds moon has been pretty gentle here in the Midwest, but I know what you mean. I'm ready for warm weather too. I heard that you were going to be able to join us for Wind's Becoming Woman ceremony and I'm calling to ask you to sit on her medicine wheel."

"Ahhh, wonderful. What space would you like me to hold?"

"The southeast. Do you remember the energy of this direction?"

"Somewhat. But, fill me in."

"The southeast is our *concepts of self*, our self-worth and self-esteem. You know that our *attitude and approach* to life affect every other direction on the wheel. The teaching of the Seven Dark and Seven Light Arrows is what I would like for you to bring to the ceremony."

"I'm remembering. The dark arrows are attachments, dependencies, judgments, comparisons, expectations, the wounded/abandoned needy child and ego self-importance, right?"

"You do have a good memory."

"I always seemed to have a big problem with ego self-importance," she laughed.

"I understand. Whenever we are shooting any of these dark arrows at ourselves, or others, it indicates that we are seeking validation from outside ourselves instead of from inside. Any time we look to others for our identity, try to gain emotional approval, mental recognition, physical security, or spiritual acceptance, we are giving away our power. The light arrows are self-awareness, self-appreciation, self-acceptance, self pleasure, self-love, self-actualization and impeccability. Shooting these arrows gives us self-reliance and a feeling that we are in harmony with the world around us."

"Yes, an amazing teaching."

"I will be doing a full teaching of this direction with Wind in the future, but for her ceremony I would like for her to understand the basic concept and for you to say a prayer that will guide her attitude and approach to life.

Chapter 26
The Dress

"Okay you guys and gals, get out of the circle. Only Wind gets to sit in the middle," laughed Wisdom Keeper. Her remarks were directed at Dogan, Tinga and Luna who were sitting back to back soaking up the energy of the wheel.

The morning of Playful Autumn Wind's ceremony was perfect. It promised to be warm and the sun was shining brightly with a few cotton candy clouds that drifted on a gentle breeze. Nature in and around the meadow seemed to hold it's breath in anticipation, while the little people flitted around like hummingbirds completing tasks that Grandmother had given them.

Wisdom Keeper had found eight large stones and performed the ritual to create the medicine wheel, by putting a prayer into each stone before she laid it in its place in the cardinal and non-cardinal directions. The finished circle was a good ten paces across. Colorful, woven blankets had been placed in front of each stone so that the person holding that space would have a comfortable place to sit. There was an extra blanket in the east and the west for Bear and Tom, the spirit guides, and a blanket and large pillow in the center for Sam. The early wildflowers of the meadow waved in the gentle breeze and poked their heads up in the midst of the colorful array to check out what was going on. Two small seashells sat on each blanket, one empty and one filled with bluish-gray cornmeal, called corn paho.

Wisdom Keeper had arranged her sacred pipe altar in the north where she would be sitting. The base was a cloth in beautiful earth tones and there was a badger skin resting on top. Several red, blue and green macaw feathers were bound together creating a fan associated with feminine energy. It rested on the left and another made of eagle feathers representing the masculine, had been placed on the right. She'd also laid out a braid of sweetgrass, a small bowl of smudge, a pouch of tobacco and several other personal items. At the front of the mesa facing inward was a small Navajo marriage basket and in it sat a clear quartz crystal skull about four inches high and three inches wide. A few tiny fractures ran through it reflecting the sun, which created a rainbow that floated above. Next to her pipe, the skull was Grandmother's most prized possession, signifying her connection to her Maya heritage. The bowl and stem of her sacred chanunpa lay in the center still protected in their soft red leather bags.

At noon Grandmother, followed by Luna, Abril and Tinga, headed over to the cabin to see how everyone was doing. Almost reverently, the trio of little people carried the dress they had made for Sam. Grandmother knew seeing the faeries and elf were going to be a shock to everyone who hadn't already been introduced to them and she chuckled imagining what their reaction would be. She'd given strict orders for the troll, gnome and leprechaun to stay behind. Griz and the other animals were also admonished to remain in the meadow. Walking up the drive to the cabin, she could see that everyone had gathered on the large front porch facing the lake.

"Grandmother," yelled Sam. "I'm so excited I can't stand it."

"Welcome…" Kari had risen to welcome Wisdom Keeper, but was suddenly speechless when the little people came around the corner. Luckily, she hadn't started walking, and managed to collapse back into her large rattan chair.

Granny laughed and clapped her hands. "Oh my, this is going to be more interesting than I ever imagined."

Jack, Nina, Tyler, Jennifer and Abriana sat stunned as Tinga ran over and Sam bent down so Tinga could give her a hug. "We brought your dress, Saaam," she grinned.

The blond and the black haired faeries flitted to the only open chair. Abril took a seat and crossed her legs while Luna took up a position standing behind her and waved. There was plenty of room for both on the flowered cushion.

Seeing the dazed look on her mom's face, Sam immediately moved over to her mother's chair. "Are you all right? You don't look so good."

Kari gave a faint nod.

"Okkaay. Everyone if you haven't already met my friends, I want to introduce you to Tinga, Abril and Luna. You guys, this is Jen…" She made a sweeping motion with her arm around the porch trying to remember who had and who hadn't met the trio. "Abby, my brother Tyler, Bear's Aunt Nina, my mom, and this is my dad. Oh, and this is my Granny. She doesn't seem too surprised to see you. I think all the rest of you know the girls."

Sam was surprised to see that Tyler looked even more skeptical than her father, but neither was as pale as her mother.

Sienna and Chloe called out a greeting.

"Surprised, but not shocked, you might say," said Granny.

Kari turned to stare at her mother and then back to inspect the tiny figure standing beside Sam. It was obvious she still couldn't speak. Tinga looked kind of like a large red-headed Barbie doll today, except for the greenish sparkling skin. She had on a filmy, green-flowered, ankle length dress and a wreath of buttercups and violets circled her head between her two pointy ears.

Luna was wearing lavender and the same vest made of white feathers that Sam had seen before. Her signature green pointy-toed slippers covered her feet. She also had flowers in her curly blond hair. Her pink wings shimmered. If it was possible to polish your wings, Sam was sure she had. Abril was as glamorous as ever in a sapphire blue, sparkling jumpsuit. She had on her gold jewelry, which contrasted with her cocoa skin and her beautiful black hair was wild and crazy like she'd just been riding in a convertible. A single daisy peaked out from behind her left ear.

"You all look beautiful today and especially you Grandmother," said Sam.

Her leather dress fell in soft folds and ended a few inches below her knees. It was cinched in at the waist with a long red, fringed sash. The yolk and long sleeves of the dress were one piece and beaded from fingers to fingers. Moccasins that extended up under the dress matched perfectly. Her magnificent silver and turquoise pendant hung around her neck.

"And you all look amazing as well," said Wisdom Keeper.

Granny had on a floor length, gauzy, rainbow tie-dyed dress with a sash similar to Wisdom Keepers, but hers was a deep teal color. She wore numerous strands of large turquoise nuggets around her neck and as bracelets. Nina had on a traditional multi-colored Navajo skirt and blouse and several necklaces as well. One had a corn-shaped ivory pendant with a face peering out between rows that Nina had said represented the Navajo deity Corn Woman. Tom and Two Crows wore ceremonial regalia, like they'd seen at the Eagle Dance. Though different, both had on tunic-style shirts with ribbons the colors of the four directions suspended from the yokes in both front and back, and long skirts with fringe on the bottom and beading down the sides. Bear was very handsome in rust-colored buckskin leggings and shirt. His attire was very simple with just an inch-wide strip of turquoise beading that traveled down the outside leg of his pants and down his sleeves from the neckline.

Wisdom Keeper came forward and asked, "May I?"

"Certainly Grandmother," said Bear Heart.

"This looks familiar." She glanced at Tom and then reached over and studied Bear's necklace. Large chunks of turquoise embedded in silver had been used to suspend eight large brown bear claws.

"It was a gift from Ol' Tom when I finished my teachings with him," he said smiling.

"It looks familiar to you, Wisdom Keeper, because I used my memories of the one your father had. I hope you don't mind," said Tom.

"It's beautiful, Tom, and it brings back wonderful memories for me."

"I got one too," said Two Crows proudly, as he lifted a silver and black jet necklace with dangling raven feathers.

She glanced at Tyler who was also wearing one of Tom's creations. A beautiful carved eagle head was the centerpiece in a long string of amber and jet beads. The eagle's eye seemed to be watching everyone on the porch.

"All three of these are amazing, Tom. Your skills as a carver and silversmith are amazing."

The tension had subsided some with the talk of the jewelry, but Kari was still looking pallid. "Everyone does look nice," she said, "but am I seeing things or are you an elf?" She indicated Tinga.

"In the flesh," she giggled, "and Abril and Luna are faeries."

"My grandmother used to talk of you little people," said Granny, "but I have to admit this is the first time I have been able to see you. I'm glad I finally can."

"Can we give Sam her dress now?" asked Luna. "She looks like the only one who still needs to get dressed."

"You're right. Is there a bedroom where you can change?"

"Yeah, come on. I can't wait to see my dress."

The women, girls, elf, and faeries left the men on the porch and headed up stairs. Kari watched as Abril flitted up the stairs in front of her and she turned to her mother who was right behind her and pointed at the faery.

Granny shrugged her shoulders and laughed.

Sam's dress was already laid out on the bed. "Oh, it is so beautiful."

"And, you have moccasins," said Abril, "I made your moccasins."

Sam couldn't quit touching the dress it was the most beautiful garment she had ever seen. She slipped it over her head and it fit perfectly. It was made of creamy doeskin with turquoise and white beading that ran around the neckline and down both sleeves, which ended in swingy fringe. A downward facing triangle with a flower pattern was in the center on the front. On the back was a beaded mandela of black and white eagle feathers and several mink tails swung freely from the shoulders and medallion. More fringe adorned the lower part of the bodice and a beaded belt cinched in the waist. The same greenish beads anchored little fringes of the leather that swirled down the front of the skirt and ended just above where the leather had been cut into six-inch fringe at the hem. Just like Grandmother's, her moccasins extended up her leg under the skirt. Tinga braided Sam's long hair as everyone admired everyone else and chatted about the ceremony. Finally, Luna added a wreath of violets with a purple ribbon that ran down Sam's back.

"I was going to give these to you after the ceremony," said Kari, "but it seems more appropriate now. You might want to wear them. They are from your father, Tyler and I." She handed Sam a small box. Inside were turquoise earrings.

"Oh, I love them, Mom. You now how I like dangly earrings. Thank you so much." She moved off the bed to give her mom a hug.

"Well, mine is a wearable gift as well," said Wisdom Keeper. "I guess I will give you mine too. From a concealed pocket in her dress Sam heard a jingling sound and then Grandmother pulled out a necklace. A turquoise cameo was surrounded by tiny silver beads. Silver feathers hung from the bottom and they were interspersed with beaded dangles and tiny silver bells. "I guess this is a ceremony for new jewelry."

Sam took a closer look at the carving on the cameo. "Is that me?"

"Yes," said Wisdom Keeper, "The Sleeping Beauty Turquoise Mine in Globe, Arizona is where the turquoise came from and then it was sent to Italy where your face was carved."

Everyone got close to stare at Sam's image on the stone.

"I can't believe it. It is you," exclaimed Nina.

"My gift is *wearable* too," cried Chloe, "Can I give it to her now, please?"

"I guess so," said Wisdom Keeper. "But the rest of the presents need to wait till after."

Chloe raced over to her backpack and pulled out a long purple box with a pink bow. Inside was a silver charm bracelet.

"This is so great," exclaimed Sam. Tiny replicas of a feather, an eagle, a wolf, and a bear hung from the chain.

"There's room for a lot more charms," said Chloe.

"Oh, my gosh. I can't believe you did all this for me. I feel just like Estanatlehi did before her Kinaaldá ceremony."

Entering the clearing, all eyes riveted on Griz who let out a welcoming roar and then rolled back on his rear, grabbed his huge feet and began his excited rocking welcome. Jack immediately stepped in front of his family taking charge, "Okay, we need to back away slowly. They say to never run from a bear. Stay behind me and don't panic."

"It's all right, Dad. It's just Griz," said Sam, pushing past and running over to give the monster a hug.

Jack frantically started to go after her, but then stopped in astonishment as the immense creature bobbed his head in recognition and then nuzzled his daughter. He and the others began eyeing the numerous animals on the outskirts of the clearing. A Red-tail hawk was perched in an oak tree and flapped his wings. Next to it sat a raven with large beady black eyes. On the ground were a red fox, a silver and black wolf, a beaver, and the mountain lion that Sam had seen when she quested for her power animal... all in a row. Standing behind them were several white-tail deer and an elk. A rattlesnake lay coiled with its head in the air, tasting the air with his tongue. Suddenly a huge eagle soared into the matrix and landed near the east stone of the medicine wheel. It nodded its head and then hopped over closer to the other animals and then swooped up into the tree and landed on a branch just above the hawk. Before anyone could say anything a flock of geese made a rather inept landing in the clearing. Sam laughed. The birds were so graceful in the air, but without a soft water airstrip they were rather clumsy. Sam thought she had greeted everyone when she suddenly heard a barking-howl and saw Coyote come strolling in. He gave her a slight bow. "I'm here. We can get started now," he chortled, laughing at his own humor.

Wisdom Keeper smiled and ignored the dazed faces. "Everyone, I think you know where you are supposed to sit on the wheel. Bear Heart and Tom, your blankets are slightly behind the east and west spaces. Tyler, as soon as everyone has taken their positions, will you begin the smudging. Jack, you and Two Crows wait over here to escort Playful Autumn Wind. Dogan will you help Tyler with the smudging?"

All eyes now turned to the troll and the elf-leprechaun. Dogan gave a little salute and went to assist Tyler. A lighter materialized in his hand and he flicked it to get a flame and then began to light the mixture in a large abalone shell. Tyler stood rigid and stared at the tiny figure with wild dark hair, dressed in what looked like the skin of a badger. His eyes nearly bugged out of his head. Dogan laughed in his deep voice at Tyler's reaction and handed him the bowl and then pulled a large eagle feather out of his wrap to use as a fan.

Dash gave a bow that strained his belt and pushed his huge belly toward his knees. He smiled through his fluffy white beard and announced that he was the official Door Guard for the ceremony. But, since there wasn't a door he was just going to stand on the path that led into the meadow. He was dressed in his usual attire of green hat, shirt and pants. He winked at Grandmother as she began walking toward the north blanket and then turned back toward Jack and Two Crows the only two that hadn't made their way to the circle.

"I think I've fallen down the rabbit hole in Wonderland," said Jack turning to Two Crows, "When do you think we will wake up?"

"You'll get used to it," he laughed.

After stopping to talk to Wolf and Cougar, Sam made her way back across the clearing to her father.

"You never told us about any of this," he said rather accusatory.

"Would you have believed me, Dad? I promise no more secrets after today."

Tyler and Dogan finished smudging the participants on the wheel and came over to perform the task on Sam, Jack and Two Crows. Suddenly they heard someone yelling and spun to look back down the trail. Gideon was running as fast as his little legs would carry him.

"I'm here, I'm here," he shouted, screeching to a halt before Dash who had stepped up to block his entrance to the meadow.

"You're late. I don't know whether I should let you in or not."

"Oh, Dash, I had some important last minute business. You're taking your job way too seriously," exclaimed Gideon. "You're a little person. You need a lesson from Wisdom Keeper. You are supposed to remind people of humor, remember?" Then the tiny gnome's eyes flashed to Sam in her beautiful dress. He kind of wilted and his mouth flew open. "Oh my, you are a vision, Wind. I never thought you could get more beautiful than the first day I saw you on the soccer field, but…."

"Soccer field, I have been meaning to ask you about all the talk about soccer. Were you spying on me?"

"Well, we had to check you out. It was a long time ago and we didn't know you then," said Gideon apologetically.

She turned toward the other little people who had taken up residence with the animals along the sidelines. "I'm not sure I can trust any of you." She playfully waggled a finger in their direction.

"Come on, Gideon. We're about to start," chuckled Wisdom Keeper. "Jack and Two Crows will you bring Sam to me?"

Sam smiled up into her father's eyes and beckoned for him to lower his face. He did and she gave him a kiss on the cheek and then turned to Two Crows and kissed his cheek.

Gideon was still standing beside them. "Where's my kiss?"

"Giddeeon," Grandmother scolded, but Sam bent down and kissed him on the top of his gray-green bald head. His face lit up and he did a little dance across the meadow to where the other little people were sitting.

Chapter 27
Wind Dancer

"Do you have something for me Wind?" asked Grandmother.

Sam reached inside a brown paper bag that she had brought along and presented Wisdom Keeper with a frayed teddy bear that she'd had since childhood.

Grandmother took it from her. "This is a symbol that our Playful Autumn Wind is ready to give up her adolescence and take her place as a woman."

Sam heard her mother gasp across the wheel.

"Wind, I want to present your Becoming Woman circle[4]. Will you take your place in the center?"

Sam got comfortable on the large pillow and then slipped out the one other item that had been in her bag, the rose quartz heart that Bear had give her for Valentine's Day. Clutching it, she slowly rotated on the pillow looking at all the smiling faces. When she got to Chloe, she noticed that she was distracted and watching Two Crows. Humm, she thought *Chloe and Two Crows haven't taken their eyes off each other all day.* When she got to her mother, she could see she was crying.

Wisdom Keeper reached into a large basket beside her and produced a box of Kleenex and then turned to Sienna in the northeast, "Will you pass this around to Kari? It may have to go around several times today," she laughed.

Sam noticed that Granny took several of the tissues before handing the box to her daughter. When she looked back, she saw that Wisdom Keeper was holding a large skein of red yarn.

"I am going to pass this yarn around and I want all the women to wrap each of your wrists a couple of times and then pass it on. Make sure you leave enough between you and the next person so you can move around comfortably. Nina, when it gets to you, please pass the ball on in to Wind." She made a couple of loops on her own wrists, leaving an ample length for her arm movement and passed the ball to Sienna.

---

[4] You will find a medicine wheel showing each participant's sitting place in Appendix E.

"There is a blood bond between women like no other. In ages past when women were on their moon cycle, they went to a special lodge called a Moon Lodge. There, over the course of several days, they shared friendship and their wisdom and much of the knowledge and tradition of our people was passed down during this time. This custom is no longer practiced, but the bond remains. This red yarn symbolizes this relationship that still binds us. As the yarn goes around, I will explain a few other things.

"In front of each of you are two small shells. One contains the blue cornmeal that is sacred to our people. It symbolizes the sustenance of Grandmother Earth and the nourishment and abundance that she unconditionally bestows upon us. As we go around the circle today and say our prayers or make our statements on Wind's behalf, I want you to take a pinch of the corn paho and hold it up so that the essence of your words is captured. After your prayer, put your pinch into the empty shell. Any questions? If not, I will begin the Pipe ceremony.

Grandmother raised the red catlinite stone bowl of her pipe in her left hand and the red cedar stem in her right. "Creator, Sacred Ones of the Universe, this is your Wisdom Keeper. I join this sacred chanunpa today in honor of this blessed Becoming Woman ceremony[5] for our daughter Samantha Playful Autumn Wind." She paused and centered herself. "In honor of the two sacred laws that everything is born of woman and sparked by man and that nothing shall harm her children or the child within each of us, and in celebration of the People, I put this pipe together." She joined the bowl and the stem and then maneuvered the pipe until the long, beaded and fringed stem pointed toward the middle of the circle. Taking a small pinch of tobacco, she began putting prayers into the bowl as she called to different entities. Sam counted thirteen pinches. When she was done, she lit the pipe and holding it with the bowl pointed toward the sky, blew seven long puffs. "Sohotahah, great As Above, I marry you to the So Below." She brought the pipe across her left shoulder and down across her chest and tapped the crystal skull before her. The magick white light followed her movement as Sam had seen it do before. Then

---

[5] This is a short version of the real Becoming Woman ceremony. For more information, contact the author using the information at the beginning of this book or see Appendix A/ *Wild Woman Rites of Empowerment Bible.*

Grandmother blew seven smokes into the eyes of the crystal skull, "Quaheytamah, sacred So Below, I marry you to the As Above." The pipe was spiraled in a sun-wise fashion this time and the energy soared back up into the sky.

Grandmother did what she called a banishing ritual to eliminate negative energies and then turned the pipe to the south, smoked seven times and began to call in the powers. The same was done for the west, north, and east and then she laid the pipe back on her altar, covered it with the red leather skin, and raised her eyes to the heavens.

Great Spirit, as I facilitate this ceremony today, may I...
See with Your eyes,
Hear with Your ears,
Speak Your words of wisdom,
Feel with Your heart,
And, touch those on this circle with Your beauty and love.
This is my prayer. It is my intention.
A-Ho.

"We are ready to begin..."

"Wisdom Keeper," said Kari, "I know that I am to represent Sam's child by sitting in this south direction, but could I read something as her mother before we start?"

"Of course, Kari."

Kari stood and Sam swiveled on the pillow to face her mother.

"Before you were conceived, I wanted you.
Before you were born, I loved you.
Before you were here an hour, I would have died for you.
This is the miracle of a mother's love."[6]

"Sam," she said very seriously, "Always know that I love you. You may not be my little girl any more, but..." she laughed through her tears and shook her finger at Sam, "but, always remember that *I am still your mother* and what I say goes."

Sam laughed and blew her mom a kiss.

---

[6] I thank Maureen Hawkins for this beautiful prayer.

"Good advice, Kari. Wind, as you have come to know native people believe that every direction has a special energy. I have spent time with each person on your wheel and helped them to understand the power of the direction in which they sit. Each has prepared a prayer for you with that intent. Kari will speak from the south and the place of the child."

After using two tissues to blow her nose, she picked up a pinch of her corn paho and began to speak. "God, Sacred Ones as Wisdom Keeper calls you, before me I see a beautiful young woman and I have prayers for her."

Suddenly Sam waved for the box of Kleenex and Chloe tossed it to her. She pulled several and held them to her eyes.

"I pray that you never lose your innocence and that you can look at all life's experiences with that same wide-eyed wonder and appreciation that you had when you were small. I pray that you will always trust in yourself, trust in your intuitions, and follow your heart in matters of love. May you always find it easy to speak from your heart. These are my prayers."

The pinch of cornmeal went into her empty shell.

"Jennifer, will you speak to Wind about her dreams?" asked Grandmother.

Sam turned slightly to face the southwest.

Jennifer took a pinch of the blue-gray powder and met Sam's eyes. "Great Mystery, I have a prayer for my wonderful friend, Samantha. I wish that you will always live your life to the fullest and go for the gusto. Wisdom Keeper says we can have everything we want, but first we have to dream it. So, I pray that you dream big and make it happen. Amen." She dropped her pinch into the empty bowl. "Oh, P.S., Great Mystery, I pray that Grandmother Wisdom Keeper will give me a medicine name. Amen."

Everyone laughed and Grandmother replied, "I think that can be arranged, Jennifer. From the west, Chloe, will you speak about relationships?"

Chloe reached down and picked up a small piece of paper. "I don't want to forget anything," she said nervously, and her eyes locked with Sam's. "God, I have a prayer for my best friend in the whole world. I pray that my sister knows that she can tug on this red yarn any time she wants and I will be there for her, and I pray that she doesn't get so busy that she forgets about me and her other friends." She smiled and then glanced down at the paper. "I pray that her powers of magick become even stronger so that she can continue to see our friends, the little people, and talk to Griz and the other animals. And, I pray that she find the power and strength to make all her dreams come true." She glanced at Wisdom Keeper and then up to the heavens, "And, if I can say one more thing like Jennifer did, I pray that I can get some more of Grandmother's teachings too, because they have already helped me a lot. Amen."

"I think that can also be arranged, Chloe. Nina, you hold the space of the northwest. What are your prayers for this daughter?"

Nina took a pinch of paho and held it up. Sam scooted around once again on her pillow. "I have prayers for the new woman among us. Creator, I pray that the lessons that she has come to learn in this lifetime are easy and quickly dealt with and that she is able to release any patterns that might keep her locked in a box of limitations. I pray that she meets the challenges that do come to her head on and that she is able to walk around the wheel and see from all directions; that she is able to understand why she is being challenged at that particular time. I pray that she closes her karmic book early and that she spends many, many years writing an empowering story for herself in her dharmic book. I also pray that she always catches minimal chance and is at the right place at the right time to laugh, love, and be her true magickal mysterious character. These are my prayers"

"Thank you, Nina. That was beautiful." Now it was Wisdom Keeper's turn. "Playful Autumn Wind, I sit in the north for you." She took a deep breath, "Wind, when you came to me in this very meadow over a year ago, my heart began to sing a very soft melody. I had waited for you for many years. Today my heart is singing so loudly that my ears are ringing," she laughed. "I am so proud that such a beautiful young woman, inside and out, will be my apprentice. So, I have prayers for you. I pray that you honor me as your teacher and are open to knowledge that I seek to give you, but that you always question everything. I pray that you never believe anything that I tell you unless it speaks to your heart. If it does, then I pray that you take that knowledge and braid it together with your own wisdom to find your own truth. I pray that you always know your own mind, but are able to walk around the wheel and honor all points of view. I pray that you feel comfortable in your naturalness and know that you are perfect at this time and at all times of your evolution. I pray that you never care what others think of you and that you draw from the energies of the Universe and know that you are never alone. A-Ho! And, now I need a Kleenex," she sniffled.

She paused for a minute dabbing at her eyes. "Sienna, you hold the space of the northeast. What prayers do you have for your friend?"

"Wow. I've heard my mother say this… Grandmother, you are a hard act to follow," she laughed and then got serious. "Samantha, I haven't known you near as long as others here today and I want you to know that I am very glad to be your friend and proud to share this day with you." She took a deep breath and held her pinch high imitating Wisdom Keeper. "Sacred Ones, I have prayers for my sister. I pray that she always has a balance in the feminine and masculine sides of herself and that when those challenges that Bear's aunt was talking about do come that she is able to relax and focus and make good decisions and choices. A-Ho!"

"Beautiful, Sienna. The next direction on the wheel is the east. Abriana?"

Abby took a pinch, blew a kiss into it and then said, "Grandmother has told me that the east is the place of visions and where your dreams come true, so I pray that you have good vision and always know where you want to go and that you are able to manifest everything that you dream about. I also, pray that you understand that not all of your dreams will happen exactly when you want them to and that you need to have patience with yourself and just let it happen. Amen. Is that right Grandmother?"

"Very nicely said," smiled Wisdom Keeper. "We have one more direction on the wheel to hear from and it is a very important direction. I have asked your Granny to hold this space, Wind."

Sam turned and looked deep into her grandmother's eyes.

"Sam, my grandmother talked to me about the Wisdom Keeper and told me that I would meet her one day. In my wildest imagination, I never guessed it would be under these circumstances. She has chosen an apprentice wisely for I have watched you grow since you were very small and have always known that you were special. This direction of the southeast is about how you see yourself in the world. She has told me that you will be receiving many more teachings and one day you will understand more why I have the prayers that I do for you today. I pray that you love yourself unconditionally, for you will never be able to love another completely until you love yourself first. I pray that your attitude and approach to life is impeccable and that you never look outside of yourself for to find who you are or to get someone else's approval. I pray that you understand that you already have everything inside of you to do whatever it is you choose in your life. These are my prayers for my beautiful granddaughter. A-Ho!"

"Wadoh, Granny. Wind, the Universe has great wisdom. In this life you chose to be a girl and then to become a woman. To help you balance your feminine energy, you and all women have been given spirit shields that are masculine. This assertive male energy is what is needed to keep our feminine receptive energy in balance. One of your spirit shields is called your cheerleader and he is your *little spirit boy*. The other is your *spirit man*, your warrior. A man would have a *little spirit girl* and a woman for a warrior. These shields are found in your luminosity or your aura and they are there for you to call upon at will. You and I will talk later about how to access these energies when they are needed. For now, I want you to understand their purpose. I have given Tom the challenge of being your *little spirit boy*."

Sam glanced to her right where she knew Ol' Tom had been sitting and barely recognized him. He looked like an overgrown five-year-old. He had pulled off his ribbon shirt and was now wearing a striped t-shirt and short pants that were held up with suspenders. He had on long socks that came up to his knees and was licking a giant sucker. But, the best part was the golden halo that was somehow suspended over his head and bounced up and down as he laughed.

Everyone was nearly hysterical when he said in a squeaky voice, "Hi, I am your spirit cheerleader. Wisdom Keeper told me I could wear a costume if I wanted. I'm not sure she had this in mind, but…" He returned his voice to normal, laid the sucker down, and took a pinch of the paho. "Seriously, Playful Autumn Wind, I will remind you of the value of humor in your life, but I am also your creative nature. I will help you to find solutions that work and bring beauty to the world. When you bring my essence to the front of your aura, you will have no fear. I will never put you in physical danger, you can trust me explicitly. But, do you remember your encounter with Old Man Coyote?" A head with two golden eyes suddenly jerked up from among the animals at the fringe of the woods and stared at Tom. "I see you Coyote. I am kind of like Coyote, I am your *trickster* and will challenge you any way I can to get you to recognize your brilliance."

"Well done, Tom. Wind, Bear Heart has agreed to take on the essence of your *spirit warrior.*"

While everyone's focus had been on Tom, Bear had also changed his appearance. When Sam turned toward the west, she truly saw a warrior. Bear's face was split down the middle, painted with red on one side and yellow on the other. A black lightning bolt zigzagged down his cheek and he carried a long spear that was decorated with fur and feathers.

Sam waited for the others to laugh, but they didn't. Bear was deadly serious. "Sam, I am your warrior. I will be with you always no matter who else comes or goes in your life, and I am talking about people," he glanced at the ground and then raised his eyes. "When you bring my essence to the front of your aura, I only have your best interest at heart, although some times it may not look that way. I will help you battle chaos and actualize your dreams. I will give you the strength to stand in the center of your own circle of power." He deposited his pinch into the empty shell in front of him.

Sam though she saw a tear, but imagine why. Her heart was beating so hard, she thought it was going to burst from her chest. She knew that Bear was only playing her warrior shield, but she didn't want to separate the words that he said from the boy that she was falling in love with. She clutched her pink crystal until her fingers were white.

"Thank you Bear Heart," said Grandmother. Gideon would you help me with something?" The little person sprang into action and was at Wisdom Keeper's side in the blink of an eye. "Do you have your gift?"

He showed her a small container of some sort.

"Good. Would you go around and gather everyone's prayers and then present them to Playful Autumn Wind?"

"I'm your man."

Sam watched as the gnome walked around the wheel. Stopping in front of every person, he helped them pour their pinches of blue cornmeal into the jar. When he'd made the full circle, he approached her.

"Samantha, these are the prayers that have been said for you today. You can now carry them with you for all time."

He handed her a small red pot sealed with a cork.

"Did you make this?"

He nodded proudly.

The tiny jar was carved of the same red stone that had been used for Grandmother's pipe bowl and he'd painted a scene of colorful native symbols around the outside. The work was so intricate and miniscule that it had to have taken days.

"It's amazing, Gideon. Thank you."

"Do I get another kiss?"

"Giiddeon!" exclaimed Wisdom Keeper.

"Well, you can't blame a guy for trying," he said, skulking off toward the trees.

"Okay, I'm going to pass a pair of scissors around and I want each of you women to cut a piece of the red yard in front of you and wrap it several times around your left wrist and tie it. Someone else on the wheel may need to help you. Wind, I want you to do this too. Even though I am going to close out the pipe next, it will not end Wind's ceremony. It is the belief of our people that a ceremony lasts for seven days. Sam, you may receive visions during this time or answers to questions that you might have. All of your sisters will wear the red yarn bracelets for seven days as a symbol of our connection and support."

The scissors started going around. "I feel we have had a very beautiful ceremony today. Sometimes I judge the effectiveness of a ritual based on how many times the Kleenex box is passed," she laughed. "It always indicates that we have spoken from our hearts. Oh, and one more thing, Samantha. During your ceremony I was told that you have a new name, which has been given to you by the ancestors. If you choose to accept, your new medicine name is *Wind Dancer.*

Note: For information on the Four Moon Cycles and to see Sam's, Bear Heart's and Grandmother's standing place at the time of Sam's ceremony, see Appendix F. This teaching is covered in more depth in the second book of the series, *Becoming the Magickal Mysterious Character.*

Chapter 28
The Kiss

After thanking the powers that had come together for Wind's ceremony, Grandmother closed out the sacred chanunpa in beauty. As she placed the bowl and stem back into their individual red bags, she announced that it was now time to feast and celebrate.

The circle was broken and everyone began mingling. Sam saw her dad eyeing the grizzly bear that was being very respectful and still laid off to one side.

"Come on Dad. You have to meet Griz."

"Oh, I don't think so, Sam."

"Come on. He's really just a big teddy bear." Jack let Sam drag him over to the edge of the meadow. "Griz this is my dad. Dad this is Griz. He's my power totem."

Griz let out a tremendous growl and his enormous head jerked up and down in his excitement. When he finally calmed a little, Jack got close enough to pat him on the head from the side, still trying to stay away from the formidable teeth. "Uhhh, nice to meet you. If you are here to protect Sam then I think that is a good thing, " he laughed.

They bid goodbye to the rest of the animals and the group made their way up the path and back to the cabin. No one had noticed that Tinga, Luna and Abril had slipped out at some point and gotten busy, but as they opened the front door the aroma of zesty lasagna and buttery garlic bread swept over them. The dining table was covered with wonderful delights and in the center sat a large vase of yellow daisies. The little trio scurried around putting the last touches on the feast.

Sam was ushered through as the guest of honor and then everyone filled plates and began to dig in.

"This is really great," said Kari. "I want you to know you girls can cook for me any time."

"Me too," exclaimed Nina.

"We just might do that," beamed Abril. "When can Sam open her presents? I can't wait to see else what she got."

"As soon as we're finished eating. Have patience," said Wisdom Keeper. The little faery's face drew up in a pout. "Well, let's say she can open them before we cut the cake. How's that?"

There was a chorus of open mine first as everyone crowded around and Sam finally took a flat box wrapped in rainbow paper from Jennifer. Inside she found a beautiful dream catcher. The leather wrapped hoop contained a spiral web of delicate cord interspersed with shiny beads and feathers hung from the bottom.

"Thank you, Jen. I'm going to hang this right over my bed to keep me from having any bad dreams."

Nina's present was next. Opening the box Sam found a golden, leather bound photo album. There was a place for a 5x7 picture on the front and Nina had inserted the photo that Kari had taken of Bear and her on Valentine's Day.

"Oh, I love it."

"There's room in there for years of pictures, Sam."

Sienna's gift was a basket full of bubble bath and lotions and potions. "Grandmother said, you might like something to pamper yourself with," said her friend.

"Mine will help you pamper yourself too," said Abby.

Sam opened the package to find a set of lavender satin sheets.

"Oh my gosh, I already feel like a princess, now I will be one. Thank you, Abby. You guys are the greatest."

Granny approached with a large sack. Tissue paper hid something inside.

"I wonder what's in here?" Sam laughed. Removing the paper she found a tooled leather quiver. The carved design on the outside was an elk. Inside were seven arrows. The feathers on the shafts were different colors and looking more closely Sam realized something was engraved on each one.

"This bag was your grandpa's. I know you don't remember him, but he was a bow hunter and used this quiver when he went deer and elk hunting. These arrows were made for you by a Cheyenne craftsman in Kalispell. They are your Seven Light Arrows from the teaching that Wisdom Keeper will give you in the future, Sam. See there's self-awareness, self-acceptance, self-appreciation, self-pleasure, self-love, self-actualization, and impeccability."

"I like the sound of impeccability. Oh, I have so much to learn. Thank you and I'm glad I have something of grandpa's." She truly meant it. She remembered her conversation with Wisdom Keeper about her future Ancestor Speaking ceremony and was looking forward to hearing what this man that she had never really known would say.

Two Crows gift was a smudging fan that he had made of Red-tail hawk's wing tip feathers. There were four feathers in a row and they had been inserted into a wooden handle that was then wrapped with rust-colored leather. She thanked him and then saw Ol' Tom approach with a beautiful hand drum. Bear had said that Tom also made drums. The tightly stretched skin cover had a picture of Griz painted in the middle.

"It's time you began learning some chants," he said.

"I still remember the first song you taught me."

Tom wrinkled his brow trying to think.

"You remember, at the crystal dig. You taught us the Wendey yah song. Wendey yah ho, wendey yah ho."

"I certainly did. That's the Cherokee Morning Song. Well, I will be glad to teach you many more real soon."

Bear had been waiting till last and now came forward with a large box with a huge purple bow on top. Everyone was getting the idea that Sam's favorite color was purple. She slipped off the top and found a soft, teal wool Pendleton blanket. A geometric pattern in red, orange, gold and white wound around the edges.

"It's a Four Winds blanket," he said. "Now you have your own medicine blanket to sit on during ceremony. We'll get Grandmother to do the Blessing and Awakening ceremony for it."

"I love it. Thank you so much." She looked up into his obsidian eyes and fought the urge to jump up and give him a big hug and kiss.

The party began winding down after the red velvet cake was served and Happy Birthday had been sung. Grandmother and Sam's parents were in deep conversation and Nina was entertaining Abriana, Sienna, and Jen with some story. Sam didn't know where the others had gone, but she slipped out the door with Bear Heart.

Once outside they saw Two Crows and Chloe laughing and sitting fairly close on the porch. They spoke for a minute and then began to walk down toward the lake.

Bear touched her hand and she paused. "I had this with me the whole time in the circle." She showed him her quartz heart. "It really means a lot to me."

"You know, you really do have my heart, Sam."

She glanced down feeling shy all of a sudden. Holding the crystal in her right hand, she slipped her left hand into his. They walked the rest of the way in silence and stood on the front of the dock gazing across the water. Grandfather Sun was almost ready to slip beneath the waves. A huge red-orange ball hung just above the trees, his face and the horizon were streaked with scattered clouds painted in oranges, pinks, and gold.

"It was a perfect day," said Sam.

"Yes," answered Bear. "There's only one thing that could make it more perfect."

"What's that?" she asked, looking over at him.

"If you'd let me kiss you."

The kiss was soft and sweet and filled with promises of many more.

As the kiss ended, Sam suddenly realized she had manifested all of this into her life.

Appendix A
Other Books by the Author

The next books in the Magickal Mysterious Character Series

Becoming the Magickal Mysterious Character

Becoming the Magickal Mysterious Character continues Samantha Wind Dancer's saga. The first book *Discovering the Magickal Mysterious Character* begins with Sam at the age of 12 and ends with her Becoming Woman rite of passage at age 13. This book tracks the next fourteen years of her life ending at age 27, as she begins a Major Chaotic Journey and moves into the Big West Moon of the Four Moon Cycles. Understanding more fully the wisdom of Grandmother, she embraces the matriarchal teachings of sisterhood, becomes engaged, married, and has a little boy, Sage McLaughlin Gaagii Begaye. When one of her friends discovers she is gay she is able to help her make sense of her life, and she finds the wisdom to help others heal the wounds of divorce, rape, and death of family members. Normal events in anyone's life are seen through the eyes of a young woman who is learning to take her own power and step into the circle of her own essence through Native American ritual and ceremony.
Due out early 2011
www.MagickalMysteriousCharacter.com
http://blog.PhyllisCronbaugh.com

Living the Magickal Mysterious Character

Living the Magickal Mysterious Character journeys with Sam through twenty-seven years of her life to the age of 54, from Wind Dancer to Wisdom Keeper. During these years Samantha begins living her Sacred Dream. Having learned the lessons that she agreed to learn in this lifetime, she expands her truth to discover the legacy that she has promised to leave to the next seven generations. She begins the crusade for justice for the people that have adopted her into their lives and to help them understand the beauty of the teachings that they have forgotten. Sun Dances and other Native American ceremonies take her deeper into the Gateway Process of the people of the Red Road.
Due out late 2011.
www.MagickalMysteriousCharacter.com

http://blog.PhyllisCronbaugh.com

Legacy of the Magickal Mysterious Character

Legacy of the Magickal Mysterious Character is the last in the series. Samantha Wisdom Keeper travels her Path of Heart to balance the chaos in her life as she searches to find her own apprentice; the one that has vowed in a previous lifetime to protect and share the sacred teachings. Only this will ensure that all women will have access to this sacred wisdom for always.
Due out early 2012.
www.MagickalMysteriousCharacter.com
http://blog.PhyllisCronbaugh.com

Other fiction:

Saving the Crystal Skull: A Mayan Metaphysical Adventure of 2012 Prophecy

Mack MacAlister is lured into the tangled rainforest jungle of Guatemala to a Maya sanctuary that has been veiled by mystifying forces for over 10,000 years. Events take him from innocence to discovering that he is integral to an ancient prophecy and has vowed in a previous lifetime to save a mysterious, life-size crystal skull. Mack is guided by Ichtaca, an old shaman who helps him in his quest to regain his powers; the intuitive magickal side of himself. And, then defying all rationality and in the midst of turmoil Mack finds his soul mate, Tlalli, and painfully realizes they have shared numerous lifetimes of unfulfilled passion. In a world where past, present and future are only separated by thin membranes, it becomes a race of wills to protect the skull from the mad Mexican magistrate, Rafael Sánchez, and ensure the portal between worlds opens at the end of the Maya Calendar on December 21, 2012. Failure could mean the destruction of the human race and Earth as we know it today.
Available NOW!
www.SavingTheCrystalSkull.com
http://blog.PhyllisCronbaugh.com

Reunion of the Crystal Skulls: An Adventure of Mayan 2012 Prophecy

Having found his partner and the love of his life, the Maya woman Tlalli, Mack MacAlister strives to resume a reality that he understands. But, his discovery that he is integral to Mayan 2012 prophecy makes this impossible. With a baby on the way, he and Ichtaca, the old Maya shaman, search for more ways to help him evolve his intuitive powers. But, Rafael Sánchez and the contingency that tried to steal the master Crystal Skull before still endeavor to defy his legacy, knowing the true source of his strength. The complete matrix of all thirteen sacred Crystal Skulls must be reunited on December 31, 2012 for the portal to the Fifth World to open and allow man's conscious evolution, and to save the Earth and mankind from destruction. The race is on to the end of days as the Maya have predicted.

Due out early 2011.

www.SavingTheCrystalSkull.com

http://blog.PhyllisCronbaugh.com

Non-fiction:

Yes, It's Possible to Change Your Past: Combining Ancient Shamanic Wisdom and Quantum Physics to Help You Consciously Create the Life You've Only Dreamt About

Have you ever wanted to change your past, knowing that if you did your future would be significantly different? Do certain events from your past influence your behavior or even haunt you today? The movie *What tHe #$*! (Bleep) Do wΣ (k)πow!?* states that it is possible to change the past. Quantum physics proves it, and many indigenous peoples have known how to do this for millennia. Implement this ancient technique called *Erasing Personal History* and your past will be changed forever, opening doors to a future you've only dreamt about.

Available NOW!

www.ChangeYourPast.com

http://blog.PhyllisCronbaugh.com

The Talking Stick: Guarantee You Are Understood and Not Just Heard

The Talking Stick is a simple tool that can be used by five-year olds or fifty-year olds… in the bedroom or in the boardroom. Promote respect and build self-esteem while settling arguments, making decisions, or brainstorming. The book contains guidelines on how to become a Certified Talking Stick Mediator and how to make your own Talking Stick. Learn the mystery of how the Iroquois Confederacy really used this secret weapon, which kept them at peace for over 700 years. Available NOW!
www.PhyllisCronbaugh.com
http://blog.PhyllisCronbaugh.com

Wild Woman Rites of Empowerment Bible

Rites of Passage, or what we call Rites of Empowerment, have helped people celebrate the natural evolution in their lives for thousands of years. Today few milestones are celebrated and those that are gloss over and fall short of addressing the emotional issues that mystify and create havoc in our worlds. Indigenous peoples have always celebrated the natural cycles of change and rites of passage promote the mourning that goes with accepting changes in our lives and closure heals the wounds of our inner child. Rites of Empowerment celebrate our growth and maturation as individuals as we travel along our Path of Heart toward enlightenment. Rituals balance our masculine and feminine energies and help us regain the Five Hauquas, health, hope, happiness, harmony, and humor in our lives, which are every human's inalienable rights. The book gives instructions on how to facilitate over 50 life-changing ceremonies. Included are numerous poems and stories to make your ceremonies personal and extra special. Available NOW!
www.PhyllisCronbaugh.com
http://blog.PhyllisCronbaugh.com

Earth Astrology: Completing What Sun Bear Started

Earth Astrology looks at what Chippewa elder, Sun Bear, started back in 1980 and combines it with knowledge she received while an apprentice to the DeerTribe Metis Medicine Society, and then elevates this amazing wisdom to a final level, by overlaying the medicine wheels

with knowledge from our Star Nation Grandmothers. Discover the messages of your totem animals as they apply to the way you consciously create every minute of every day of your life. The Elders say that life is not meant to be hard, but easy, if we will only align with the energies of nature around us. They say that the only reason we have stress in our lives is because we are resisting the changes in life that are inevitable. Animals are perfect in the Great Mystery's plan, with no thoughts of the past or future. They live in the NOW, enjoying life to the fullest and you can too. Understanding the messages your animal allies have for you will allow you to enjoy the five Hauquas, health, hope, happiness, harmony and humor, which are every sacred human's inalienable rights.
Due out in 2012.
www.PhyllisCronbaugh.com
http://blog.PhyllisCronbaugh.com

Appendix B
The Earth Astrology Medicine Wheel

What you see above are Sam's totem animals on a medicine wheel. You can discover your animal totems on the next page. First find your birth date or astrological sign of the zodiac in the center circle. You'll see that Sam's sign of Aries (Mar 21 – Apr 19) is one of two in the northeast quadrant. The words Red Hawk are written just below the word Aries. All Sam's animals can be found using the smaller circle with Red Hawk in the south (bottom). It is the top most one on the right side of the page. Bear Heart's sign of the zodiac is Sagittarius (Dec 22 – Jan 19) and is found in the northwest quadrant of the main circle. His main animal totem in Earth Astrology is the Elk and his small circle showing all his totems is the top most one on the left side of the page. I hope you lean a lot about your animals and the messages they have for you.

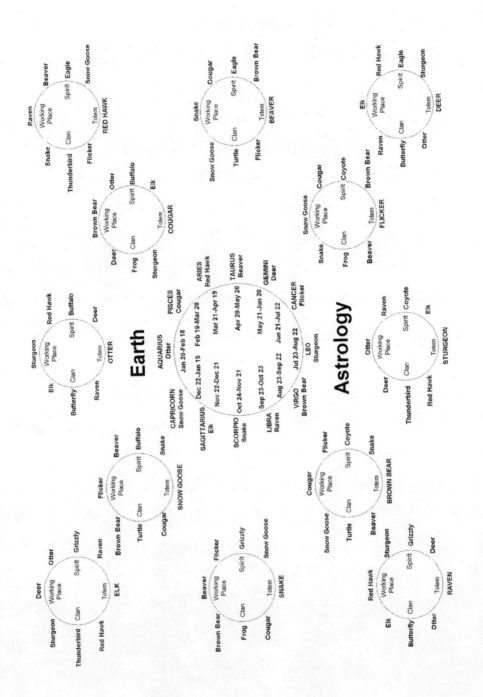

Earth Astrology Months

December 22nd to January 19th – Earth Renewal Moon
January 20th to February 18th – Resting Moon
February 19th to March 20th – Big Winds Moon
March 21st to April 19th – Budding Trees Moon
April 20th to May 20th – Frogs Return Moon
May 21st to June 20th – Corn Planting Moon
June 21st to July 22nd – Strong Sun Moon
July 23rd to August 22nd – Ripe Berries Moon
August 23rd – September 22d – Harvest Moon
September 23rd to October 23rd – Ducks Fly Moon
October 24th to November 21st – Freeze Up Moon
November 22nd – December 21st – Long Snows Moon

Appendix C
Making a Talking Stick

**Talking Sticks embody the wisdom-heart
of the group, and are often artifacts
of great beauty, simplicity, or significance.
They spiritually empower the holder to speak
his or her heart-truth as an offering
to another person or the group.**

There are no rules for making a Talking Stick. They are as individual as the speakers and listeners who will use them. If a situation arises and you feel the need to have a Talking Stick immediately, a pen or pencil or some other object at hand can work. It is your intent that brings magick to the implement.

But, many feel the ceremony has more meaning if they are using a tool that has been designed as a Talking Stick. If you feel this way and would like to create your own Talking Stick, here are some ideas. Use them to spark your own imagination.

Use a stick between 15" and 18" in length. You can use a dowel rod or a stick you have found in the woods or your backyard. Driftwood or dead branches make beautiful Talking Sticks. The stick can be straight or gnarly with lots of knotholes. I don't recommend cutting a live branch from a tree, but if that is your only choice ask the tree before cutting and thank the tree for its gift when you are through. A Native American way to thank the tree would be to leave it a gift of tobacco (not a cigarette with a filter, just the tobacco), some corn meal, a hair from your head, or some spit or saliva.

My late husband was a woodcarver and the first Talking Stick I ever made used the top half of a walking stick that he had made. It had a wonderful carving of a mountain man and I began a beading pattern using circular peyote stitch right below the carving. It became a present for my stepdaughter and her family. I used the bottom half to create my own Talking Stick so I could keep the connection.

I made another interesting Talking Stick from a saguaro cactus spine and decorated it with porcupine quills and leather. I've made numerous Talking Sticks from ¾" diameter dowel rods beading them with the peyote stitch. They became gifts for friends. A friend of mine went into a thrift store one day and found a long carving of a snake. He gave it to me thinking it might be a nice medicine gift to thank someone for doing a sweat lodge ceremony. When I saw it I knew I wasn't going to give it away for a long time. I beaded the black snake using a rattlesnake design and still have it. Maybe I will give it away someday or maybe not. My father was given a real Irish shilalie years ago. Shilalies were actually weapons of old. When he crossed over, I took the stick and made it into a Talking Stick using a rainbow bead pattern. It's a great conversation piece. It will never be used again in war. While walking the shores of a lake one day I found an interesting stick. The top is bent over and looks exactly like the head of a dragon. It didn't take much to make it into a Talking Stick. All I had to do was add a large red crystal stone for the eye. I bought my most recent Talking Stick from a special artist. It is made of a very thick grapevine (about an inch and a half in diameter). It is very gnarly, and has nooks and holes for wonderful stones and treasures. Attached to one end is an amazing crystal of some variety and a smaller clear quartz crystal finishes off the other end. I have had a number of people jest that it just might be missing at the end of the circle.

In making your own Talking Stick, you may want to include something from the Four Worlds of Grandmother Earth – Mineral, Plant, Animal and Human. You might even add something that you feel represents the Spirit World. The stick itself is a representation of the Plant world, but you can certainly add something else that is a plant if you choose. Dried grasses or flowers would be beautiful. When you hold the stick and pass it, you are adding the Human world.

Here are some ideas for the Mineral world. Use a pointed crystal the same diameter as the stick for the top. They come in many different colors. Crystals amplify energy and many feel it increases the connection between what native peoples call the *As Above* and *So Below*, bringing a powerful aspect to the ceremony. The crystal can be attached with a little glue and then by wrapping the stick with a long leather strip or sinew. To secure it, begin the wrapping at least an inch below the crystal on the stick and continue up making sure to wrap at least and inch on the crystal. I have seen them attached with sinew and copper wire as well. Almost any kind of stone that has meaning for you can be attached with good hearty glue.

I have mentioned that I beaded a number of sticks. Use seed beads, usually size 11, to create intricate circular patterns in what is called peyote or brick stitch. Most craft stores have books that can teach you how to do this beading stitch. You may choose to bead straight onto the stick or add leather first and then secure your beading to it. Beading straight onto the stick allows you to move the beading up and down, if you aren't sure where your pattern may take you. Beading onto leather is more permanent. You can also use a beading loom to create a long strip and then wrap it around the stick. Both are beautiful. Since most seed beads are glass, they are a representation of the Mineral world.

Another idea for the ends of the stick is stone cabochons glued onto a ninety-degree or forty-five degree mitered cut. Cabochons are stones that have a flat surface on one side and can be found at rock, gem and mineral stores. Turquoise is especially sacred to native peoples and is a representation of the land for Hopi Indians. The Hopi use red coral as a representation of the sea. You might use a piece of turquoise on one end and coral on the other. Many tribes utilize seashells in their decorations and small ones make beautiful ornaments. If you use a stick with a lot of knotholes, tuck large beads or stones into the holes with a touch of glue.

Many animal fetishes or stone animal carvings can be purchased at gem and mineral stores. Metaphysical and native stores normally have a wide selection as well. If you find one that represents one of your power animals, you might want to attach it to the top in some fashion. A friend of mine has one with a large turquoise bear attached to the top with copper wire and leather. A stone animal fetish would actually be a representation of both the Animal and Mineral worlds.

Leather is a common representation of the Animal world. If you choose a dowel rod, a nice affect is to wrap the entire stick with the leather in a spiral fashion. Leather cord or laces can be purchased in many colors as well as regular leather, allowing you to cut your own strips. If your stick is an uneven branch, you can wet the leather and stretch it onto the stick. This helps it mold to the surface. A friend of mine has a beautiful stick wrapped in rattlesnake skin. The rattles were attached at the top with a leather thong.

If you fancy turtles, you can use a turtle or tortoise shell on your stick. Insert a stick into the rear of the shell and let it extend out through the neck hole. Shape the end of the stick to look like the turtle's head. You might decorate the rest of the stick with green beading, or paint and shells.

Sticks can also be wrapped with jute or other materials. Yarn is a very inexpensive, colorful way to decorate a stick and even kids can create their own using yarn. Several layers of yarn in different colors can create a very interesting pattern. Choose wool yarn if you are trying to keep your stick natural.

Leather fringe attached somewhere on the stick is a nice touch. Cutting fringe can be difficult, but some stores like Tandy Leather have fringe already cut. You might want to thread glass or stone beads onto the fringe at intervals and secure with glue. They add a little weight and help create a nice swingy effect. Attach small bells to the ends of the fringe also. Native peoples use bells to call to the Tolilahqui or Little People, the elves, gnomes, leprechauns, elementals, etc. When you use your Talking Stick, they can remind you to not take yourself too seriously.

Feathers are a popular addition as representation of the Animal world. Natives feel all birds are a connection to the *As Above* and Great Spirit. Before using any feathers, you might want to wrap the feather base with red thread. This is an honoring of the bird and signifies giving the bird back its lifeblood. If you do this, consider adding a looped string to the base of the feather. Do this with several feathers and then attach them to the stick with a leather lace so they hang free. You can cover the thread with leather or if you are beading your stick, you can bead the base of the feathers as well. The best time of the year to find feathers is in summer when birds are molting, but feathers can be purchased at most craft stores any time of the year, if you are unable to find your own.

Instead of feathers, I have seen interesting sticks that utilize the tail of a raccoon, fox, or some other animal. Another nice representation of the animal world would be to add a band of rabbit fur or some other type of fur or hair. Rabbit skins are available at most craft stores. I have seen horse hair used and buffalo or bear would be especially nice, because they are sacred to indigenous peoples.

Adding color by painting your stick is a great idea and quite inexpensive. Here are two color schemes that have a native connotation. One is what native people use to represent the four original races of man. Some call this the colors of the Four Winds. There are variations, but most traditions use red for the south, black for the west, white for the north and yellow for the east. Some tribes switch the red and white, putting the white in the south and the red in the north. The As Above or heaven is generally blue and the So Below or Earth is green. The point where the As Above and So Below meet can be amethyst (purple).

Another color scheme you might consider is a rainbow (red, orange, yellow, green, blue, purple and indigo). Start at the bottom and paint one-inch wide stripes of each. Of course, you can also paint the stick with any colors that mean something to you.

These are just a few ideas that I hope will get your imagination flowing. When your stick is complete, you can ask someone to Bless and Awaken it for you or, do it yourself. Use the sage stick or smudge that was mentioned previously to banish negative energy and cleanse. Separating the elements in smudge and using them individually can create a special intent. The sage represents banishing negative energy, the sweetgrass is for blessing, cedar is for balance and lavender is for beauty. Speak your own thoughts as you run your stick through the smoke created by each ingredient. I also suggest that you say a prayer or indicate in some way, your intent to always use your stick in a sacred manner.

Lastly, keep your Talking Stick in a place of honor and NEVER use it as a weapon.

Walk in beauty, my friend. Awanestica!

Appendix D

Star Maiden's Circle

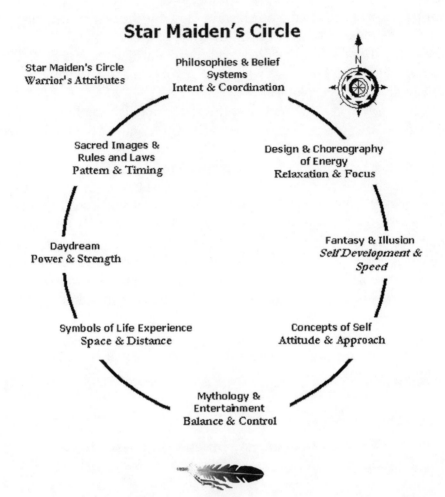

Star Maiden's Circle
Warrior's Attributes

Philosophies & Belief
Systems
Intent & Coordination

Sacred Images &
Rules and Laws
Pattern & Timing

Design & Choreography
of Energy
Relaxation & Focus

Daydream
Power & Strength

Fantasy & Illusion
*Self Development &
Speed*

Symbols of Life Experience
Space & Distance

Concepts of Self
Attitude & Approach

Mythology &
Entertainment
Balance & Control

Appendix E

Sam's Becoming Woman Ceremony

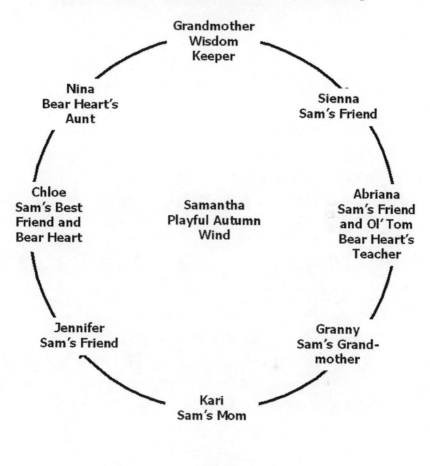

Appendix F
Four Moon Cycles

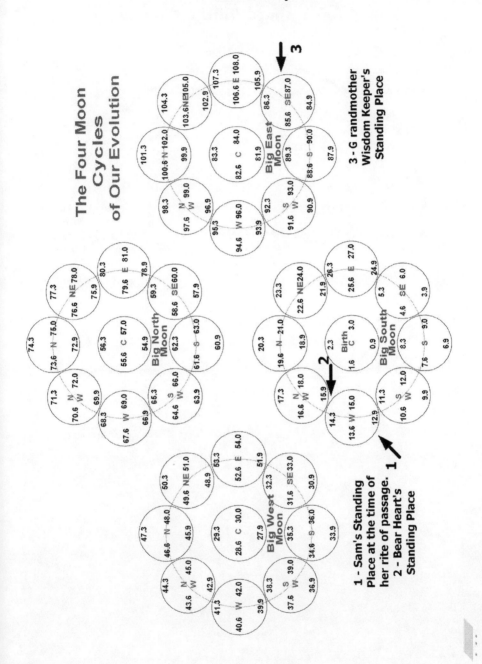

The Four Moon Cycles of Our Evolution

3 - Grandmother Wisdom Keeper's Standing Place

1 - Sam's Standing Place at the time of her rite of passage.
2 - Bear Heart's Standing Place

At the time of Sam's rite of passage her *standing place* was in the southwest of the west of the big south moon. The number 1 on the diagram above designates this place. The number 2 is Bear Heart's standing place and the number 3 is Grandmother Wisdom Keepers. On the small wheel of Sam's standing place, you can see the numbers 12.9 are at the bottom (south) and the numbers 13.6 are in west). Sam's age fits between these two in the southwest. The number 12.9 means twelve years and nine months.

The second book in the Magickal Mysterious Character series, *Becoming the Magickal Mysterious Character*, goes into more detail about how to read this diagram.

I thank the Deer Tribe Metis Medicine Society of the Sweet Medicine SunDance Path for this teaching.

Made in the USA
Charleston, SC
08 March 2010